Dead in the Water

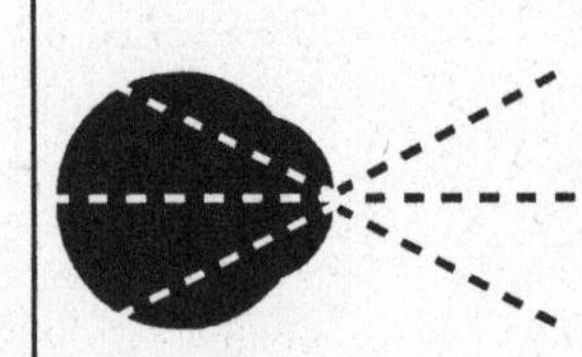

Dead in the Water

Denise Swanson

THORNDIKE PRESS
A part of Gale, a Cengage Company

Farmington Hills, Mich • San Francisco • New York • Waterville, Maine
Meriden, Conn • Mason, Ohio • Chicago

Welcome Back to Scumble River.
Thorndike Press, a part of Gale, a Cengage Company.

Thorndike Press® Large Print Mystery.
The text of this Large Print edition is unabridged.
Other aspects of the book may vary from the original edition.
Set in 16 pt. Plantin.

LIBRARY OF CONGRESS CIP DATA ON FILE.
CATALOGUING IN PUBLICATION FOR THIS BOOK
IS AVAILABLE FROM THE LIBRARY OF CONGRESS

ISBN-13: 978-1-4328-4535-3 (hardcover)
ISBN-10: 1-4328-4535-7 (hardcover)

Published in 2018 by arrangement with Sourcebooks, Inc.

Printed in Mexico
1 2 3 4 5 6 7 22 21 20 19 18

This book is for all the survivors of the Coal City tornado. And for the wonderful volunteers who appeared as if by magic and helped my mother so much.

Mega thanks to:
Ronette and Mike Ksiazak
Bob and Joelle Elberts
Jim and Angie Hutton
Darla Hutton
Tiffany Votta
Traci and John Curl
Gene and Naomi Bianchetta
Gina, Vince, and Jacob Piatak

Travis, Joe, JT: Orland Fire Protection District firefighters who turned up with their trusty chainsaw just in time to clear away all the downed trees.

I apologize if I've forgotten anyone.

Dear Readers,

To those of you who have journeyed to Scumble River before, thank you for traveling with me down my rocky road to publication. To those of you who are first-time visitors, come on in and sit a spell. I hope you enjoy getting to know my sleuths, Skye Denison-Boyd and her husband, the chief of police Wally Boyd. I promise you that you will be able to pick up this book and feel right at home.

A lot has changed in Skye and Wally's lives and in mine since I first met them back in 2000, which is why I felt it was time for a restart. In *Dead in the Water,* I'm so excited to launch a new incarnation of their hometown in the Welcome Back to Scumble River series.

Because the Scumble River series is being reborn as Welcome Back to Scumble River, I've decided to reboot the timeline of the books going forward. It is now present day. Although the characters haven't aged and only a few months have passed since Skye and Wally's adventures in *Murder of a Cranky Catnapper,* it is now 2017 in Scumble River.

I also hope you all will forgive me for this leap in time — figuring out how to handle the years passing is just one challenge that comes with writing such a long-running, well-received series, and I have to thank you, my wonderful readers, for supporting Skye, Wally, and all the rest for so long that I have to make these kinds of decisions! There are a lot of new adventures waiting for Skye and Wally, and I promise you exciting things to come for them and the rest of the gang in Scumble River.

Chapter 1

"There's a cyclone coming, Em."

— Uncle Henry

School psychologist Skye Denison-Boyd woke with a start. She jerked upright, nearly falling out of the brown leather recliner, and her black cat, Bingo, hissed his displeasure. With a glare in her direction, the fuming feline settled back on what little lap Skye still had at nearly thirty-four weeks pregnant.

Rain hammered against the glass of the sunroom windows and when lightning ripped open the darkness outside, the table lamp flickered. Skye had been reading the first book in a new mystery series set in a nearby college town, Bloomington-Normal, when she'd dozed off and awakened to a dark and stormy night. The cliché didn't escape her notice.

Skye shivered when the air conditioner

suddenly kicked on and goose bumps popped up on her bare arms. Although it had been hot and muggy all day, the television meteorologists had promised that a cold front was headed their way. However, Scumble River was seventy-five miles south of the city and the Chicago weather forecasts were rarely accurate for her tiny corner of Illinois, so Skye wasn't convinced that relief from the heat was on its way.

When her stomach growled, she wrapped her arms around her huge baby belly and whispered, "Patience, sweet pea. Daddy's not here yet."

Skye had been waiting for her husband, Wally, to get home so they could have supper together. Since their marriage eight months ago, she'd gotten used to eating later. But the more advanced her pregnancy, the harder it was to delay a meal. And now she was ravenous.

Wally had called around four to say he would be late because the officer scheduled for the afternoon shift had, at the last minute, called in sick. As the chief of police, Wally needed to find a replacement for the guy before he could leave the station. The town's population might be only a little over three thousand, but someone still had to be on duty at all times.

What time was it? Skye glanced at her wrist, frowning when she discovered her trusty Timex was missing.

Shoot! After her first day back at work after summer vacation, she'd been so warm and sticky that she'd stripped and showered as soon as she got home. The high school's AC had been on the fritz and Skye's office had felt like a sauna.

Because her job included working with students at all three schools in the district, she could have moved over to one of the other buildings. But it was highly unlikely any of them would have been much better. Before she'd claimed the space, her offices at the elementary and junior high had both been storage closets. Even in the best of circumstances, those rooms were usually hot as heck or colder than Antarctica.

Instead of seeking a cooler place to work, Skye had ignored her discomfort and spent the majority of her time getting her calendar set up for the rest of the year. She'd had her testing and counseling schedule mostly in place before she'd left for summer break, but there were always transfer students to accommodate.

She had wasted a good half hour trying to figure out how to pronounce the name of one of the new girls. It was listed as Le-a, and initially, Skye had assumed it was pronounced Leah, but she hated to call the teen by the wrong name. It could be Lee-a, or Lay-a, or even Lei.

Finally, Skye had just telephoned the student's mom to ask, and she was really glad she'd made the call. The girl's mother had explained that her daughter's name was Leedasha. Evidently, the dash in Le-a wasn't silent.

Paying attention to details such as correctly pronouncing names was one of many tidbits Skye intended to pass on to her new intern, Piper Townsend. In fact, she'd hoped to use today, before the students started school, to familiarize the woman with her duties, but Piper had had car trouble and wouldn't arrive until tomorrow.

The woman really should have been better prepared and moved to town over the weekend. Her lack of planning made Skye wonder if she'd hired the right applicant. Of course, there hadn't been that many candidates to choose from. A ridiculously low stipend and the promise of a heavy caseload hadn't exactly been enticing to the new grads.

Plus, there was the fact that Skye would have six weeks at the most to help Piper get settled before going out on maternity leave.

In theory, during Skye's absence, a school psychologist from the Stanley County Special Education Cooperative would supervise the woman. In practice, Skye feared that even if it meant she had to guide the intern via telephone while cradling her newborn, she would end up with the brunt of the responsibility.

At that disquieting thought, Skye bit her lip. She really hoped there wouldn't be any crises until after she got used to being a mother. Coping with —

Oomph! Everything below Skye's waist tightened as if a giant fist had closed around her uterus. She dug her nails into the smooth leather armrest while she tried to breathe through the pain. The first time she'd felt the squeezing sensation, she'd panicked and called her ob-gyn, convinced she was going into labor.

Dr. Johnson had reassured Skye that the baby wasn't about to make an early appearance. Instead, she was experiencing Braxton-Hicks contractions. And although uncomfortable, unless the contractions grew consistently longer, stronger, and closer together, everything was fine.

Now, as she panted through the contraction, Skye gripped the wooden lever on the side of the recliner and pushed until the footrest lowered. Then, risking the wrath of Bingo, she picked up the cat, put him on the floor, and struggled out of the chair.

She shoved her swollen feet into a pair of flip-flops and began to pace. Walking usually provided some relief from the Braxton-Hicks throbbing, but as Skye marched the length of the sunroom, the pain continued. Her doctor had warned her that dehydration could worsen the discomfort and she'd been sweating all day. Maybe water would help.

Heading into the kitchen, Skye snagged a bottle of Dasani from the refrigerator and chugged it. As she drank, she checked the microwave clock. It was five thirty. She'd been asleep for more than an hour. Where was Wally?

When the contractions eased, Skye glanced at the telephone hanging on the wall near the stove. The tiny light on the base glowed a steady red, indicating there was no voicemail. Pulling her cell out of her pocket, she saw she'd missed a text. Wally had sent a message at 4:55, saying he was having trouble finding someone to work.

While Skye contemplated calling him for an update, she hurried to the hall bathroom. Along with all the other joys of her pregnancy, it seemed that the baby was nearly constantly kung fu fighting on Skye's bladder and she always had to pee.

She had just lowered herself onto the toilet when she heard tires crunching over the gravel of the driveway. She assumed it was Wally, but a few seconds later, the sound of two car doors slamming instead of one convinced her she was wrong.

Darn! Why was it that the only time she ever got company was when she was in the bathroom? Of course, since she had been expecting, she had been spending a lot of time in there.

Skye hastily finished her business, straightened her clothes, washed her hands, and hurried into the foyer. She reached for the dead bolt but jerked her hand back. Granted, they lived in a rural area near a small town, but Wally had drummed into her head the need for caution enough times to make Skye peer out the side window rather than fling open the door.

She squinted through the pouring rain. Trudging toward the house were two people huddled under a neon-yellow umbrella. The halogen lamp attached to the garage didn't illuminate the sidewalk and it was too dark to make out their faces.

Flipping on the porch light, Skye frowned when she saw her visitors were Frannie

Ryan and Justin Boward. What in the world were those two doing slogging up her sidewalk?

Skye had become extremely close to the pair during their high school years, and after their graduation, that professional relationship had grown into a personal one. Normally, she would have been happy to see her friends, but the young couple should be at college, not on her front porch.

Frannie and Justin both attended the University of Illinois, and the fall term had started last Monday. Before they'd left to drive down to Champaign, Skye had had breakfast with them. And as far as she knew, there was no good reason they'd be back in Scumble River so quickly. Something bad must have happened.

Her pulse racing, Skye threw open the door and demanded, "Why are you here?"

She winced as the words left her mouth. She sounded like her mother. It was a good thing Frannie and Justin were no longer her students, because that wasn't a very empathetic greeting. But between the weather, her advanced pregnancy, and Wally's absence, Skye was spooked.

"Can we come in?" Justin asked, closing the umbrella and leaning it against the outside wall.

"Sure." Skye stepped aside. "Sorry. I'm just surprised to see you."

Justin allowed Frannie to enter first, then followed her into the foyer. At twenty years old, Justin seemed to have finally reached his full height of six feet two. And although he'd probably always have a slender build, his weight was finally catching up with his last growth spurt.

Justin pushed his damp brown hair off his forehead and reached into his pocket for a handkerchief to wipe off his glasses. As he cleaned the lenses, his long-lashed brown eyes blinked, adjusting to the brightness inside the house.

Skye smiled. Justin hadn't been an attractive or socially comfortable teenager. But he was turning into a nice-looking young man who appeared finally to be comfortable in his own skin.

"Let's sit in the kitchen." Skye started down the hallway, forcing herself to be patient. Frannie and Justin would tell her what was up in their own good time. "How about a soda or some tea?"

"A Diet Coke would be great." Frannie caught up to Skye and gave her a one-armed hug.

Frannie was tall and solidly built. Skye had spent most of Frannie's high school years trying to raise the young woman's self-esteem. She'd attempted to help Frannie navigate a world dominated by media that insisted anything above a size four was huge. Unfortunately, much of that work had been undone during Frannie's first semester at a Chicago university.

After a couple of months of feeling like an outcast and missing home, Frannie had returned to Scumble River, completed her freshman and sophomore years at a local community college, and then transferred to U of I. Unlike her previous university experience, U of I's journalism program was more concerned with a student's abilities than her appearance or clothes. It had been just what Frannie needed and she'd thrived.

Justin had also lived at home while getting his associate degree at the same local community college as his girlfriend. Being nine months younger than Frannie, this was his first year joining Frannie in Champaign.

"Any chance of some chips with the pop?" Justin asked, dropping into a chair as if exhausted. "We haven't had dinner yet."

"Sorry," Skye said. "Not much in the way of snack food around here since the doctor gave me heck for gaining fifteen pounds almost overnight. Her exact words were: 'Thou shalt not be bigger than thy refrigerator.' " She patted her gigantic belly and made a face. "I've got salsa chicken in the Crock-Pot for dinner and there's plenty if you'd like some."

"That would be awesome." Justin straightened and reached for the bowl of fruit in the middle of the table. "I'm starving."

Skye took two cans of Diet Coke from the fridge and handed them to Frannie, then reached back into the refrigerator and grabbed the Tupperware container with the Mexican rice. After spooning half into a covered Pyrex bowl, she popped it into the microwave and pressed the reheat button.

Waiting for the side dish to get hot, Skye put plates, silverware, and napkins on the table. Although Justin had already devoured a pear and was gnawing at the core of an apple, Frannie was only chewing on her thumbnail and staring into space.

When the microwave dinged, Frannie jumped, then shot a worried glance at Justin. Something was definitely up. Skye just hoped whatever the problem was, it was fixable.

Justin dug into the chicken as if he were a squirrel and his plate of food was the last acorn on earth. Frannie never lifted her fork to her lips.

Having decided she was too hungry to

wait to eat with Wally, Skye helped herself to a serving of the casserole. After pouring herself a glass of milk, she took a seat across from Justin and Frannie.

She waited to see if either of them would start the conversation, but when they both remained silent, Skye said, "Now tell me why you're here and not at college."

"My parents weren't answering their phone and I got worried," Justin mumbled through a mouthful of chicken.

Justin's father was in constant pain due to degenerative arthritis of the spine and his mother suffered from a debilitating depression. Neither was able to hold down a job or handle the minutia of everyday life. Until Justin had left for school last week, he'd been the one to take care of those details.

"Are they all right?" Skye asked, then took a bite of rice.

"As good as they ever are." Justin pushed away his empty dish. "They only have the one cell phone, no landline, and Mom forgot it was in her pocket and tossed it into the hamper." He shrugged. "They don't get many calls, so they didn't miss it until we showed up."

"Luckily it was on and the battery wasn't dead." Frannie rolled her eyes. "We found it by calling the number and zeroing in on the ringing."

"That was clever," Skye murmured. It didn't explain why Justin and Frannie had come to her house, but at least it hadn't been a true emergency. She tilted her head and asked, "So, Justin, your parents were otherwise fine?"

"Yeah." He paused and drained the can of Diet Coke. "But the thing is, I've been wondering for a while if I can leave them on their own."

"I see how that would be a concern." Skye nodded. She hated that Justin might feel he needed to give up college to take care of his parents, but she understood his feelings.

"You can't just stay here and take care of them," Frannie snapped. "You're too good a writer to drop out of school and take a job at a factory."

"It would only be until Mom and Dad were able to get their act together." Justin didn't lift his eyes from the tabletop.

"Which will be never." Frannie's brown eyes flashed. "They need to step up to the plate and be the adults for once. Yes, they both have issues. But they certainly should be able to handle their own lives and allow you to be able to follow your dreams."

Justin scowled and said, "I know that's what you think, Frannie." His lips thinned.

Clearly, this was an argument they'd had before. "And yeah. I wish had a father like yours. Someone who cared enough about me to deal with his problems. But my parents aren't ever going to be like him."

"Sorry, sweetie." Frannie scooted her chair over, laid her cheek on her boyfriend's shoulder, looked at Skye, and said, "Isn't there some kind of assistance available to help people like Mr. and Mrs. Boward?"

"Your parents receive social security disability benefits, don't they?" Skye asked.

Justin nodded. "Uh-huh."

"Tomorrow, I'll call the co-op's social worker and see if she can refer me to an agency that is able to provide a caregiver to check on them a few times a week."

Skye got up and made a note on the pad by the phone, then walked into the foyer, grabbed her appointment book from the tote sitting on the coatrack bench, and stuck the slip of paper inside it.

When she got back to the kitchen, the table had been cleared, and Justin was lining up the fruit bowl, napkin holder, and salt and pepper shakers as if there were going to be an inspection.

Frannie poked him and giggled. "You are so OCD."

"I'm not obsessively compulsive." Justin

grabbed her finger and kissed it. "I'm just super meticulous."

Justin turned to Skye and said, "It's nearly seven, so we'd better hit the road. We both have early classes tomorrow."

Skye recoiled as a flash of lightning illuminated the kitchen window, immediately followed by an explosion of thunder. "The storm seems to be getting worse."

"I'm sure we'll be fine." Justin put his arm around Frannie.

"Let me call Wally and see how the roads are." Skye snatched the receiver from the base, then repeatedly poked the on button.

"Something wrong?" Frannie wrinkled her brow.

"There's no dial tone." Skye replaced the handset in the holder.

"Try your cell," Justin suggested.

Skye took it from her pocket and blew out a frustrated breath. "No bars."

Frannie and Justin checked their cell phones with no better luck.

"Shoot!" Now Skye really didn't want them to leave. If the phones were all out, the rural roads between Scumble River and Champaign might be flooded.

As she stared at her cell, there was another blinding bolt of lightning, then the distinctive smell of smoke and the crunch of metal being smashed.

Justin, Frannie, and Skye rushed to the front door and peered outside. One of the enormous oak trees that lined the driveway was split down the middle, with the largest part lying across Frannie's car.

"Guess we're not leaving after all." Justin sighed, then shrugged and asked, "Do you have anything for dessert?"

CHAPTER 2

"That is because you have no brains."
— Dorothy

"Son of a bitch!" Chief of police Wally Boyd slammed down the telephone. It looked like he was working a double.

Zelda Martinez had been his last hope, and his call had gone directly to her voicemail. Zelda, as Scumble River's youngest and only female officer, was usually eager to work a double shift, not only for the money but also for the experience.

When Tolman had called in sick at the last minute, Wally had known it was going to be tough to find coverage for him, but he hadn't counted on the storm's interference. The Scumble River Police Department had only six full-time officers, including Wally, so it just took one case of the flu or someone on vacation to create a staffing problem.

With two guys stuck on the wrong side of

a flooded underpass, two others not answering their phones, and the part-timers, who were supposed to fill in the gaps, unavailable due to their other jobs, Wally was out of options. And as usual, to solve the problem of being short-staffed, he would have to sacrifice time with Skye. He had to figure out a way to employ additional officers before the baby came, because he wasn't going to be an absentee father.

Wally walked over to the dartboard on the back of his door and flipped it over, then returned to his desk, opened a drawer, and took out a handful of darts. Taking careful aim, he released the projectile and watched in satisfaction as it landed smack-dab in the middle of the mayor's forehead.

The police department needed more personnel, but the city council had frozen hiring for all local government services. Although Wally had been begging for an exemption for the PD, with Mayor Dante Leofanti behind the moratorium, he knew he didn't have a chance at getting the council to allow him to take on another couple of officers.

Hizzoner was throwing a tantrum because his plot to outsource the town's law-enforcement services to the county sheriff's department had been thwarted. He had wanted to use the money saved on police salaries to finance building a mega incinerator on the edge of town so he could charge other communities to burn their trash and funnel the money into his mayoral salary. But once his plans became public, Scumble Riverites had protested, and Dante had been forced to give up his scheme. Which meant the police department would be the last city service the mayor would excuse from the freeze.

Although Dante was Skye's uncle, her mother's brother, their relationship hadn't ever been particularly cordial. It had deteriorated even further when Skye and Wally had exposed the mayor's incinerator plans. And because Hizzoner held on to his grudges like a tick stuck to a hound dog, there would be no more money for the PD until he was booted from office.

However, in order for that to happen, someone needed to run against him. Currently, he was running unopposed in the November election, leaving only a little over two months for a write-in candidate to appear.

Hell! Wally threw another dart. This one landed on the mayor's beaky nose. The police department hadn't even been allowed to replace the idiot who had been fired for dealing drugs. Hizzoner had brushed off Wally's reasoning that replacing an officer wasn't the same as a new hire, all the while insisting that the budget didn't have room for another salary.

Wally had hoped the city council members would override the mayor, but they were all either in his back pocket or afraid of his wrath. Even Zeke Lyons, the newest council member and the only one who wasn't one of Dante's old cronies, was too much of a milquetoast to speak up.

When Zeke had been appointed to fill in the vacancy created after Ratty Milind had a stroke while he was screwing his little side dish in the Dollar or Three store's parking lot, Wally had hoped Zeke would change the way the council did business. From what everyone had said about Zeke, he had seemed like a stand-up guy who would put the town's interest before his own. But so far, Zeke hadn't even opened his mouth at any of the council meetings.

Which just proved what Wally's father, Carson, always said — politicians and babies have one thing in common: they both need to be changed regularly and for the same reason. Of course, Carson Boyd was *sarchotic* — so sarcastic that his targets weren't sure if he was joking or a whack job.

Blowing out an exasperated breath, Wally threw the remaining darts, then removed them from the board and flipped it back over. It wouldn't do for the mayor to come visit and see his own face, impaled by the sharp projectiles, staring back at him.

Checking that he had his portable radio and flashlight, Wally turned off the lights in his office, stepped into the hallway, and locked the door behind him. If he couldn't find anyone to cover the afternoon shift, he'd better get his ass out on patrol.

As he ran down the stairs, Wally grabbed his cell from his shirt pocket and dialed Skye to tell her he wouldn't be home until midnight. His wife wouldn't be happy, but he knew she wouldn't complain. She was employed by the department as a part-time psych consultant and understood the demands of the job.

When his call didn't go through and there were only clicks and pops, then a strange buzzing on the landline, he stopped his descent and tried Skye's cell. That number went to voicemail after the first ring.

Since Skye had gotten pregnant, she'd faithfully kept her phone turned on and charged up. Maybe she was in a dead zone.

Their house was full of mysterious spots where their cells didn't work.

Frowning, Wally left a message and headed toward the attached garage. A few steps from the exit, he turned and hurried to the front of the station instead. His mother-in-law, May Denison, was the afternoon dispatcher. She could keep trying to reach Skye while he was out on patrol.

When Wally walked into the dispatch area, he stopped to stare out of the rain-streaked window. His office was windowless and he was momentarily stunned by the intensity of the howling wind and flashing lightning. He'd been following the weather alerts for the past couple of hours, but clearly the storm was growing worse than had been predicted.

May pointed outside and said, "It's getting really bad." Her forehead wrinkled. "A lot of phones are out and cells aren't working too well either."

At sixty-three, his mother-in-law had the energy of a twenty-five-year-old. She kept her house immaculate, exercised at a nearby community's fitness center three times a week, and worked the afternoon shift at the PD as a police, fire, and emergency dispatcher. As far as Wally could see, May's only flaw was her over-involvement in her children's lives.

Skye was thirty-six and her brother, Vince, was forty. Neither needed nor wanted the intense nurturing their mother was determined to provide, which made Wally asking May to check up on Skye a little awkward. His wife wouldn't be happy that he was siccing her mom on her. But for the past several days, Wally had had an uneasy sensation about Skye's pregnancy, and he didn't like the idea of her being alone for the next eight hours.

"The alerts didn't make it seem as serious as it looks."

"Did you find someone to cover for Paul?" May asked. "I hope he's okay."

"A hot appendix is nothing to mess around with and I'm glad he went to the ER, but I sure wish he would've called me when he first felt sick, rather than waiting until the last minute." Wally scowled. "And no, I wasn't able to get anyone to work for him."

"So you're staying until Zelda comes on at midnight?" May asked.

"No choice." Wally shoved his hands in his back pockets. "But I don't like the idea of Skye being by herself. Do you think her dad or Charlie would run over and stay with her until I get home?"

Charlie Patukas was Skye's godfather. He'd never married or had any children of his own, and he had been like a father to May, whose real dad had died when she was young. He owned the Up A Lazy River Motor Court, but was knee-deep in most of what went on in Scumble River.

Wally pursed his lips. Maybe Charlie could be talked into running for mayor. It sure wouldn't hurt to ask. If anyone could win as a write-in candidate, Charlie was that person.

"Why are you worried?" May's frantic voice yanked Wally from his musing. "Is something wrong with her or the baby?" She clutched her chest. "What is she hiding from me?"

"Nothing," Wally assured his mother-in-law. "It's just she's only a few weeks from delivery, and she's gotten so big it's hard for her to move."

"She can barely fit behind the wheel of her car." May's mouth flattened. "That old Bel Air isn't going to work when she has a baby to haul around. I wish she would have let you buy her that SUV."

Wally fully intended for Skye to have a safer vehicle, whether she wanted one or not. In fact, he'd ordered her a Mercedes G-class. It was being delivered to their house this Friday and he couldn't wait to see her face. The SUV was an extravagant car, but his wife and child deserved the best.

Unwilling to ruin the surprise, Wally mumbled something noncommittal to May and repeated, "So, do you think either her dad or Charlie would be free?"

"Jed won't answer the phone, so let me try Charlie." May dialed, then said, "It's busy. Hopefully that means he's home and the telephone is working. I'll keep trying. And I'm sure when I reach him, he'll be happy to go visit his goddaughter."

"Great." Wally glanced out the window. "I need to hit the streets. Let me know if you aren't able to reach Charlie within the next half hour."

"Will do." May frowned. "I have a bad feeling. Maybe I'll call someone in to cover for me and go over to your place myself."

"Don't!" Wally realized he'd shouted and modulated his tone. "Skye's going to be mad enough that I sent Charlie to babysit her. If you take off work to do it, she'll be upset with both of us."

"Well . . ." May narrowed her eyes, their emerald green the same brilliant color she'd passed on to both her children. "Okay." She shook her finger at Wally. "But nothing better happen to my daughter or grandchild while I'm stuck here."

"If Charlie can't go over, I'll stop by and check on her." Wally's jaw clenched. "Worse comes to worse, I'll ask County to cover for me."

Wally started to leave but halted when the phone rang. May answered it, then held up a finger, indicating he should wait. She listened for a few more seconds, then frowned and tried to speak.

Finally, May put her hand over the receiver, looked at Wally, and said, "Myra Gulch called a few minutes ago. Seems her neighbors were playing their music too loud and she wanted the police to make them stop. She's just called back and is threatening to shoot them."

"What's her address?"

"1900 Kansas Street," May read from the computer monitor.

"Call County for backup!" Wally shouted as he ran toward the police station garage.

Once he was in his squad car, he raced toward the crazy woman's address, thankful that the rain had momentarily stopped. Arriving a few minutes later, he leaped out of the cruiser, unsnapped his holster, and hurried up the sidewalk.

When he knocked on the screen door, it crashed open, clipping him on the side of the head. A woman stood just inside with her hands on her hips, glaring at him.

Without apologizing, she snapped, "I thought the idiot dispatcher said that nobody was available."

"Myra Gulch?"

"Of course." Myra was a plain woman in her late seventies. She wore her gray hair scraped back into a bun and her dark eyebrows formed a disapproving line across her forehead. "I knew threatening to shoot my horrible neighbors would get your attention."

"I'll need you to hand over your gun, ma'am." Wally kept his fingers on the butt of his weapon.

"I don't have a gun, you moron," she sneered. "I just said that to get your attention."

"Threatening to shoot someone is a serious offense." Wally kept his voice even.

"And driving me crazy isn't?" Myra huffed. "If it's not that stupid dog barking, it's that awful classical crap. Just listen."

"I don't hear anything," Wally said.

"Are you deaf?" Myra pulled her white cardigan closed. "The thumping is awful."

"You can hear it right now?" Wally asked. The only sound he could make out was the howling of the wind and the water dripping from the house's eaves. "You know sometimes, if you're having a panic attack, your heartbeat can thud like a bass line pounding."

"I'm not mentally ill." Myra's large nose twitched in disapproval. "Go make that noise stop."

"Ma'am." Wally's patience was wearing thin. "There is no music."

"You lazy, good-for-nothing —"

"Your crazy is starting to show," Wally said, keeping his voice calm. "You might want to tuck it back in."

"I'll have your job!" Myra ranted. "The mayor is a personal friend of mine."

"Glad to hear it." Wally shrugged. Sometimes you had to burn a few bridges to keep the lunatics away from you, and he was fine with that. "He can post your bail if you do shoot someone."

He turned to leave, and when something hit his shoulder, he looked back and saw the witch had thrown a book at him. He picked it up and gently tossed it inside the open door.

Shaking his head, Wally stared at Myra and said, "Just be aware that falsely reporting a crime wastes the police's time, and you could be prosecuted."

"You'll be sorry you treated me this way,"

she screamed. "I'm going to talk to the mayor about your cavalier attitude."

"Join the crowd," Wally muttered, getting into his squad car. "Join the crowd."

After canceling the county call for backup, Wally began his patrol of the town's streets. When the rain started up again, the windshield wipers nearly hypnotized him. His eyelids drooped and he powered down the window, hoping the air and droplets blowing in his face would keep him awake.

He was tired and hungry. Maybe after the next loop around downtown, he'd go through the McDonald's drive-through and get something to eat. Or, better yet, he could stop at his own house for dinner.

The roads were quiet. Folks must have decided to stay home because of the weather. Even the bars along the main drag were empty. Everyone must have been hunkered down waiting for the storm to pass.

Having made the decision to take his meal break at home, Wally steered the cruiser out of the business district. He crossed over the river and made a left. Now that he was on the edge of town, there were no streetlights, and he could see only a few feet ahead on the narrow asphalt.

A right turn on Brooks Road and Wally

was less than a mile from his house. He had just reached for the radio, intending to tell May he would be out of service for the next thirty minutes, when he spotted a Chevy Silverado parked on the shoulder.

The pickup didn't have on its emergency lights, and the rear end was sticking out onto the blacktop. If the driver couldn't be located, Wally would have to call and have the truck towed.

Sighing, Wally pulled the cruiser behind the Chevy and studied the scene. There didn't appear to be anyone in the Silverado, but he couldn't see fully into the cab from where he sat.

Keying the radio, Wally said, "I've got a vehicle stopped alongside Brooks Road near Rood. The plate is muddy and I can't see it from here. I'm getting out to take a closer look."

After May acknowledged his transmission, Wally exited the squad car, easing the door shut without a sound. He unsnapped his holster and rested his hand on his weapon.

Wind rustled the cornstalks in the fields on either side of the road. The rain held the scent of fresh earth and a trace of smoke. Where was that coming from? It was too hot for anyone to have their fireplace going, and the weather was too bad for a bonfire.

The moon was hidden by a huge bank of low-lying clouds and the night sky was completely dark. The cruiser's headlights illuminated the area immediately behind the pickup and Wally moved forward until he was a few steps from the Chevy's rear bumper.

He trained his flashlight's beam on the license plate, but it was still too obscured to read. As he reached out to wipe off the mud, his radio crackled to life and Wally straightened.

"10–75!" May screamed. "A twister just made an unexpected turn and is heading this way. It's less than five minutes out. I'm going into the basement. You need to find shelter."

"Is Charlie with Skye?" Wally asked. His heart thudded and fear formed a sour ball in his stomach.

The radio was silent and Wally heard the tornado siren blaring. His pulse pounded in his ears. What if Skye was asleep and didn't hear the alarm? Could he make it home?

He had to. There was no way he was leaving the welfare of his wife and child to anyone else.

Chapter 3

"Run for the cellar!"

— Aunt Em

Skye, Justin, and Frannie were just finishing their ice-cream sundaes when the alarm sounded. Skye froze, the last spoonful of caramel-topped vanilla goodness a millimeter from her lips. *Shoot!* Was that really the tornado siren? They should have had the radio on.

The three of them stared at one another for a nanosecond, then Skye blinked, jumped to her feet, and ordered, "Get into the basement and stay away from the windows."

Justin and Frannie stared at her.

"There." Skye pointed to a closed door between the trash can and the cat-food bowl. "Move your butts!"

As she rushed into the sunroom to grab Bingo, she yelled, "Don't wait for me. I'll be right behind you."

Even though it was a tight fit for a feline of his bulky proportions, the black cat had managed to wedge himself beneath the sofa. And with the law of cat inertia — a cat at rest will remain at rest — how in the world was she going to get him out from under there? With her ginormous baby bump, if she got down on her knees, she'd never get up.

Treats! He'd come out if he heard the rustle of the package. Of course, that was how he'd become the size of a small Saint Bernard.

Skye grabbed a bag of Temptations from the end-table drawer, perched on the edge of the chair next to the couch, and called, "Here, kitty, kitty."

Nothing. Why was it that neither teenagers nor cats came when you called them?

Fear clogging her throat, Skye shook a few treats into her hand and tried again. "Here, kitty, kitty."

A long moment later, Bingo's head emerged from under the couch. He narrowed his golden eyes and refused to budge. When Skye crinkled the package, he crept forward, but in order to escape the tight confines of his haven, the cat had to do a military crawl.

The black cat looked as if he were emerging from a foxhole and she swallowed a giggle. If Bingo thought she was laughing at him, he'd return to his hideout.

Finally, assured that she wasn't offering him anything remotely healthy, Bingo stepped closer. As soon as he dipped his head to nibble on a treat, Skye thrust out her right arm and grabbed him by the scruff of his neck. He yowled and tried to twist away, but she held the squirming cat's back flush to her chest with both hands, hoping to avoid his claws.

The tornado siren continued to shriek as she jogged, okay, waddled, across the hallway. Justin and Frannie were still in the kitchen, rather than going into the basement as she had instructed. Not that she was surprised. The pair had rarely followed her recommendations when she was their school psychologist; why would they do what she told them to now that she was only their friend?

"Forget the lecture." Justin snatched the wiggling feline from her arms and shoved him into a black canvas case. "We found Bingo's carrier in the broom closet, and we weren't leaving you up here alone."

"Come on." Frannie seized Skye's wrist and dragged her toward the basement. "The air feels funny and the sky's gotten all green."

"Wait." Skye dug in her heels. "We need the emergency radio."

It was sitting on the windowsill above the sink, and as she turned to get it, with Frannie still hanging on to her arm, the front door slammed.

They all looked toward the hallway.

"Skye, where are you?" Wally's anxious voice accompanied the sound of running footsteps. "Sugar, are you all right? Answer me!"

Wally's frantic shout jolted Skye out of her trance, and she called out, "We're in the kitchen."

When he raced into the room, Skye broke free from Frannie's grasp and threw herself into his arms.

"Basement!" Wally was breathing heavily as he herded Justin and Frannie down the steps, then half dragged, half carried Skye right after them.

"Under the pool table," Wally ordered, dropping to his knees and helping Skye down to hers. "Everyone move, move, move!"

Pushing Skye, Justin, and Frannie beneath the old pool table, he grabbed a laundry basket full of linens from the top of the washing machine and tossed it to them.

Joining the trio, Wally ordered, "Wrap yourselves in the towels and sheets. Use everything. Make sure your face and any exposed skin is covered."

"Protect Bingo's carrier, too," Skye called out, fearful for her pet.

Wally pulled Skye into his arms and quickly surrounded her stomach with towels, then draped sheets and blankets around them both.

Skye snuggled against her husband's chest, grateful for the miracle of his presence. As she took a moment to catch her breath, she said a prayer of thanks.

From her unique perspective — she didn't usually sit on the basement floor — she noticed that the concrete cinder blocks near the ground were stained and uneven. Maybe when she was home on maternity leave, she'd find someone to come in and renovate down here.

As it was now, they used the basement only for laundry and storage. The pool table had been there when Skye inherited the house, and although it was unusable in its present dilapidated condition, it had been too expensive to restore and too heavy to haul away. Tonight, she was glad she'd kept it. At least it provided them with another layer of protection.

Suddenly, it started to hail. The sound of frozen missiles hitting the basement windows was earsplittingly loud, and Skye's head began to throb.

Putting her lips to Wally's ear, she raised her voice and asked, "How did you get here so fast?"

"I was coming home for supper when your mom radioed me that a tornado was headed this way. I was less than a mile down the road." Wally smoothed a hand down Skye's hair and said, "Don't worry. Your mom went into the PD's basement right after she alerted me."

"We're definitely in the tornado's path?" Skye shuddered, cold sweat gluing her T-shirt to her back. What about all of her relatives and friends and students who were in danger? Had they taken cover?

Skye hoped that, like so many other times, this was a false alarm. In the past, when neighboring communities had tornadoes wreak havoc in their municipalities, Scumble River had always somehow managed to escape unscathed. Evidently, her hometown's luck had run out.

As the power went out and the basement was plunged into darkness, Wally tightened his arms around her and said, "Afraid we're in for it, darlin'."

Skye's scalp prickled. She turned her head toward her friends and screamed, "Are you two all right?"

She couldn't see Frannie and Justin, and she was barely able to hear their assurances over the noise of the hail and wind. Chills chased up and down Skye's spine. It felt as if the storm were sucking the electricity from the walls of the house and leaving something evil in its place. The hair on her arms and the back of her neck stood on end, her heart raced, and she cradled her stomach. Would her baby be okay?

As her ears popped, Skye flinched. Suddenly the wind and hail stopped. Then, just as she thought they'd been spared, the wind returned and she could feel the walls of the house vibrating.

Wally tucked her head into his chest and said, "I love you more than anything."

"Being married to you these past eight months has been the happiest time of my life." Skye pressed a kiss to his chest. "No matter what happens, I'm glad we're together for this."

Wally tightened his grip on her and braced them both. There was a deafening roar, followed by a thunderous rushing sound, and

Skye clutched her belly, praying for them all.

CHAPTER 4

"The house must have fallen on her. Whatever shall we do?"

— Dorothy

Skye's eyelids flew up and she wasn't sure whether she'd dozed off or fainted. She extended her hand in the darkness. Had it been a nightmare?

No. She wiggled her butt. It felt like she was sitting in a bathtub. She reached down. There was at least six inches of water beneath her.

It was all coming back to her. She was huddled under the old pool table in her basement with Frannie, Justin, and Wally. And she was pretty darn sure their house had been hit by a tornado.

The previously deafening roar was now silent and the only sound she heard was water dripping from the ceiling. With a final squeeze, Wally released her. At the loss of his warmth, a chill swept over her and her teeth chattered.

Suddenly, the beam of a flashlight illuminated the area and Skye blinked. Wally would have had the Maglite on his duty belt and it was clear he was using it to inspect the situation and formulate a plan. Reaching out, she grasped his leg and he immediately scooted in front of her.

"Are you and the baby okay, sugar?" Wally's voice was husky.

"I think so." Skye didn't mention the Braxton-Hicks contractions, which had started up again. They'd probably be gone in a few minutes. She was sure that once she got up and stretched, she'd feel better. "How about you?"

"Other than a wet rear end, I'm fine, sweetheart." Wally swept the flashlight beam over Justin and Frannie. "You two hurt?"

"Nope." Justin had his arm around Frannie, who was holding the cat carrier on her lap. "And despite his complaints, Bingo's okay, too."

As the cat's indignant meows rang in her ears, Skye blew out a relieved breath. She'd been afraid that, in the commotion, Justin might have forgotten about him. Although the water wasn't high enough for Bingo to drown, at his age, getting soaked might have the same result.

"Is it safe to get out?" Frannie asked, plucking at the damp material of her jean shorts.

"Whether it is or not, we need to leave." Wally helped Skye crawl out from beneath the table. "I'm afraid it's dangerous to stay here." He took both her hands and raised her to her feet. "This is an old house and I think it took a direct hit."

"Time to bounce." Justin nudged Frannie, and using the illumination Wally's flashlight provided, they joined Skye and Wally.

Frannie held the cat carrier against her chest and cooed to the fussing feline.

As the four of them trudged through ankle-deep water to get to the staircase, odds and ends that had accumulated for the past hundred years in the basement floated by them. When Skye had inherited the house, she'd never fully cleared out the attic or the cellar, and the debris hitting her legs was from another era.

She absently noted that a tattered Spiegel catalog, a veiled hat, and a plastic box full of McCall dress patterns were drifting through the dark water. How many vintage treasures were now destroyed?

"How bad do you think it is?" Skye asked Wally, hanging on to his arm.

"We'll soon see." Wally grabbed the door-knob and twisted, but nothing happened. He shoved at the unyielding wood with his shoulder and grimaced. Turning to Justin, he said, "It's stuck. Get up here with me and see if our combined strength will move it."

The two men managed to create a small opening, and as the skinniest of the four, Justin wiggled through it. Skye heard the sound of something dragging across the kitchen floor, and then the gap widened.

Wally passed Skye and Frannie through first, then joined them. As Skye stared upward, rain pelting her face, she clasped her husband's hand and gasped. Instead of the ceiling, clouds rolled over her head. The second and third floors were completely gone.

A weight pressed on Skye's chest and she couldn't catch her breath. The house she had inherited and painstakingly repaired had disappeared, as had the nursery that she and Wally had lovingly decorated and furnished. It was too much. Skye whimpered, hugged her stomach, and wept.

She knelt on the debris-strewn tile and sobbed. "It's gone. It's all gone."

"Everything will be all right, darlin'," Wally murmured into her ear as he gently drew Skye to her feet and wrapped his arms around her. "The four of us are fine, the baby's fine, Bingo's fine, and the rest can be replaced."

"But how about the town?" Skye's voice rose and she wiped at the tears running down her cheeks. "Our family? Our friends? Everyone?"

"The siren went off in time." Wally stroked her hair and kissed the top of her head. "With the stormy weather, people would have been listening to their radios and watching for alerts on TV. Around here, folks know to take cover."

Skye glanced at Frannie and Justin. Both looked dazed. She'd always been the strong, calm one in their young lives. They'd never seen her lose her cool before, and if she didn't pull herself together fast, her out-of-control emotions would become contagious.

Taking a deep breath, Skye gazed up at her wonderful husband and said, "You're right." She took the handkerchief he offered and wiped her face. "What do we do now?"

"At the moment, we need to get out of the house and find shelter." Wally twined her fingers with his. "There might be structural damage. This place is really old and we don't want to get trapped if the walls start to collapse."

He jerked his chin at Frannie and Justin, and the four of them hurried down the hall. As they neared the front door, Skye nabbed her purse from the hall table. She was slipping the strap over her shoulder when she stepped outside. The rain had stopped, but the night air was thick with moisture, and there wasn't even a hint of a breeze to relieve the mugginess.

"I've got to check on my parents," Justin said as Wally hustled the group down the sidewalk. "They don't have a basement."

"Thank goodness Dad's at the Vietnam Vet's rally in Springfield," Frannie said, awkwardly clutching Bingo's carrier to her chest. "But I need to see if our house was damaged."

"First things first." Wally urged Skye toward his squad car. He'd parked it behind Frannie's now-tree-crushed Ford and it was miraculously intact. Even better, the driveway between the cruiser and the road was clear.

Justin gazed at his cell phone. "There's still no signal."

Frannie juggled Bingo as she dug her cell from her pocket. "Mine either."

"Get into the squad car," Wally ordered the couple, helping Skye into the front passenger seat.

As Wally jogged around to the driver's side, Skye saw that most of their beautiful trees were toppled over and one had landed against the door of the garage, smashing the heavy double door onto both of their cars. They didn't really need two vehicles, since Wally almost always drove his cruiser between home and the station, but his Thunderbird convertible had been a fortieth birthday gift from his father, and Skye mourned the loss of the beautiful car.

About to inform Wally of the additional damage, she heard him say, "May, do you read me?"

Wally had the police radio mike in his hand and was trying to reach the PD. When there was silence, Skye's chest tightened and sweat trickled down her back. Had her mother made it into the basement? Was she okay?

A couple of long seconds later, Skye let out a relieved breath when a panicky voice demanded, "Are my daughter and grandbaby all right?"

Skye grabbed the mike and said, "The second and third floors of our house are gone, but we're all okay. Are you okay? How about Dad and Grandma Cora? Have you heard from Uncle Charlie? How about Vince and his family?"

"I'm fine," May answered. "Cora is with your uncle Wiley and his family, visiting relatives in California. No word from Charlie or Vince yet, but I see your father's truck pulling into the parking lot, so he must be okay." There was a pause, then May added, "Heck. Jed's got that darn dog with him. He can't bring that smelly beast in here."

May's aversion to animals was legendary. And her husband's affection for Chocolate, his Labrador retriever, was a constant source of irritation.

Wally took the mike back from Skye. "Was the station hit?"

"Not that I can see. I don't think the tornado came through this part of town."

"Do you have phones and electricity?"

"No phones," May reported, "but the generator came on, so we have power."

"Call in all the officers, including the part-timers," Wally said. "Do you have cell reception?"

"Let me find my purse and turn the dang thing on," May muttered. After a couple of minutes, she said, "I've got two little bars."

"Great." Wally gave Skye a thumbs-up. "Put the order out over the radio for all officers to report to the station, then start making calls. I'll be there as soon as I can."

"You know she won't have her charger

with her," Skye warned. "Maybe we should grab ours before we leave." She glanced at the wreckage of their house. "We could also get Bingo's food and litter box and —"

"I have a couple of extra chargers at the station. The rest we'll deal with later." Wally dug his cell phone from his pocket, tossed it to Skye, and asked, "Anything?"

"Nope. Mine either."

"Shit!" He started the engine, glanced into his rearview mirror at Frannie and Justin, and said, "If the streets are clear, I'll drop you two at your respective houses on the way to the station."

As Wally reversed onto the road and drove toward the station, the squad car's headlights revealed debris littering the asphalt. He had to maneuver the vehicle around downed limbs and power lines, dodging a refrigerator that looked as if it had been placed upright in the dead center of the road. When they were a few miles from town, Wally's officers started checking in on the radio.

"It sounds as if Mom was able to get ahold of everyone," Skye said with a smile. "Or they came in on their own. They'd do anything for you and Scumble River."

One of the best parts of small-town life was the strong bonds that formed among the residents. They were especially evident during tough situations when the stress of the circumstances put a lot of strain on these ties, yet time after time, the citizens came through for one another.

"They are a loyal bunch," Wally agreed, never taking his eyes from the road.

She frowned. "Wait, I don't hear Paul."

"He's the one whose shift I was covering," Wally explained. "Tolman had to have an emergency appendectomy over in Laurel Hospital."

After dropping Justin at his house and Frannie at hers, both thankfully undamaged, Wally headed to the station. Frannie had volunteered to keep Bingo until Skye and Wally found a place to stay and Skye had gratefully accepted. The elderly feline would not enjoy being confined at the PD.

Noticing for the first time that the streetlights were working, Skye gestured to them and asked, "If the power's out all over town, why are those still on?"

"When the grid's off, they use the solar cell backups," Wally explained.

Skye nodded, then said, "From what your officers are reporting, it sounds as if most of the worst damage is north of town by our house and east where my parents, Vince and Loretta, and Trixie and Owen live. I hope they're okay."

Trixie Frayne was Skye's best friend and the high school librarian. She and her husband, Owen, lived in an old house nestled among the acreage he farmed.

"I'm sure May will have found a way to check on your brother and his family by now." Wally pulled the cruiser into the station's garage, retrieved a duffel from the trunk, then came around to help Skye out of the car. "And Trixie and Owen will have taken cover as soon as the sirens sounded."

Wally and Skye walked to the door connecting the garage to the station, and when he opened it for her, the cacophony of voices nearly pushed her back out. The parking lot hadn't been that crowded. Where had everyone come from?

Resting his palm on the middle of Skye's back, Wally gently nudged her inside. They made their way down a short hallway that led to the interrogation/coffee room. Opposite the break room were several workstations, all occupied by people talking on the telephones.

"Looks like Mom called in the dispatchers as well as the officers," Skye said. "And it's a good thing, since the landlines seem to be back in service."

"Thank God!" Wally dug in his duffel,

handing Skye a pair of his sweatpants. "I've got an extra uniform upstairs, so you can use these." Once she nodded, he continued. "Sugar, after you get out of those wet shorts, call my dad and tell him we're okay."

"Of course." Skye thrust her purse into the open duffel bag and said, "I don't want to lose this, so take it upstairs with you."

"You got it." He kissed Skye's cheek, and as he sprinted toward the steps, he yelled, "I'll be in my office. I need to get ahold of the ILEAS and put a plan into place."

"What's the ILEAS?" Skye asked his retreating back.

"The Illinois Enforcement Alarm System," one of the dispatchers translated. "Nearly seventy agencies are involved. In a disaster situation, it provides a mobile field force for additional law enforcement services."

"Oh. Good. We'll need them." Skye nodded her thanks to the woman, then retreated to the restroom to change into the sweatpants Wally had given her. After using the facilities, because of course she had to pee, Skye went to find her mother. As she neared the front of the station, the noise level increased and she wished she had earplugs.

Once she stepped out of the back hallway, she had her choice of two doors. The one leading out to the lobby was closed, but a chorus of frantic voices was still clearly discernible. People were demanding information and assistance, neither of which were likely available right at the moment.

The second door was partially open and Skye could see Thea, the daytime dispatcher, sitting at the desk with a phone to her ear as she frantically typed on the computer keyboard. May was standing at the counter, attempting to soothe an extremely agitated middle-aged woman.

Skye stepped into the room, walked up to her mother, and hugged her. May ran an expert eye over Skye, held up a finger, then turned back to the petite woman who had begun knocking on the bullet-resistant acrylic barrier separating the lobby from the dispatch area.

"Ma'am," May said, speaking through the small hole cut into the partition, "Scumble River was hit by three separate tornadoes. Presently, we are assessing damage and securing the streets. Once we have more available personnel, we'll begin searching homes for survivors."

"If you can't send someone, let me go look for my husband. He has a heart condition." The attractive woman gripped the edge of the counter. "The officers forced me to leave. Just make them let me go back to hunt for him."

"I'm sorry, ma'am." May shook her head. "The worst-hit neighborhoods are all being evacuated and no one will be permitted to return until the structures are deemed safe."

"Safe by whom?" The slender woman's voice rose. "My husband is Zeke Lyons, a member of the city council. Surely, locating him is a top priority."

"No, ma'am." May's cheeks reddened. "It is not. No one is more important than anyone else. I haven't been able to reach my own son!"

Skye put her arm around her mother's shoulders as they began to shake. May turned and pressed her face in her daughter's chest. She gripped Skye's waist and sobbed.

For a second, Mrs. Lyons seemed shocked, then an older woman who had been standing silently at her side said, "If this ninny won't help you, we'll talk to the mayor. I've told you never to deal with peons."

May whirled toward the counter, her eyes narrowed.

Skye quickly clapped her hand over her mother's mouth and whispered, "Watch that quick temper of yours."

"I do not have a quick temper," May

snapped after removing Skye's palm. "What I do have is a quick response to idiots." Her shoulders suddenly drooped and she cried, "Why is God doing this to us?"

"I'm pretty certain if the tornado is God's punishment, he has a badly researched sinners list." Skye moved her mother out of the dispatchers' office and said, "I'm sure Vince, Loretta, and the baby are okay. They have a safe room and would have heard the sirens."

"I know." May hiccupped. "Your dad tried to get to them before he came here, but the road was blocked by an overturned combine." She straightened and shook her head. "Who in their right mind would be harvesting in the middle of a storm?"

"It was probably sitting in the field and got blown onto the road." Skye patted her mother's back. "Is Dad here?"

"No." May reached into the pocket of her uniform shirt, took out a tissue, and wiped her eyes. "Once he heard you and Wally and the baby were okay, he went home to get the John Deere. He said if he had to, he'd go through the fields to get to Vince's."

Skye smiled at her father's ingenuity. Jed might not say much, but his mind kept working until he had a solution to the problem.

"Did you guys have any damage?" Skye asked. "From what I heard on the radio, your road was right on the path of the tornado."

"We lost some trees and the back door was blown out, which ruined the utility room, but the garage is completely gone." May shut her eyes. "Thank goodness your dad's truck was in the driveway and my car was here in the parking lot. Since they don't make them anymore, I'd never be able to replace my Oldsmobile. It's less than ten years old and only has twenty-five thousand miles on it."

"It's one of a kind, all right," Skye agreed with a grin.

May cupped Skye's cheek. "Is your house fixable?"

"I doubt it." Skye blew out a breath. "All that's left is the first floor and Wally says it's likely the walls will collapse."

"I'd say you could stay with us, but with no power to run the pump for the well, we don't have water." May smoothed her hair. "But I talked to Charlie and the motor court wasn't hit, so he's saving you and Wally a room."

"Does he have power?" Skye asked.

"He's got a big generator that can handle the whole motel." May's expression was sheepish. "I guess I should have let your dad buy one after that last outage."

Skye hid her smile. May had been all for the generator until she'd found out the electrician would have to run conduit on the wall next to her back door. At the thought of the ugly pipe marring her beautiful redbrick exterior, she'd put the kibosh on the idea.

Wisely refraining from reminding her mother of that fact, Skye instead asked, "Have you heard anything about Trixie and Owen?"

"Not yet." May stepped back in the office and glanced at the hoard of people lined up at the counter. "I better get back to work."

"I need to call Wally's father and try to get ahold of Trixie," Skye said, looking around. "Are there any free phones?"

May tapped her chin. "There's a second outlet in Wally's office." She jerked her thumb downward. "You could grab one of the old rotaries from the basement and plug it in upstairs."

"Great idea." Skye kissed her mother. "Let me know as soon as you find out about Vince and Loretta or if you hear anything about Trixie and Owen or anyone else."

"I sure will, honey." May hugged Skye. "Love you."

"You too, Mom." Skye took a deep breath. "Wally and I were sure lucky today."

"Yeah." May frowned. "I wonder how many folks weren't as fortunate."

CHAPTER 5

"There, now you have a heart that any man might be proud of."

— The Wizard

Wally placed the handset back in the base, thankful for his private line. He'd contacted ILEAS and help would be arriving soon. The supplemental law enforcement personnel would take care of perimeter security, traffic control into town, and enforce the curfew that, once the disaster had been declared, would automatically go into effect.

ILEAS assistance would allow Scumble River's officer on duty to respond to regular 911 calls, as well as continue routine patrols. The remaining officers would be organized to help with search and rescue.

Wally unfolded a map of the town and picked up a yellow highlighter. From the accounts he'd received, three separate twisters, each up to three-quarters of a mile wide, had cut through Scumble River. Reports stated that twelve tornadoes had come from the same super cell and most of central and southern Illinois had in some way been involved. A few areas had been spared from tornadic activity, but the high winds and torrential rains still caused enormous problems for those populations.

According to preliminary estimates, 25 percent of Scumble River had sustained extensive destruction and another 30 percent had less severe damage. First responders were guessing that as many as fourteen hundred or more properties might be affected.

Wally had been in touch with the fire chief and the firefighters would partner with the police to conduct immediate search and rescue operations. It was highly likely a good number of folks were trapped in the wreckage, and they needed to be found sooner rather than later.

Wally was deeply absorbed in plotting out the search grid when a light tap on his partly opened door caught his attention. Before he could respond, Skye walked into the room, carrying an old rotary phone.

Actually, at thirty-four weeks pregnant, walk wasn't exactly the right word for her movement, but he didn't even dare to think *waddle* or she would go ballistic. No matter how hard he tried, he couldn't convince Skye that to him she would always be the most beautiful woman in the world. Having experienced ridicule for her curvier than acceptable figure as a young woman, she was having trouble dealing with the added baby weight.

He'd been attracted to Skye since she was sixteen, but at the time, he'd been twenty-four, too old to do anything about his feelings. Then when she'd turned eighteen, she'd moved away and hadn't come back for nearly twelve years.

He'd never forgotten the sweet, smart teenager who had enchanted him, but he'd tucked her memory away and settled for someone else. That had been a huge mistake, trapping him in an unhappy marriage. Darlene had been a fragile woman he had never truly loved but couldn't, in good conscience, divorce.

When she had run away with another man, he'd nearly danced for joy. He'd finally been free to pursue the woman he'd always wanted.

However, although he was no longer married, Skye had been dating the town funeral director and local coroner, Simon Reid. But soon afterward, Reid screwed up. When Skye dumped him, Wally quickly made his move. It had taken him a while to convince her that he was the right man for her, but they'd been married for eight months now and it had been the happiest time of his life.

When Skye had told Wally she was pregnant, his heart had nearly burst with joy. He'd never thought he'd be a father — Darlene had blamed him for her infertility — and to have Skye and their baby was all he'd ever wanted.

Shaking off his musings, Wally hurried to his feet, rushed to Skye's side, and asked, "Everything all right, sugar?"

"Uh-huh." Skye kissed his cheek as he escorted her to a chair and held her arm while she sat down. "It's a madhouse down there, so I thought I'd come up here to make some calls." Holding up the old-fashioned phone, she said, "Mom told me you had an extra telephone line in your office."

"She's right. I almost forgot about that. The new system didn't need it, but the outlet is still there. I wonder if it works." Wally plugged the cord in and picked up the receiver. "Yep. You're good to go."

"Awesome."

Skye's emerald-green eyes sparkled and

Wally leaned over to tuck a chestnut curl behind her ear. He pressed his lips to her soft, pink ones and sighed in satisfaction. Even in a disaster, she made him feel content.

"I need to complete the grid assignments so I can get the search and rescue started," Wally explained as he reluctantly straightened and resumed his seat.

"Will my talking on the phone bother you?" Skye asked. "I could go somewhere and try my cell."

"You stay put, sweetie," Wally assured her. "I like being able to keep an eye on you."

As Wally continued working on the grid, he half listened to Skye. Her first call was to his father, and hearing her part of the conversation, Wally's mouth twitched upward. Even before their wedding, Carson had fallen hard for Skye and asked her to call him Dad.

With the exception of Skye, no one in Scumble River knew that Wally's father, Carson Boyd, was a Texas oil millionaire. Wally kept quiet about his wealthy background because he didn't want people to see him as a rich man's son. He wanted to be judged on his own merits.

Although Carson had always wanted Wally to take over the family empire, Wally had no interest in running CB International. For many years, this decision had caused considerable tension between himself and his father, but from the very beginning, Skye had charmed Carson and made him understand his son's point of view. Then when she'd become pregnant, the tough tycoon had become putty in her hands.

"Hi, Dad." Skye's greeting was perky. "You may have heard that this evening, Illinois was hit by some pretty bad tornadoes. Scumble River was one of the communities on the twister's path, but so far there have been no fatalities or critical injuries reported." She explained their situation, listened, then said, "Tonight we'll be staying at Uncle Charlie's motel. After that, I guess we'll have to look for a house to rent until we can rebuild. It's too bad Wally sold his bungalow last month or we could live there."

At Skye's long silence, Wally glanced up from the map he'd been studying.

When he raised his eyebrows at her, she covered the receiver and said, "Your dad wants to send us a huge motor coach to live in."

"What!"

"He says we can park it near our house and it will be here by tomorrow night. He'll arrange to buy it from a Chicagoland dealer and fly in a driver who will set it up for us." She wrinkled her nose. "I always forget how rich he is. I know you don't like taking too many gifts from him. Should I say no?"

Wally rubbed the back of his neck. He hated to accept, but he suspected there weren't going to be many rental places available anywhere near Scumble River. And it didn't seem right to take an apartment or house from someone else when they had another option.

"Go ahead and tell him we'll take it, sugar." Wally saw the relieved look in his wife's eyes. "I'm sure the RV will be more comfortable than a lot of our other choices, and I don't want you any more stressed than you already are."

While Skye concluded her conversation with his dad, Wally radioed his officers with their assignments, then contacted Fire Chief Eaton to coordinate their efforts. The plan was to pair a cop with a firefighter or paramedic. As Skye had told Carson, so far, no serious casualties had been reported, but he suspected, in the long run, their luck wouldn't hold out.

"Oh my gosh, Trixie. I'm so glad to hear your voice." Skye's cry of relief interrupted his thoughts. "Are you and Owen okay?"

Skye listened, then beamed and gave Wally

a thumbs-up.

"How about your house?" She frowned and asked, "Can it be fixed?" She glanced at Wally and mouthed, "A good part of their roof was torn off."

He grimaced.

"Owen thinks it can be repaired and he's already tarping it?" Skye repeated, clearly for Wally's benefit. "That's great. It looks as if we'll be building from the foundation up." She listened, then asked, "Do you have a place to stay?"

Wally watched his wife's expression as she listened to her friend.

After a second, she instructed, "Call Charlie immediately. Mom said out of his twelve cabins, only two are presently occupied and those folks are from out of town. He's going to ask them to check out tomorrow so he has room for people displaced by the tornado. Get ahold of him and nab one of the vacant ones now."

Once she disconnected, Skye looked at Wally and said, "Is there anyone else I should call?"

Wally scratched his chin and considered his wife's lengthy family list. "Vince and Loretta?"

Skye paled and blinked back tears. Cursing himself, Wally shot to his feet and hurried around the desk.

"Dad's trying to get to them," Skye explained. "They aren't answering their cells and the road is blocked." She sniffed. "Mom is supposed to let me know as soon as Dad comes back with any news."

Drawing Skye out of her chair, Wally wrapped his arms around her and rested his chin on the top of her head. "They'll be okay. Loretta will have made Vince get in their safe room."

"Yeah." Skye gave him a watery smile. "No guy will mess with a frantic pregnant woman." She arched her brow at Wally. "Right?"

"Absolutely," Wally murmured into her ear, then kissed down her neck.

Suddenly, the office door slammed open and someone shouted, "We don't pay you to make out with your wife!"

Skye jumped back. Wally looked at the man lumbering over the threshold and growled. Just what they needed, Mayor Leofanti on the warpath.

"Uncle Dante, glad to see you're okay," Skye said, then added, "And thank you for asking, even though our house was completely destroyed, we're fine, too."

"Yeah. Good." The mayor tugged his green T-shirt down over his protruding stomach and pulled up his matching sweatpants.

Wally was struck by how much Dante resembled a pear. A malevolent pear, but a pear none the less. His small head, narrow shoulders, and concave chest expanded to a bulging stomach and rounded hips that seemed more suited for childbearing than any other occupation.

"Is Aunt Olive okay?" Skye asked. "Have you heard from Aunt Minnie and the cousins?"

"Everyone has checked in and is just dandy. Can we move on to town business now?" Dante sneered at Skye, then marched up to Wally and poked him with his index finger. "You need to get your ass over to Zeke Lyons's house and find the city councilman. His wife and mother-in-law just ripped me a new one because no one is looking for him."

"Where does he live?" Wally asked, grabbing the mayor's finger and shoving it away from his chest.

"Kansas Street."

Wally glanced at the map on his desk. "Martinez has that neighborhood. I'll radio her to keep an eye out for him."

"Hell no!" Dante squawked. "You do it right now. Those damn women are camped in my office and I want them gone."

"How did the councilman and his family get separated?" Wally asked.

"Lyons doesn't have a basement, and although the folks across the road offered shelter, the moron wouldn't leave his dog. The neighbor's kid is asthmatic and highly allergic, so the pooch wasn't welcome. The idiot sent his missus to take cover but stayed with the hound."

"Pets are important, too, Uncle Dante." Skye glared at him.

Ignoring his niece, the mayor continued. "Your cops made his wife get out of the neighborhood before she could find Lyons." The mayor narrowed his beady, black eyes. "Did you tell your officers to do that?"

"Standard procedure in a situation where structures may not be safe and when there's the possibility of looters." Wally lifted his chin and stared at the mayor. "Allowing people to remain in a dangerous situation is a lawsuit waiting to happen."

"Right. Which is why I'm going to have Scumble River declared a disaster area." Dante grabbed Wally's arm. "Now move your butt and go find the missing councilman." When Wally didn't budge, he said, "If you ever want another budget approved, you'll take care of this for me right now."

Wally hesitated. Refusing Dante just because the man pissed him off was stupid. He needed to get out and do some recon anyway, and it wasn't as if he had anything urgent he had to do at the police station. He might as well try for some mayoral brownie points.

After grabbing an extra flashlight and handheld radio from his bottom drawer, he hugged Skye and said, "If you need me for anything, have your mother radio me."

"Will do." She gave him a soft kiss. "You be careful. Baby Boyd needs his or her daddy."

"Not a chance in hell I'm missing that." Wally glanced at the mayor and said, "Are you coming with me?"

"No!" Dante backpedaled toward the door. "I have to stay here to direct operations."

"What's the house number?"

"1902." Dante gripped the knob. "As soon as you find Lyons, let me know so I can get his entourage out of my hair."

"Sure." Wally kissed his wife goodbye and headed toward the garage.

Sliding behind the wheel of his squad car, he turned on the engine and threw it into reverse. A few minutes later, he turned into Zeke Lyons's street and shook his head.

Every single house was severely damaged and there wasn't a tree left intact in any of the yards. Several homes were completely gone, with only the foundations remaining. Others were collapsed or missing walls or roofs.

Debris filled the lawns and the road, and power lines stretched across all the driveways. Spotting a parked Commonwealth Edison truck, Wally pulled over, exited the squad car, and walked over to the man gathering equipment from the back of his vehicle.

When the workman looked up, Wally said, "I'm Chief Boyd. What's the status?"

"Seventy-five percent of the town is without power." The guy shrugged. "It's only been three hours since the tornadoes hit, so right now, our priority is making sure the downed lines are safe. I told your officer that she and the firefighter couldn't cross them until I was finished with my inspection."

"Good to know." Wally thanked the man and left him to his work.

Fortunately, once again, the streetlights were still functioning. Wally left his car where he'd parked it and made his way down the road, studying the situation as he maneuvered around the rubble. There was no sign of Martinez or the firefighter, but he spotted several houses on the left side of the street with red *X*s spray-painted on their doors or siding, indicating that residence had been checked. Martinez and her partner must be circling around and accessing the buildings through the backyards.

Zeke Lyons's place was several blocks down and on the opposite side of the road. Wally knew he should call for backup, but he hated to interrupt Martinez and the firefighter. They'd have to get out of whatever residence they were currently clearing and make their way to his location.

No. He wouldn't bother them. There wasn't enough manpower to waste it. He'd be careful and stop if it was too risky.

Retracing his steps, Wally followed his officer's method of avoiding the downed electrical lines and approached the councilman's house from the rear. The front of the structure hadn't looked too bad, but the back of the building was demolished. If Lyons was inside, he very well could be trapped in the wreckage.

Edging around an overturned fishing boat, a couch missing its cushions, and a washing machine lying on its side, Wally made it to what looked to have been the family room. An empty bracket for a flat-screen television was attached to the only remaining wall and a lounge chair was positioned facing it.

Cupping his hands around his mouth, Wally yelled, "Zeke, are you here?"

Nothing.

Wally stepped over an upended coffee table, moved farther into the room, and tried again. "Zeke, it's Chief Boyd. I came to help you."

The same silence that greeted his first shout accompanied his second.

It looked as if, before its demolition, the rear of the house had contained a family room and two small bedrooms. Wally continued to call out the councilman's name as he checked under every piece of furniture and in all the standing closets.

There was no sign of Lyons. Wally moved on to the fairly intact front of the residence, which held the kitchen and master bedroom. Maybe the councilman had taken shelter in one of those places.

Wally could see what remained of a hallway, and pushing debris out of his path, he made his way down the corridor. The carpet squished under his shoes as he walked and he realized that even possessions spared by the tornado would have severe water damage. Peering into the kitchen, he saw the windows were blown out, but otherwise, the room appeared untouched.

If Lyons was in the master suite, there was a decent chance the guy was okay. He wasn't in the bedroom or the closet, but as Wally approached the attached bath, he heard a noise.

"Are you there, Zeke?" Wally tried the bathroom door. It was ajar, but the gap was too small for him to get through. "It's Wally Boyd. Can you hear me?"

This time, Wally was able to identify the sound as an animal's whimper.

Hell! He should have asked Dante the dog's name.

Putting his shoulder to the wood, he shoved until the opening was large enough for him to squeeze through. Facing him was a toilet, tub, and separate shower stall. To his left, there was a countertop containing a double sink.

The partially opened door concealed the right side of the room and the animal's whine was coming from that area. Unable to move the door any farther, Wally walked around it and stopped when a German shepherd raised its head, peeled back its lips, and growled.

The dog was lying next to what Wally assumed was the barefooted body of Zeke Lyons. He was wedged facedown against the door. And if Wally were a betting man, he'd wager the guy wasn't ever getting up again.

CHAPTER 6

> Jumping down, he watched it until the long legs stopped wiggling, when he knew it was quite dead.
>
> — Cowardly Lion

Skye yawned, stretched, and tried to find a comfortable sitting position on the narrow office chair. Wally had left the police station two hours ago to go look for Zeke Lyons and she hadn't heard from him since. She'd give him another fifteen minutes, then she was going to have her mother radio Wally for a status update.

To start the countdown, she checked the time on her newly charged cell phone. Thank goodness the station had a generator and Wally had a couple of spare chargers in his desk drawer. Skye's watch, along with her clothes and almost every other thing she owned, was gone with the same whirlwind that had destroyed her home.

Yikes! With the house in ruins, what would happen to Mrs. Griggs? When Skye had first inherited the place from the elderly lady, she hadn't realized that, along with a leaky roof and rusty pipes, the building came with a resident ghost.

She'd discovered that the previous owner, Alma Griggs, had never really left. Mrs. Griggs's spirit hadn't begun making an appearance until after Skye and Wally began dating. Then, whenever they attempted any kind of intimacy beyond an innocent kiss, the apparition would make her presence known in as destructive a manner as possible — fire and explosions were among the ghost's favorite diversions.

Having spent a small fortune on remodeling, and with the home improvement loan to show for it, Skye had been determined to live there once she and Wally were married. She, along with her BFF Trixie, had even attempted to purge the house of the mischievous spirit.

However, the ritual Skye had found on the internet hadn't worked, and instead of leaving, Mrs. Griggs had pushed the television off its stand, smashing it to smithereens. After the ghost's little temper tantrum, Skye had been afraid to try another cleansing.

Happily, once Skye and Wally were husband and wife, the apparition quit destroying things. She occasionally still made an appearance. But now, instead of causing problems, she left little gifts. On their wedding night, she'd scattered rose petals around their bedroom, then when Skye got pregnant, the occasional vintage baby toy began to show up in the antique crib they'd brought down from the attic and put in the new nursery.

Now that her home was destroyed, would Mrs. Griggs finally go toward the white light? Or would she stick around the wreckage, waiting for Skye to rebuild?

Having no ready answer regarding the ghost's continued existence, Skye turned her thoughts to the chaos downstairs in the PD. She'd offered her help, but assuring her that all the phones were manned and the counter covered, May had sent her back to Wally's office to rest.

With her offer of assistance declined, Skye had used her time waiting for Wally's return making a list of priorities for the next day. Contacting their insurance company, shopping for clothes, and borrowing a car were her top concerns. However, figuring out what to do about her intern was a strong number four.

The poor thing certainly hadn't signed on for this kind of training. But now Piper was stuck with it. Skye sure hoped the woman had had a good crisis intervention course.

Although none of the three school buildings were in the path of the tornado, Skye had heard that their roofs had sustained damage from the high winds and many of their windows had been broken by the hail. Rumor had it that the superintendent had canceled classes until the extent of the destruction was determined. One of the school psychologists employed by the special education cooperative would have to agree to take charge of Piper until things in Scumble River were sorted out, because Skye certainly couldn't do anything with her.

Glancing at the time, Skye was surprised that only ten minutes had gone by. She had five more to kill until she would allow herself to ask May to check on Wally.

Squirming, Skye tried to find a position that didn't aggravate her backache. The cheap office chair was an odd height that made her thighs ache and had a barely padded seat and metal arms that dug into her sides. Thankfully, the Braxton-Hicks contractions had stopped. Now if she just didn't have to run down the stairs to the restroom every half hour, she'd be in good shape.

Skye shook her head and reminded herself to be grateful that she, her family, and her friends were alive. So far, there hadn't been any fatalities in Scumble River from the tornado and the injuries had been relatively light. Mostly only superficial cuts, scrapes, bruises, and a few broken bones.

Another reason for thankfulness was that when her father had made it to Vince's, her brother, pregnant sister-in-law, and niece had been fine. Their road was still blocked with the overturned combine on one end and a live power line across the other, but their new house had weathered the storm with only minor damage. Their roof was missing some shingles, and like almost everyone else, they didn't have electricity. However, their generator had kicked in, leaving Vince, Loretta, and their daughter, April, in comfort and none the worse for wear.

If it wasn't for their home's current inaccessibility, Skye and Wally could stay with them. With five bedrooms and bathrooms, they had plenty of room.

On the other hand, Skye was glad Carson was sending the motor home, because sharing a house, even with people you loved, could get awkward fast. And between taking care of a toddler and Loretta's difficult pregnancy, Vince's family had enough on their plates.

Speaking of families, where was Wally? Why was it taking him so long to check out one residence? He'd warned Skye about the dangers of a structure hit by a tornado. What if a wall had collapsed on him? Considering the current state of confusion in Scumble River, how long would it take for anyone to notice he was missing?

Using the arms of the chair, Skye managed to hoist herself to her feet. She was tired of waiting patiently. Her hormones were screaming that it was past time to have her mother radio Wally for a wellness check.

Before Skye reached the office door, the knob turned and May stepped over the threshold. Her usually immaculate hair was standing on end, her typically crisply pressed uniform was wrinkled, and her face was pale. Whatever lipstick she had applied earlier was long gone and the only hint of its color was smudged in the wrinkles around May's mouth.

Skye's chest tightened at her mother's serious expression and she demanded, "What's wrong? Why do you look like that? Did something happen to Wally?"

May shook her head tiredly. "No. I promise you he's fine. He just asked me to get you to the motor court."

"Why can't I wait for him?" Skye asked, narrowing her eyes suspiciously.

"Wally can't leave until the coroner comes for the body," May explained. "And Simon is having trouble getting back from Laurel. He and Emmy were eating at Little Mario's when the storm struck and now all the usual routes are flooded or blocked with debris."

At the mention of Simon's name, she wondered if his mother, Bunny, who managed the bowling alley he also owned, had made it through the storm okay. Skye was fond of the feisty redhead and sorry that she rarely saw her anymore. She needed to make a point to call her and chat. Surely, now that Simon was seeing Emmy, all was forgiven.

After Skye's marriage to Wally, Simon had started going out with Emerald Jones, a dance instructor at Olive Leofanti's studio. Olive was both the mayor's wife and Skye's aunt. Saying that life in a small town was a tangled web of relationships would be an understatement. And adding an ex's family to the mix made for a delicate balancing act.

"What body?" It had taken a second for May's words to get through Skye's tired brain, but she finally realized what her mother had said and asked, "Who died? Did someone get killed in the tornado?"

"Zeke Lyons." May's voice was low and she glanced nervously over her shoulder through the open doorway and down the empty corridor. "Wally found Zeke in his bathroom, but he's not sure the guy's death was due to the twister."

"Oh?" Skye raised an eyebrow, and then, when her mother didn't elaborate, she prodded, "Why doesn't Wally think it was due to the tornado?"

"He didn't say." May glanced over her shoulder again. "He just told me not to mention his suspicions to Dante or Zeke's wife."

"Do the mayor and Mrs. Lyons know Mr. Lyons is dead?" Skye asked.

"Wally spoke to Dante about an hour ago." May's lips thinned. "I'm surprised you didn't hear your uncle screaming."

"Screaming?" Skye wrinkled her brow. "Was Uncle Dante close to Mr. Lyons?"

"Not at all. Zeke was only appointed to the city council last month."

"So why was Hizzoner upset?"

"Dante was pitching a fit because Wally refused to come back to the station and tell Zeke's wife that he was dead." May rolled her eyes. "Your uncle didn't want to deal with the poor woman's grief."

"Ah. Now I get it." Skye finally understood. Her uncle's ability to weasel out of unpleasant tasks was legendary. "So did the mayor end up breaking the sad news to Mrs. Lyons?"

"Of course not," May said. "He talked Thea into doing it for him. Dante claimed that Billie would take it better coming from a woman."

Thea, the dispatcher who worked the weekday morning shift, was notoriously softhearted, and Dante never hesitated to use that against her. He was a wizard at finding people's weaknesses and exploiting them.

"Mom, your big brother is a creep of the worst magnitude," Skye muttered in disgust.

"Tell me something that I don't know." May shrugged, then said, "Let's go before he tries to make one of us do something yucky."

"I'd really rather just wait here for Wally," Skye said, her voice hitching. "What's the difference where I am? I don't have any pajamas or clean underwear or even a toothbrush."

May wrapped Skye in a hug and said, "We'll get all that for you tomorrow. But right now, for the baby's sake, you need to rest." She patted Skye's back. "Charlie told me that he'd give you one of his T-shirts and the toiletry pack he keeps on hand for folks who forget stuff."

"I'm not sure his shirt will fit me with this enormous belly." Skye rubbed her stomach.

"Oh, please." May snickered. "Charlie's gut is way bigger than yours."

Well, that was a first. Skye's mom wasn't usually so tolerant of her daughter's less-than-skinny appearance. May really was mellowing now that Skye was married and expecting.

Smiling, Skye picked up Wally's duffel, which contained her air-dried shorts and purse, then followed her mother down the steps. As she walked through the police station, she noticed that the bedlam had died to a dull roar.

In the five hours since the tornadoes had ripped through Scumble River, the huge, new Methodist church on the south edge of town had opened its doors, welcoming people with no other place to go for the night. As the news spread, volunteers had assembled, bringing cots, air mattresses, and sleeping bags. Soon afterward, the displaced families had begun leaving the PD and making their way to the shelter.

Although there were far fewer folks in the interior of the station, the parking lot was more crowded than it had been when Skye and Wally had arrived. Vans from all the major television networks were lined up along one side and Dante stood in front of the vehicles, waving his arms. With his chest puffed out, he was clearly pontificating about the disaster.

Skye shuddered at the thought of her uncle in the spotlight. Dante tended to speak impulsively and later deny what he had said. Did he realize denial was a lot harder if your statement was recorded for posterity?

After getting into her mother's white Olds Eighty-Eight, Skye asked, "Is Wally aware that the PD has been invaded by the media?"

"After a reporter barged into the station, asking how I 'felt' about the devastation, and I sent him packing, I radioed Wally." May glowered. "He warned the PD employees not to make any statements to the press, and told Roy that he was the public information officer."

"Interesting choice." Skye leaned back and closed her burning eyes.

"I just hope Roy doesn't lose it," May said. "That boy has a short fuse."

Sergeant Roy Quirk had been Wally's right hand since before Skye returned to town, but he wasn't exactly an easygoing man. Before Wally had insisted Roy see a therapist, there had been a few times that Skye had been on the receiving end of his temper and she still had the emotional scars to prove it.

The sergeant had been doing better, but having microphones thrust in your face could try the patience of a saint. And no one had ever suggested that Roy Quirk be canonized.

"Mmm." Skye was too tired to discuss the sergeant's issues. "If those vultures get a hint that Zeke Lyons's death might not be due to the tornado, there would be an even worse feeding frenzy than now."

"It'll get out." May's tone was glum. "There are no secrets in Scumble River."

May was wrong. There were plenty of secrets in town, and as a school psychologist, Skye knew a lot of them.

Keeping that interesting tidbit to herself, Skye asked, "Did you hear if any other communities around us were affected by the tornadoes?"

"We seem to be the worst hit in this general vicinity," May answered. "But Brooklyn has significant damage near the highway and Clay Center had a couple of neighborhoods demolished." She sighed. "And there's a lot of downstate areas that were hit."

Skye felt the car turn and opened her eyes. They'd arrived at Up A Lazy River. It was located on Maryland Street, which was part of historic Route 66, and just across the bridge from the center of town.

The motel's usual guests were fishermen taking advantage of the motor court's placement on the banks of the Scumble River. Occasionally, a tourist traveling down the Mother Road checked in for a brief stay, but this evening, Skye guessed that Up A Lazy River was full of evacuees from the storm.

The big sign near the road usually flashed a red vacancy sign adorned with a neon-blue river. Tonight, the sign was dark and there were vehicles in front of all the cabins. Evidently, a few lucky families had quickly snatched up all the available rooms.

May parked the Oldsmobile and met Skye as she got out of the car. There were no lights in the office, but the windows in Charlie's attached apartment glowed invitingly. May and Skye climbed the two steps leading to his place, but before they could knock, Charlie flung open the door and swept them inside. Somehow managing to hug them both simultaneously, he said, "You and Jed okay, May? How about Vince and his family?"

"I told you when we talked before that we're all fine."

Charlie nodded and turned to Skye. His intense blue eyes under bushy, white brows scrutinized her face as he demanded, "Everything all right with the baby? You and Wally were fully insured, right?"

"I feel good," Skye assured him. "But just to be safe, I'll keep my doctor's appointment tomorrow and let her check me out." She patted his arm. "And yes, the house and cars were insured."

Despite the late hour, Charlie was dressed in his standard uniform of gray twill pants; limp, white shirt; and red suspenders. His face was red and the beads of sweat dotting his forehead concerned Skye.

At seventy-seven, he had high blood pressure and a fondness for steaks, beer, and cigars, which made Skye worry about his health. Especially when he was under stress. Which was often, since he liked being in control and the world didn't always acquiesce to his wishes.

"Good." Charlie gripped Skye's elbow. "I'm getting too old for this kind of BS."

He sighed. "Since stuff is supposed to get better with age, I must be darn near magnificent." Grimacing, he added, "Too bad nobody told my body."

"You need to take care of yourself," Skye admonished, a flicker of fear running down her spine. Her godfather rarely admitted to feeling old.

"Yeah. Right," Charlie said, then took her arm. "Come on. I put you in the cabin right next to me. Trixie and Owen are on the other side of you."

"So they made it here?" Skye beamed. "That's great. I'm so glad you had space for them."

"Hell yes, I had a place for them." Charlie frowned at her. "I waited until I heard from friends and family before renting out any of my empty rooms."

"Of course you did," Skye murmured, then covered her mouth when she yawned.

"That does it." Charlie shoved a paper grocery sack in Skye's left hand; her right hand was clutching the strap of the duffel bag. "Time to get the little mother-to-be in bed. We can talk in the morning."

As May turned to leave, Skye asked, "Are you and Dad staying at the house?"

"Not tonight." May blew out a breath. "I'll stop home for some clothes, but we're staying at Minnie's place, since she has a generator. We'll be there until either the power comes on or Jed can find a generator to buy."

With a final kiss goodbye, May left and Charlie showed Skye to her cabin. It was a typical 1950s motel room. The walls were paneled in knotty pine, the bed was only a double, and a television sporting rabbit ears sat on a metal stand. Skye stared at the aluminum-foil-wrapped antenna, realizing that the old-fashioned rabbit ears might be a good thing, since cable and satellite were probably not working.

Charlie turned on the light and waved to the bag in Skye's arms. "I put in one of my T-shirts, a robe I got for Christmas and never wore, and a complimentary toiletry kit. If you give me your clothes, I'll wash and dry them and have 'em for you in the morning."

Skye flung her arms around his neck and said, "That would be so awesome." She let him go and added, "Thank you so much for the room and clothes and everything. I'll bring my stuff over to you in a few minutes."

The bathroom wasn't any more modern than the rest of the cabin. The walls were a lemon yellow, while the sink, toilet, and tub were an odd shade of green. Thank goodness she no longer woke up each day feeling the need to vomit or this color scheme would literally make her sick.

Skye turned on the shower, stripped off her maternity top, bra, sweatpants, and underwear, then stepped under the warm water. It wasn't hot, but it wasn't ice cold, so she couldn't complain. It was way better than what a lot of Scumble Riverites had right now.

All too soon, Skye forced herself to get out of the shower. She didn't want to overtax Charlie's generator by having to run the water heater too long. She wasn't sure if that was how it worked, but just in case, she wanted to make sure she didn't hog the resources.

Skye walked into the main room, thankful that Charlie was so big and tall that his T-shirt made it over her baby bump and still hung nearly to her knees. She didn't mind sleeping in the altogether with her husband, but if there was a fire, she certainly didn't want the entire motor court to see her naked.

As she rubbed her wet curls with a towel, the cabin door opened and Wally stepped inside. His expression numb, he gave her a tired smile and took off his duty belt. His tie was missing and his dark hair stood on end as if he'd run his fingers through it again and again.

Although Skye had a million questions, she didn't ask any of them. Instead, she quickly led him into the bathroom, unbuttoned his shirt, and said, "Charlie offered to wash and dry our clothes so we'd have something to wear tomorrow. I'll run them over to him while you shower."

"That'd be wonderful, darlin'." Wally stepped out of his pants and boxer briefs. "Do you think he might have a spare beer and something to eat? I never did get supper."

"Absolutely." Skye dug her shorts out of the duffel bag and gathered the rest of the dirty laundry from the bathroom floor. Then as she turned to go, she said, "I'll be right back with food and a cold Sam Adams for you."

"Great. I need a drink." Wally's voice was muffled from the water. "Reid finally made it into town and it's likely that Zeke Lyons was murdered."

Chapter 7

"The road to the City of Emeralds is paved with yellow brick," said the Witch, "so you cannot miss it."

Skye woke slowly the next morning, and when she stretched, her joints creaked as if she were eighty-six instead of thirty-six. Hearing Wally chuckle, she turned her head and saw him grinning at her.

He leaned over and kissed her forehead, then said, "You know it's a good stretch when it sounds like you've just poured the milk on a bowl of Rice Krispies."

She snickered when Wally swung his legs over the side of the mattress and groaned as he got to his feet. Giving her a dirty look, he walked over to the door and picked up a plastic sack with their freshly laundered clothes neatly folded inside. A note attached to the bag informed them that breakfast would be ready at seven and scrambled eggs weren't good cold. Evidently, Uncle Charlie had used his passkey.

While Wally took his turn in the bathroom, Skye checked her phone. Before going to sleep last night, she had sent a quick text to the intern, instructing her to report to the Stanley County Special Education Co-operative administration building in Laurel. Skye'd had to leave a voicemail for the co-op's lead school psychologist, since she didn't have the woman's cell number, and now she saw that both the intern and psychologist had left messages for her not to worry about them. Skye was beyond relieved to have at least one item removed from her to-do list.

Once Wally and Skye were dressed, they walked next door to Charlie's apartment for breakfast. He ushered them into the kitchen and ordered them to sit. A mountain of toast was already on the table and he slid plates of eggs, bacon, and hash browns in front of them. After pouring Skye a glass of milk and himself and Wally coffee, Charlie took his seat and they began to eat.

Taking a healthy swig of milk, Skye swallowed and said, "I don't know how we can thank you enough for saving us a cabin and doing our laundry and feeding us, Uncle Charlie."

Picking up his fork, Charlie pointed it at Skye and said, "If there's one thing that I've learned, it's that as you get older, life is like a roll of toilet paper. The closer it gets to the end, the more essential it is not to waste a single bit of it. You and your family are the most important things in my life. I will always do what needs to be done to make sure you all are taken care of."

Skye swallowed the lump in her throat, reached for her godfather's hand, and kissed his knuckles. "Right back at you, Uncle Charlie."

Waving away the emotionally charged atmosphere, Charlie asked, "When's your doctor's appointment?"

"Eight thirty. I took the first one so I could get back early for school." Skye snickered. "Guess I don't have to worry about that now." She glanced at Wally. "I thought I'd get Mom to take me so you can stick around here. You probably don't want to be out of town today."

"Sugar" — Wally put an arm around her shoulder — "nothing is more important than you and our baby."

"But we're fine." Skye squeezed his fingers. "And afterward, I'm going to need to go shopping." She wrinkled her nose. "Do you really want to spend several hours at

Target and Walmart?"

"Well, if your mother is available, I'm sure she'd enjoy taking you," Wally said quickly. "But you should probably check with her right now, since you'll have to leave by quarter to eight to get to Kankakee on time."

Skye nodded, fished her cell from her shorts pocket, and made the call. Her mother was ecstatic and promised to pick her up in half an hour.

When Skye hung up, Charlie turned to Wally and asked, "How's Scumble River look?"

"Bad." Wally cradled his mug. "Lots of homes will have to be rebuilt from the foundation up and even more have varying amounts of damage, mostly to roofs and windows. ComEd tells me there are outages all over Illinois and that it might be several days to a week before our power is fully restored. Last night they were still trying to make sure the lines weren't live before allowing people to cross them."

"Hell's bells!" Charlie swore. "That's even worse than I thought."

"With the tornadoes hitting Brooklyn and Clay Center, assistance from other communities is spread thin."

"I imagine the media jackals won't have

the same lack of personnel." Charlie slathered a triangle of toast with butter and grape jelly.

Neither Skye nor Wally mentioned that the press had already descended.

"I spoke to the superintendent last night." Charlie took a sip of his coffee. "He's trying to figure out some option other than canceling classes."

"How about the Hutton dairy farm out by I-55?" Skye suggested. "The country music guy renovated the barn and a few of the outbuildings, but then when Suzette was murdered, the theater never opened."

"By Jingo, that might work." Charlie pounded the tabletop. "We'd have to get in some room dividers and such, but we can probably scavenge those from our own buildings. I wonder who owns the farm now."

"Check the tax records at the county courthouse," Wally advised.

"Before Mom gets here" — Skye grabbed a pen and paper from the counter underneath Charlie's wall phone and looked at Wally — "is there anything I need to buy for you besides some clothes and basic toiletries?"

"Let me think." Wally scratched his chin, which, lacking his usual morning shave, had a dark layer of stubble. "An electric razor, jeans, shorts, shirts, and a belt. A pack of underwear and socks." He paused and snapped his fingers. "A good pair of sneakers."

"Do you think your dad really will be able to get a motor coach here by this afternoon?" Skye asked. "Should I buy household stuff and groceries?"

"Go ahead and get the basics." Wally flicked glance at Charlie. "If Carson Boyd says he can, he can."

Skye hurried to cover her slip. "It's great that your father's employer allows him to use the company resources when he needs them."

Because no one in Scumble River knew that Wally's family had money, their cover story was that Carson's boss was very generous with his top management.

"Will you be able to contact the insurance or should I try to do it?" Wally asked.

"I can make those calls while Mom is driving me to Kankakee."

"Don't let them give you the runaround," Charlie ordered. "You pay your premiums on time and you want a check in the same timely manner."

"Yes, sir." Skye saluted her uncle, then turned to Wally. He'd fallen asleep before she could question him last night, but she didn't want to say too much in front of Charlie. "Have there been many fatalities from the tornadoes?"

"So far, the only body we've found is Zeke Lyons," Wally answered carefully. Then he caught Skye's gaze and gave an infinitesimal shake of his head. "Let's hope there aren't any more."

"Well, old Zeke doesn't really count, since he wasn't a victim of the storm, does he?" Charlie raised a bushy, white brow. "I heard he was murdered. And you can't really blame a twister for that, can you?"

"Who told you he was murdered?" Wally demanded, narrowing his eyes.

"A little bird at Laurel Hospital might have chirped in my ear." Charlie's expression was smug. "Son, do you actually think anything goes on in this town that doesn't get reported directly to me?"

"Not really. But although it's likely Zeke was murdered, we don't have an official cause of death yet and I was hoping to keep it quiet until then," Wally muttered. "I don't want the media to get wind of it before the medical examiner has a chance to finish the autopsy and send me his report."

"I'll put the word out to keep a lid on it." Charlie crossed his arms, then glanced out the window of his kitchen and announced, "May's here."

"Thanks for breakfast, Uncle Charlie." Skye stood and kissed the top of her godfather's head, then hugged Wally and said, "I'll call you when I get out of the doctor's office. Love you! Bye!"

Skye hurried outside, waved to her mom, then rushed into her cabin to grab her purse. She was going to need her credit cards for today's massive shopping expedition. It was a good thing Wally had added her to his Amex, which had a huge credit line, because her Visa would never cover all they needed.

Sliding into May's Oldsmobile, Skye said, "Thanks for taking me, Mom."

"I can't wait." May put the car in gear and pulled out into the street. "I've been dying to go to the ob-gyn with you. I have lots of questions."

Skye rolled her eyes. She appreciated her mother's enthusiasm, but knew May was going to try to trick Dr. Johnson into revealing the baby's gender. Skye's mom hadn't been a happy camper when Skye and Wally had decided they wanted to be surprised. This was May's chance to try to weasel the information from the doctor.

"I hope you don't mind." Skye powered

up her cell. "I need to call our insurance company and get the ball rolling on our claim."

"Go right ahead." May kept her eyes on the road. "I did that first thing this morning. Supposedly, a claims adjuster will be at our place between nine and twelve. I left your father sitting in a lawn chair in front of what's left of the garage, cleaning his rifle."

"Subtle," Skye said. "I suppose that would give the appraiser a little added incentive. It certainly worked with my teenage boyfriends."

May smiled serenely, then as Skye gasped, she yelled, "What's wrong?"

"The Feed Bag. It's gone. It's completely gone." Skye pointed. "No one told me the Feed Bag was hit."

"Oh yeah." May swallowed. "Everyone is devastated."

The Feed Bag was Scumble River's only real restaurant. Diners at the Feed Bag felt as if they were part of an extended family. For the elderly, it was a comfort knowing the staff would notice if they varied from their normal routine, and someone would check up on them if they didn't show for their customary coffee, bowl of soup, or game of chess.

For young families, it was reassuring that

no one would frown if their kids were loud or messy. Not to mention that when the check arrived, they wouldn't have to take out a second mortgage.

And for singles, it was a safe place to go on a first date. Or a comfortable spot to meet up with other like-minded people looking for a love match. The restaurant was the heart of Scumble River. Without it, there would be a huge hole.

As they continued past the wreckage, May and Skye were quiet. Finally, Skye turned back to her cell and dialed the insurance company. As she listened to the endless menu of "push one for this" and "push two for that," she wondered if the town would ever be the same.

It took Skye the rest of the drive to get through to both the homeowners and then the automobile department. And by the time May parked at the medical complex, Skye was afraid that when the nurse took her blood pressure it would be so high the doctor would put her on bed rest until she had the baby.

When they entered the doctor's office, May accompanied Skye to the counter. Skye signed in and was given a specimen cup. May started to follow her to the bathroom, but Skye pointed to the waiting room and refused to budge until her mom took a seat.

After producing the required sample, Skye was shown into an examination room. The nurse perched on a stool in front of a laptop situated on a shelf attached to the wall and began asking Skye the same list of questions they went over at the beginning of every single visit.

Just as they finished, the door opened and May stepped inside. With a smug grin, she said, "When the nice receptionist found out you were my only daughter and this was your first pregnancy, she told me your room number. She said she was sure you'd want the grandma of your baby with you and wouldn't deprive me of seeing the sonogram."

"Of course she did." After that little speech, Skye would look like the worst daughter on the planet if she insisted May leave. "But I don't think we're doing a sonogram. Dr. Johnson and I agreed only to do them if there's a good reason."

May took a seat and mumbled, "Finding out if I'm going to have a grandson or granddaughter is a pretty darn good reason."

The perky nurse smiled sympathetically at May, then looked at Skye and said, "Let's get your weight."

"Let's not," Skye muttered under her breath, glancing at her mother.

Could she ask May to step out? Her mom would have a coronary when she heard how many pounds Skye had recently gained.

The nurse stood by the scale. "No need to be shy."

"Sure. Why don't we just do this in the middle of the waiting room?" Skye retorted, then kicked off her flip-flops, stepped on the scale, and closed her eyes.

"All done." The nurse evidently had finally clued into Skye's discomfort and walked over to the computer without comment.

As the nurse entered Skye's weight on the electronic chart, May leaned forward and Skye glared at her mother. Pasting an innocent expression on her face, May shrugged, relaxed back into her chair, and crossed her legs.

Next, the nurse took Skye's blood pressure and temperature, then, after recording that information, she handed Skye a shapeless, green gown and said, "Once you've changed, flip the switch by the door to indicate that you're ready. The phlebotomist will come in to draw your blood, and the doctor will be with you after that."

"Could you step out, Mom?" Skye asked.

"Why?" May frowned. "It's not as if I've never seen you naked."

Skye tapped her toe. "Mom, we've talked about you giving me some space."

"Fine."

As soon as May left, Skye removed her clothes, put on the gown, and flipped the switch. A split second later, May reentered and resumed her seat.

Skye sat on the examination table and tried to calm her nerves. She loved her obstetrician, but having any kind of medical exam still made her nervous.

May studied her and asked, "Are you still afraid of doctors?"

"A little." Skye wrinkled her nose. "But Dr. J is great. I just need to keep reminding myself she isn't like the mean ones that I've had in the past."

Before May could respond, the phlebotomist arrived to draw Skye's blood, and as the tech left, Dr. Johnson walked into the room. The obstetrician was an attractive woman in her early forties with short, blond hair and warm, blue eyes. Under her white jacket, she wore a cute pair of geometric-print cotton slacks and a pink T-shirt.

"Skye, good to see you." Dr. Johnson turned to May and held out her hand. "And you are?"

"Skye's mom." May shook the doctor's hand.

"Nice to meet you." Dr. Johnson moved to the sink and washed her hands. "Everything going okay? Any problems or concerns?"

"Let's see." Skye paused, then said, "Last night, our house was destroyed in a tornado."

"Oh my gosh!" Dr. Johnson gasped. "Are you and your husband okay?"

"Yes. We took shelter in the basement. But the Braxton-Hicks contractions didn't help matters, and the baby has been bouncing all over the place. One minute I feel a kick here" — Skye pointed to her right side — "and the next second a punch in another spot. I thought you told me that closer to the due date, the baby would slow down."

"Hmm." Dr. Johnson threw her used paper towel into the trash and tapped her password into the computer. Peering at the screen, she frowned and said, "You've gained another ten pounds since your last visit two weeks ago."

"I truly haven't been stuffing my face." Skye bit her lip and glanced at her mom.

May's forehead was wrinkled and she seemed uneasy rather than exasperated.

"I'm sure you haven't been overeating."

Dr. Johnson opened a drawer and took out a tape measure. "Please lie down." The obstetrician helped Skye recline, then said, "I'm going to measure your fundal height. The height of your fundus should roughly equal the weeks of your pregnancy."

"Okay." Skye took a deep breath. "You've done that before."

After a few seconds, Dr. Johnson said, "You're measuring a little large."

"Does that mean her due date is closer than we thought?" May asked.

"Maybe, but I need to do a sonogram before I can say for sure." Dr. Johnson warmed up her stethoscope, then moved Skye's gown aside and pressed the instrument to her stomach. Instead of her usual smile, she nodded to herself and said, "I'll be right back."

"I've only had the initial sonogram and the one at twenty weeks," Skye murmured worriedly to her mother as the doctor disappeared. "Since we didn't want to know the sex and the pregnancy was going well, our insurance didn't cover any more."

May got to her feet and moved next to her. "I'm sure everything's fine," she reassured her, then said, "Delivering sooner wouldn't be so bad, right?"

"But the tornado took all the baby stuff."

Skye frowned. "At least, I'm guessing it's gone, since the nursery was on the second floor, which is no longer there."

"We'll buy new things." May stroked Skye's hair. "And I have clothes and furniture in the attic from when I had you and Vince." She brightened. "Good thing we didn't have the baby shower yet."

Before Skye could respond, Dr. Johnson returned, followed by a woman pushing a cart holding a machine. The sonographer stopped by the examination table, introduced herself, then squirted Skye's stomach with a clear gel. As the tech moved the wand, Dr. Johnson leaned toward the screen, which today was turned away from Skye.

During the previous two sonograms, Skye could look at the monitor and the doctor had explained what she was seeing. Her silence shot Skye's anxiety through the stratosphere. She gripped her mother's hand so tightly May yelped.

Once the test was finished and the tech left, Dr. Johnson swiveled the screen and Skye blinked. There were two heads, one pointed up and one pointed down.

"Does that mean what I think it means?" Skye's voice cracked.

"Yep." Dr. Johnson grinned. "You, my

dear, are having twins."

"What the . . . You've got to be kidding me!" May shouted. "Six weeks before my daughter is due and you only now realize she's having twins. What kind of doctor are you?"

Dr. Johnson smiled, apparently unruffled by May's accusation. "It seems your grand-babies have been playing hide-and-seek during the previous sonograms. It's unusual to find out this late in a pregnancy, but far from unprecedented."

"But you only heard one heartbeat," Skye protested. "Is the other baby okay?"

"Yes." Dr. Johnson beamed. "Now that we know how tricky the babies are, I found the other heartbeat today."

"Give me my cell, Mom," Skye ordered. "Wally will be so upset he missed this appointment. I need to call him right away."

"You might want to tell him in person." Dr. Johnson pointed her pen at Skye. "In case he passes out, you want to make sure he's sitting down. You can tell him to sit down over the phone, but my experience with men is that they say they are when they aren't. The last one who claimed to be seated when his wife telephoned him with the news she was pregnant keeled over and ended up with a nasty concussion."

"That's good advice," May said.

Skye mutely nodded her agreement. She really did want to see Wally's face when she told him the news. That way she could tell if he was happy or upset about her having twins.

As the doctor walked out the door, she said, "Call me immediately if anything changes."

"Absolutely," May said, her bright-green eyes shiny with happy tears.

Skye dressed, then she and her mother headed for the parking lot. Sliding into the car, Skye looked at May and said, "What if I can't handle two babies?"

May snorted. "Like you have a choice."

CHAPTER 8

"I am Oz, the Great and Terrible," said the little man, in a trembling voice. "But don't strike me — please don't — and I'll do anything you want me to."

"Sorry, Mrs. Lyons, I still haven't received the ME's report." Wally kept his voice level. The woman had already telephoned him three times, wanting to know how her husband had died. She seemed heartbroken and Wally wished he had some answers for her. "Give me your cell number and I'll call you as soon as I know anything."

"I don't have a cell phone," Billie Lyons said softly.

"Then give me the number where you'll be staying," Wally suggested.

"I'm not sure of that yet," Billie answered.

"Then how about you wait two or three days, then touch base with me again?"

"I can call you Thursday?"

"Make it Friday," Wally countered. "I promise to have some answers by then."

Disconnecting, Wally pushed aside the lists, maps, and files on top of his desk and took a long drink from the water bottle Thea had placed by his elbow an hour ago. The liquid was now lukewarm, but he didn't care. His throat was as dry as West Texas and he could swear his tongue had turned to sandpaper.

The police station's thermostat was set at eighty-five and Wally's second-story office felt several degrees warmer than that. Air-conditioning was a huge drain on the generator and ComEd continued to warn everyone that the power might be out for as long as a week.

At least the station wasn't the madhouse it had been last night. Still, there were a lot of people wanting help and only so many employees available to assist them. First thing this morning, after grabbing only a few hours of sleep, all of Wally's officers, with the exception of Tolman, who remained on the disabled list, had reported for duty and been assigned to search and rescue teams.

The dispatchers were another story. May was with Skye at her appointment, and Char, who, thank the Lord, had decided to postpone her retirement until the mayor's hiring freeze was lifted, would be here at midnight. Which left the three part-timers and Thea dealing with the multitude of calls and in-person requests.

Between looky-loos, looters, and the fear that the motorcycle gang that had been breaking into houses all around the county would take advantage of the chaos, access to the decimated neighborhoods had to be tightly regulated. Volunteer police from all over the state were providing traffic control along the major roads into town, as well as in the most devastated areas.

As blocks were cleared, residents who could verify that they lived or had relatives in that section were allowed in to start sifting through what remained of their possessions. But no one else was permitted past the barricades.

Fighting the urge to ignore the paperwork and get out into the field, Wally ran his fingers through his sweat-dampened hair. He felt useless sitting behind a desk when there were so many people missing and so many more buildings to search. Logically, he knew someone had to be in charge, but his gut didn't buy that excuse. Making lists wasn't his idea of serving or protecting.

And even if he could persuade himself that he didn't need to coordinate the efforts, someone had to look into Zeke Lyons's death. Wally pondered the oddities. The lack of shoes might be explained, although most folks choose not to handle an emergency barefoot. But the position of the body was suspicious. Why was he wedged behind the door instead of taking shelter in the bathtub, which was standard procedure for someone caught in a tornado?

It was frustrating that although there were several fresh pairs of small, round burn marks on the councilman's chest, which indicated probable foul play, the medical examiner hadn't yet been able to verify the cause of death. The ME had promised a preliminary report by noon, and without it, Wally was at a loss as to where to start his investigation.

Time of death had been narrowed down to between seven thirty and eight thirty, which was during the height of the storm. It was possible that Lyons had surprised a looter. But the thief would have had to be somewhere nearby to get there so soon after the tornado hit.

Unfortunately, from what Wally had been able to gather, Zeke wasn't the type of guy anyone would care enough about to bother to kill. He wasn't wealthy. He didn't have a glamorous job or a fancy house. And his only interest, outside of his wife, seemed to be his dog.

The sole activity Wally had been able to connect to Zeke had been the city council, and he sure hadn't stirred up any trouble there. Wally had never even heard him speak at one of the meetings.

Zeke Lyons seemed like a guy who could fade into the background rather than stand out in a crowd. His murder would probably turn out to be a case of being in the wrong place at the wrong time rather than a crime of passion.

As Wally finished the bottle of water and tossed it into the recycle bin, he caught a glimpse of his watch and frowned. It was nearly ten o'clock. Skye's doctor appointments usually were over in less than a half hour. Why hadn't she called to tell him what the doctor had to say?

Maybe she couldn't get through on the landlines. Had he accidently muted his cell? Fishing the device from his shirt pocket, he saw he had indeed missed a text from Skye.

He tapped the icon with his thumb and read the message. Everything fine. XXOO.

Narrowing his eyes, Wally stared at the screen. Granted, this was the first ob-gyn visit he'd missed, but why hadn't she given him any details? For that matter, why had she texted instead of calling?

Was Skye hiding something? Surely if something was wrong, she wouldn't hesitate to call him. Knowing his wife, she would want him with her, if for no other reason than for him to handle her mother. So what could it be?

Pressing her speed dial number, he pursed his lips when it went directly to voicemail. Maybe she was still in the obstetrician's office. It was possible Dr. Johnson was running behind schedule. Just because they'd never had to wait in the past didn't mean it couldn't happen.

He tapped his fingers on the desktop, trying to decide what to do. There really wasn't any way to reach her if she wasn't answering her cell. He'd just have to wait for her to return his call.

Staring at the mess in front of him, he started to pull Lyons's file toward him, then remembered that the mayor had called a meeting for ten thirty. Representatives from the Multi Agency Resource Center, Department of Insurance, and city officials were invited to discuss who would do what as they moved forward.

Shit! Just what he needed. Another of Hizzoner's endless BS sessions where nothing would really be decided.

Sending Skye a text instructing her to call him ASAP, he made sure his ringtone was loud enough to hear from his pocket, then grabbed a legal pad and marched into the hallway.

The police station, city hall, and library were all housed in the same building. The city hall and PD shared the ground floor. The town's small library took up the back half of the second story, with the chief's and mayor's offices sharing the remainder of the space.

A couple of years ago, Dante had ordered that an opening be cut in the wall between the city hall and the police department. While Wally wasn't fond of Hizzoner's ability to stroll over anytime the urge hit him, Wally had to admit it was a hell of a lot easier to walk through the archway rather than go downstairs, out the PD's door, enter the city hall, and climb the steps to the mayor's office.

A few seconds later, when Wally strolled into Dante's lair, he was surprised that no one else was there. Hizzoner was on the phone and, by the looks of it, wasn't getting the response he wanted from whomever was on the other end of the line.

"I have nothing to say to you." Dante's voice vibrated with outrage. "You misquoted me last night. I never said that anyone who was too stupid to take shelter deserved whatever happened to them."

Wally took a seat and settled back to enjoy the show. The mayor was more proficient at the sidestep shuffle than Dante's wife, Olive, who had been a professional dancer.

"Shit," Dante said under his breath, then cleared his throat and barked, "I did not give you permission to record our conversation. That comment was off the record."

Wally chuckled and the mayor glared at him.

"Leave me alone!" Dante screeched. "You're all out to get me." Banging the handset into the holder, he scowled at Wally. "What are you staring at?"

"I'm trying to imagine you with a personality." Wally crossed his legs.

"I have a damn good personality." Dante thrust out his chin. "Maybe you're confusing it with my attitude and that depends on other people."

Wally just stared, knowing his silence would drive the mayor crazy.

Less than a minute later, Dante caved and demanded, "What do you want?"

"I'm here for the meeting." Wally

shrugged.

"It's been canceled." Dante shoved his chair back so hard it hit the wall behind him. "I've got better things to do than listen to everyone's plans. I told 'em all just to do what they're supposed to do."

"Great." Wally stood.

"Wait." Dante leaped to his feet and demanded, "What's this I hear about Councilman Lyons's death not being an accident? And why wasn't I informed?"

"I'm waiting for word from the ME before I make any official announcement."

"Screw that!" Dante advanced on Wally. "From now on, I want to be kept informed of anything like, like" — he flailed his arms — "like dead people."

"Gotcha. You want to know about any stiffs that turn up." Wally barely stopped himself from rolling his eyes. "Anything else?"

"One more thing." Dante puffed up his chest. "My very good friend Hollister Brooks owns various buildings around Stanley County. He's been able to reach all of his renters but one. I want you to check out that property. It's an old farmhouse on the east side of town." Dante dug in his pants pocket and withdrew a slip of paper, read off the address, then threw the Post-it

Note on the desktop.

"I suppose this is something you want me take care of myself," Wally drawled. "Not have one of my few officers handle it?"

"Of course." Dante glowered. "I told Hollister you'd contact him personally before noon today."

"I won't do it." Wally crossed his arms, waited for Dante's face to turn the shade of a ripe tomato, then added, "Unless you give me a signed statement allowing me to hire an officer to replace Zuchowski."

"You're blackmailing me!" Dante squawked. "At a time like this?"

"Yep." Wally handed the mayor the legal pad he'd been holding. "You better get writing if you want me to get to the house by noon."

Bellyaching the entire time, Dante scribbled the agreement Wally dictated. He signed the paper, shoved it at Wally, and ordered him to leave.

"Why can't this Brooks character inspect his own property?" Wally asked, tucking the agreement into his shirt pocket.

"He's enjoying a well-deserved retirement."

"Where?"

"He has an amazing waterfront estate in Tampa."

"I should have known that he'd be living in God's waiting room." Wally walked toward the door. "You know Texas is a much better place to retire."

Hizzoner glared, then before Wally made it over the threshold, Dante yelled, "You'll be sorry you forced me to sign that paper."

Ignoring the mayor, Wally headed to the garage, slid behind the wheel of the squad car, and backed out, making a right onto Maryland. As he drove, he realized Skye still hadn't called him. What could be taking so long at the doctor's office?

Hell! If he didn't hear from her by the time he'd checked out the Brooks property, he'd try May's cell.

Worried about his wife, Wally nearly missed his turn onto Basset Street. Shortly after crossing one of Scumble River's three narrow plank bridges, he made a left onto Harvester. There were no buildings along the dirt road, and even the cornfields looked neglected. The land on the north was in Wilson County and out of the Scumble River police's jurisdiction, but just his luck, the Brooks property was on the south side.

The place was easy to find, one of only two structures on Harvester Road between Basset and the next intersection. The other building was an abandoned barn across the road from the Brooks place that was leaning to one side as if a giant had given it a good shove.

Pulling into the driveway, Wally studied the old farmhouse. The two-story, gray asphalt-shingled dwelling had seen better days, but it didn't appear to have suffered any recent damage. The tightness in his chest eased. This might be a wild-goose chase, but at least he wouldn't find another body.

The absence of vehicles in the driveway and the rundown condition of the house's exterior made Wally wonder if Brooks's tenants had flown the coop. Getting out of the squad car, Wally walked toward the ramshackle machine shed out back. The harsh sunlight showed every rust spot and dent in the ancient metal building.

Noting that the shed's only window was in the pedestrian entrance, Wally approached the door cautiously. When he couldn't see anything, he leaned closer. That was odd. It wasn't apparent at first glance, but something had been set up on the other side of the glass to block the view inside.

Suddenly, the hair on the back of Wally's neck rose and he whirled around. Shortened shadows and washed-out colors created an eerie picture. Something was off about this setup.

He examined the various tire tracks in the muddy ground. More than one type of vehicle had driven between the driveway and the shed. And the marks were fresh. Several people had been in and out since last night's storm.

As Wally headed toward the squad car, he checked his phone. Still nothing from Skye. He scrolled through his contact list, frowning when he didn't find May's cell number. Why didn't he have her number? Probably because she rarely thought to turn her phone on. Still, maybe with everything in such turmoil, she would remember.

Thea might have it. But Wally didn't want to tie up either the radio or the police station line with a personal call. He'd wait until he returned to the PD to ask her for the number.

But first he'd check the house's perimeter. Sweat dripped down Wally's back as he walked around the dwelling. There was no wind, and the heat felt like a branding iron pressed against his spine.

Wiping his forehead with his handkerchief, he continued his inspection. Warped flower boxes clinging to the bottom of the windows were filled with rusty beer cans rather than summer blossoms. Several cracks in the glass were sealed with duct tape and it looked as if mold was growing between the panes. Heavy curtains were pulled closed and sagged on their rods.

The lawn was badly in need of mowing, and dandelions had all but taken over. Around back, next to the boarded-up kitchen door, enormous piles of black, plastic garbage bags were strewn around a huge generator chugging away on the concrete pad.

Returning to the front, Wally took out his cell and tapped in Hollister Brooks's number. When the guy answered, Wally identified himself, described what he'd observed, and assured the man that there was no visible tornado damage to his property.

Brooks thanked him and asked, "Chief, since you're on the scene, would you check to see if my tenants are still there?"

"Sure," Wally agreed. If he didn't find out now, Dante would probably demand he come back and do so. "Should I let you know at this number?"

"Thanks. But I'm about to get on my boat and won't have cell reception for a while," Brooks explained. "I'll call you sometime next week."

Disconnecting, Wally approached the front

door. A couple of weather-beaten two-by-fours, resting loosely across stacked cinder blocks, functioned as the front steps. He tested the wood, and although they squeaked loudly in protest, the boards held his weight. Gingerly easing past a variety of rusty folding chairs and an old sofa that decorated the porch, he rapped on the weathered wooden door.

When no one responded to his polite knock, Wally banged harder. Suddenly, the door was yanked open and a scrawny-looking guy in his late teens stood in the doorway.

"Shit!" the skinny teenager squeaked, then turned his head and screamed, "5–0's here!"

In the blink of an eye, the teen grabbed a gun from his waistband and pointed it at Wally.

"Whoa there." Wally held his palms up. "Put down your weapon."

The young guy's hand was shaking and it was clear he wasn't a stone-cold killer. Unfortunately, Wally wasn't as sure about whoever had come up behind him and yanked some kind of sack over his head.

The teenager with the gun spoke to the person behind Wally. "Tin, look what I caught."

"Give me the gun, Boo-Boo," Tin ordered

the teen, then pushed Wally through the door and said, "Go get the duct tape."

"Listen, man," Wally said, keeping his voice even, "this doesn't have to get ugly. I'm only here checking out the place for your landlord."

There was no response, and a few seconds later, Wally's arms were jerked behind his back and tape was wrapped around his wrists. He felt his duty belt being removed. Then a gun was pushed into his side and a hand around his biceps dragged him forward.

Wally listened closely as he was marched through the house. He could hear feet shuffling and someone cursing, but nothing else.

When they came to a stop, hinges squeaked and Tin commanded, "Down."

Wally slowly shuffled from step to step. It smelled like the devil's room service and he figured they were descending into a dank basement or cellar that had been used to store food and whatever remained had been left to rot. When they reached the bottom, Tin pushed Wally onto what felt like a wooden chair. He taped Wally's feet to the legs, then he looped more tape around Wally's chest, securing him to the chair's back.

Suddenly, whatever had been placed over

Wally's head was whipped off and he blinked in the dim light of the overhead bulb. His pulse raced. If the guy wasn't worried about revealing his face, that meant he didn't intend to allow Wally to leave the place alive.

His captor stood frowning down at him and Wally quickly said, "Seriously. If you let me go right now, no harm, no foul."

Tin was a big guy, over six foot and well muscled, with long, dark hair held back by a skull-and-crossbones do-rag. Strangely enough, his eyes narrowed slightly, as if he might actually be considering it.

"Wish I could, man. But that will be up to Veep."

"You're not in charge?" Wally was surprised. He would have sworn Tin was giving the orders.

"Nah. I'm the sergeant-at-arms."

Wally tried to bond with the guy. "So sort of a cop, like me."

Tin shrugged and said, "Sorry about this."

Before Wally could figure out what the guy meant, Tin reached over and backhanded him with such force that his head snapped back.

When Wally didn't make a sound, Tin advised, "You need to scream," and hit him again.

Ignoring his throbbing jaw, Wally forced his voice to sound undisturbed and asked, "Why?"

Tin looked upward toward the closed door to the kitchen and said softly, "For them," and he hit Wally again.

Unsure of why he thought he should do as Tin said, Wally bellowed. This time instead of smacking Wally, Tin punched a leather-covered bag hanging from the ceiling. Catching on, Wally cried out each time the guy pummeled the bag.

When Tin stopped, Wally mouthed, "What's going on?"

"Keep quiet and I won't have to gag you." Tin fished Wally's keys and cell phone from his pants pocket, then roared, "That'll teach you to spy on us, you lying sack of shit!"

"Hey," Wally said as the guy started up the steps. "Why do they call you Tin?"

"It's short for Tin Man," the biker answered, " 'cause I got no heart."

As Wally heard the door to the kitchen close and lock, his mind worked furiously. His cheekbone throbbed, blood dripped down his jaw, and his right eye was almost swollen shut. Tin may not have hit him as hard or as much as he could have, but he'd still done a number on Wally's face.

Was that the point? Did Tin want Wally to

look as bad as possible? Why had the guy held back? The whole situation didn't add up. Didn't these men know that as soon as someone realized he was missing, they'd check out his last location?

Son of a freaking bitch! He'd made a rookie mistake and never called in his 10–20. He'd been so preoccupied about Skye, he'd forgotten.

Wally blew out a breath. At least Dante knew where he was. He'd just have to survive until the cavalry showed up or he could escape. There was no way in hell he was going to die in this shithole and leave Skye and his baby all alone.

CHAPTER 9

> "You people with hearts," he said, "have something to guide you, and need never do wrong; but I have no heart, and so I must be very careful. When Oz gives me a heart of course I needn't mind so much."
>
> — Tin Woodsman

After leaving the doctor's office, Skye and May hit Target and Walmart for the basic necessities — household goods, toiletries, underwear, and socks. Several hours later, they stopped at Olive Garden, her mother's favorite restaurant, for lunch.

As Skye slid into the booth, she groaned. It felt so good to sit down. Although she'd changed into her newly purchased tennis shoes, her ankles were still swollen and her feet were killing her.

Sighing in relief, she contemplated slipping off her sneakers but knew she'd never get them back on her feet. Instead, she dug through her purse and retrieved her phone. Wally had left her both a voicemail and a text, demanding that she call him ASAP.

Skye bit her lip, looked at her mom, and said, "Wally wants me to call him."

"Not a good idea." May shook her head firmly as she used an antibacterial hand wipe to clean off the already immaculate tabletop. "You'll spill the beans if you talk to him. You're not good at lying."

"Yeah. I guess." Skye shrugged. "I have a hard enough time remembering the truth." She paused. "But I could probably keep the twins a secret by just not mentioning them."

"Secrets aren't your strong point either." May didn't raise her eyes from the menu. Skye snickered softly. May was studying the selections as if she'd never been to the restaurant before and wasn't going to order her usual soup, salad, and breadsticks. Or maybe her mother was looking at the drinks. She rarely ate out without having a cocktail.

"I can, too, keep secrets," Skye protested, then added, "Just not my own."

"Just send him a text saying you'll talk to him when you get home." May straightened the salt and pepper shakers. "And then turn off your phone."

Before Skye could answer, the waiter approached. "Hi. My name's Auggie and I'll be serving you today. Are you ready to order?"

Once they made their selections and the server left, Skye texted Wally and took a sip of ice water. "We probably should head back to Scumble River soon. Wally's dad is sending us a motor coach to live in and he said it would be delivered sometime between two and four."

"What?" May yelped. "Carson is giving you a camper? Why am I only hearing about this now?"

The waiter returned with their drinks, salad, and breadsticks. He assured them their soup would be out soon and hurried away. The restaurant was crowded and the poor man was nearly running between tables.

"I forgot you didn't know." Skye nabbed a breadstick and took a big bite of the warm, garlicky goodness. Once her mouth was no longer full, she said, "He's just loaning us the RV and his boss is the one picking up the tab."

Because she and Wally had agreed not to tell anyone about his father's wealth, including May, Skye stuck to the story they'd told Charlie.

"Must be nice to work for a company like that." May sipped her Bloody Mary. "The city doesn't even give me a present at Christmas."

"Hmm." Luckily, Skye's mouth was filled with salad because she wasn't sure how to respond. If she agreed, her mom would defend her employer; if she didn't, her mom would claim Skye never took her side.

Changing the subject, Skye swallowed and asked, "Have you heard anything more about Zeke Lyons? Wally wasn't at all happy that rumors of his murder are already floating around Scumble River."

"Nobody has said anything to me about him being murdered." May moved her hands out of the way, allowing the server to put the bowl of hot chicken-and-gnocchi soup in front of her. "Minnie did mention that his death was a shame, since he was practically a newlywed."

After serving Skye's minestrone, the waiter asked, "Anything else I can get for you ladies?"

"More breadsticks," Skye said just as her mother made a similar request.

As they ate, May filled in Skye on which of their friends and family had tornado damage and the severity of the destruction. Many of her first, second, and more distant cousins had trees down, roofs in need of repair, and windows broken. It was shocking to realize just how many Scumble Riv-erites were affected.

As she and her mother chatted, Skye thought about what her aunt Minnie had said to May about Zeke. When Skye had seen Billie Lyons at the dispatcher counter, she'd estimated her to be in her late forties or even early fifties. Billie might not be the first Mrs. Lyons. An acrimonious divorce could provide a motive for his murder.

Skye wiped her mouth with her napkin. "Was it a second marriage for Mr. Lyons?" Shoving her empty bowl away, she patted her stomach. She and the babies were nearly full and she wanted dessert.

"I have no idea." May motioned the server over. "Zeke is new in town. I think he lived in Brooklyn before he got married. And Billie always kept to herself."

When the waiter approached the table, May started to ask for their check, but Skye interrupted and said, "I'll have a slice of the lemon cream cake."

"I thought the doctor warned you about gaining more weight." May scowled.

"Your point?" Skye raised a brow and shot a significant look at her mother's empty Bloody Mary glass. "I'm pregnant; sugar is my booze."

"Well, far be it for me to interfere," May

said, then she handed the server her credit card and told Skye that lunch was her treat.

After the waiter brought the cake, May didn't comment as Skye finished every crumb. Finally, pushing the plate away, she scooted out of the booth and told her mom that she was going to the restroom. She definitely needed a potty break before they headed to the mall.

As May drove the short distance to the shopping center, Skye made a mental list of what she needed to buy. Although she didn't want to forget anything vital, she really wanted to get just the bare essentials.

There were several reasons Skye didn't plan on purchasing too many clothes for herself today. First, she didn't have the time to look around. Second, she'd need maternity clothes only for another couple of months. And third, shopping for herself with her mother was always a challenge. Not because May didn't want Skye to get anything, but because her attention span was so short and she tended to wander away.

When Skye and May entered JC Penney, Skye draped her purse strap across her body, glanced around until she spotted the men's department, and said, "I'm going to get Wally's stuff first."

"Maybe I should buy Jed a new shirt?"

May tapped her chin. "I bought myself those sandals at Target and I didn't get him anything."

"Didn't you tell me you needed to get an outfit for Maggie's son's wedding?" Skye asked, trying to distract her mother.

The last thing Skye's father needed was another "guilt" shirt. Every time May bought something for herself, she felt the need to even the score. Maybe if she got Jed a six-pack of beer or a new model tractor, he'd appreciate the thought. But he rarely wore anything other than work clothes and his closet was already stuffed with garments he didn't need.

"Well, the wedding *is* only a few weeks away," May said, clearly tempted. "No. A few months ago, when we had our little talk, one of the things you said that bothered you was that when we go shopping, it seemed that no matter what we start out looking for, we usually end up getting clothes for me. Today is going to be different."

"Wow." Skye hugged her mom. "You actually listened to me. Thank you."

"I'm trying." May grabbed Skye's elbow and attempted to tug her in the direction of the maternity department. "Let's get you some outfits."

"How about while I shop for Wally, you

look for yourself?" Skye freed her arm from her mother's grasp. "Then, I'll grab some maternity clothes and meet you at the dressing room near the petites."

"Great." May beamed. "We can try on what we've found together. I'll buy you an outfit."

"Thanks, Mom." Skye waved and hurried away, feeling touched that her mother had not only understood her concerns, but was also trying to change for the better. "I'll see you in about half an hour."

It took less than fifteen minutes to buy Wally shorts, jeans, shirts, and a belt. She'd already gotten both of them sneakers at Target. Next, she made a quick trip through the maternity section, grabbing a pair of jeans, black slacks, knit capris, shorts, a dress, and several tops before heading toward the dressing room.

May was waiting with her own armload and they quickly chose adjoining cubicles. Skye had already tried on and approved most of her selections when she heard her mother calling for her.

May stood in front of a three-way mirror at the end of the row of dressing rooms. She wore a pair of flowy, cream slacks with a brown-and-beige silky top that poofed out over an elastic band that rested on her hips.

She twisted around, looking at herself, and asked, "What do you think?"

"It's nice," Skye said, not mentioning the fact that it looked like an outfit her mother already owned. "It fits you well."

"I don't think it's right for the wedding." May frowned. "It looks cheap."

"Okay." Skye felt her eye start to twitch and reminded herself she'd been the one to encourage her mother to shop. "I guess I don't understand what you want."

May screwed up her face in thought, then said, "It can't be too fancy, but it shouldn't be too casual either. Dressy, but not formal."

"I'll keep that in mind." Skye's head was spinning with the conflicting descriptions. "Do you have something else to try on?"

"Two more outfits," May said and disappeared into her cubicle.

Shopping for clothing for May was always mind-boggling. She wanted an outfit to make her look ten years younger, ten pounds slimmer, and she wanted it for less than twenty bucks. Too bad Skye didn't have a magic wand.

While Skye waited for her mother to reappear, she checked the time. It was one forty-five. There was no way they were going to make it back to town by two. Sighing, she dialed Wally. She had to make sure he would be at their place when the motor coach arrived. Surely, she could keep her mouth shut about the twins for a two-minute conversation.

Wally's cell went directly to voicemail and Skye left a message. Before she could try his landline at the PD, May walked out of her dressing room wearing navy-blue slacks and a frilly, red, white, and blue top.

"That's pretty," Skye said.

"No. The shirt is too fitted. It shows all my rolls of fat." May twirled on her heels and disappeared again.

Skye bit the inside of her cheek to keep from screaming. Her mother wore a size six, occasionally an eight, and the only bulges were in her imagination.

May liked the third outfit, but before she could stop herself, Skye said, "The blouse is too big." The top hung loosely on May's small frame, the shoulder seams drooping halfway down her upper arms. "Let me get you a size smaller."

"Then it would be too tight." May's expression was stubborn. "I'm getting this one."

"Fine." They needed to get going, and although Skye knew May would end up returning the shirt, instead of indulging in a futile argument, she followed her mom to the register.

After Skye and May paid for their purchases, they walked out to the parking lot. Skye was loading the bags in the Oldsmobile's trunk when she noticed Billie Lyons get out of a car the next row over. She stood near the open door, looking as if she couldn't remember where she was or how she got there.

As May drove away from the mall, Skye saw Billie's mother take her daughter by the arm and lead her toward the entrance. Skye's heart broke for the shattered woman. Shopping may have been a chore for Skye and May, but at least they hadn't been dealing with the tragedy of their husbands' deaths.

After a long, contemplative moment of sadness, Skye reached for her purse. Digging out her phone, she dialed Wally's cell. But once again it went straight to his voicemail. She got the same result when she tried his private line at the police station.

Frowning, she sent him a text, then looked at her mom, and said, "Wally isn't answering his cell or landline. I need him to be at our house in case the motor coach from his father arrives before we get home."

"Call Thea," May suggested. "If he's out of the station, she can get him on the radio."

"I hate making her do that for our personal business," Skye said.

"Don't worry." May waved away Skye's concern. "It's not as if you're asking her to contact him to pick up a gallon of milk. These are unusual circumstances and everyone needs to cut everyone else a little slack."

"True." Skye dialed the police station's nonemergency number, and when Thea answered, she relayed her request to the dispatcher.

A few minutes later, Thea came back on the line and said, "The chief's not responding on the radio. I just checked in the garage. His squad car is gone, but he never gave us a location update."

"Oh." Skye felt lightheaded. "When you reach him, please tell him to call me immediately."

May glanced at her daughter and wrinkled her brow. "What's wrong?"

Skye repeated what Thea had told her, then said, "Where could he be?"

"He's probably helping with the search and rescue efforts and the batteries in his handheld radio are dead." May patted Skye's knee. "It isn't very often that those radios get this much use."

"I guess." Skye chewed her thumbnail. "But I have a really bad feeling."

"He's fine," May assured her, but pressed her foot down on the gas and honked at a slow-moving Chevy pickup.

"I hope you're right." Skye gave her mother a forced smile. "This is one time that I'd be happy to hear you say 'I told you so.' "

"And I'll be happy to say it," May muttered, riding the truck's bumper.

"Maybe you should slow down a little, Mom." Skye clutched the dashboard.

"How about this?" May ignored Skye's suggestion. "I'll drop you at the PD so you can check Wally's office and then go wait for the motor coach at your house. My shift starts at four, so I can stay until then."

"That would be great." Skye inhaled. "Maybe he left me a note or something on his desk." She hit her forehead with her palm. "Shoot! I should have arranged to rent a car when we were in Kankakee."

"Oh." May made the turn that would take them into Scumble River. "I forgot to tell you that your dad is borrowing a car for you from his brother. He might already have it waiting at your house."

"When does Uncle Wiley get back from California?" Skye asked.

"Sunday. So that gives you a few days to figure something else out." May pulled up in front of the police station. "I'll call you when the motor coach gets to your place or if Wally shows up at the house."

"Thanks, Mom." Skye leaned over to kiss her mother's cheek. "Can you put all the stuff I bought today in the RV when it gets there?"

"No problem. I'll pick up some groceries for you, too." May gave Skye a one-armed hug. "Try not to worry."

Skye watched her mother drive away, then hurried inside the station. She used her key to let herself into the back, then went looking for Thea. She found the dispatcher talking on the phone at her desk and shot her a questioning glance.

When Thea shook her head, Skye's chest tightened. It was extremely unusual for Wally not to check in with the dispatcher when he was out of his office. Even more uncommon for him not to immediately return Skye's calls and texts.

When Thea hung up, she said, "I've checked with everyone I can think of — all the officers, the ILEAS coordinator, and the fire chief. No one has seen or heard from the chief since before eleven o'clock."

"That's about the time of his last text to me." Skye rubbed her belly.

"All the officers are keeping an eye out for

his squad car," Thea said.

"Could he have run over to Laurel to talk to the ME about Zeke Lyons?"

"That's a thought." Thea reached for the phone. "Let me check with the medical examiner and the crime scene lab." She pressed the buttons on the receiver. "First thing this morning, the chief requested the techs look at the scene. He said he doubted they'd find anything in the rubble, but wanted to cover his bases."

While Thea made her calls, Skye tried to think of anywhere else Wally might be. The only option she could come up with was their house, and if he was there, her mother would have already let her know.

Thea disconnected and said, "The chief isn't at the ME's or the lab." The dispatcher pressed her lips together. "I don't know what else to do."

"Let me look in his office," Skye said walking toward the stairs. "If there's nothing there, we need to have Sergeant Quirk put out an APB."

CHAPTER 10

"Dear me," said the Voice, "how sudden! Well, come to me tomorrow, for I must have time to think it over."

— The Wizard

As Skye climbed the steps to the police station's second floor, she whispered to herself, "Wally's fine. There's no need to panic. There'll be something on his desk that will explain his absence."

Using her key to unlock the door to his office, Skye hurried across the large room. Wally's desktop was strewn with documents and she sank into his leather chair. It would take a while to go through everything and she was beyond tired. Dealing with the tornado, adjusting to news of the twins, and shopping had already exhausted her. Wally's absence was the final straw.

Thirty minutes later, Skye had listened to his voicemail — nothing helpful — studied every scrap of paper, and examined every folder. She separated the documents into two piles — tornado and murder — but there hadn't been any hint as to Wally's location.

Snatching the silver-framed photograph of their wedding from the desktop, Skye leaned back in the chair and stared at the portrait. Her gown had been gorgeous and Wally had been even more handsome than usual in his tuxedo. They'd been so happy that day. Years of obstacles and missteps were behind them and they were finally together. If something had happened to Wally, she wasn't sure she could go on.

Skye traced a finger over his image and set the picture aside. She wasn't giving up. There had to be a clue somewhere. She glanced at the computer. Maybe there was something on his schedule.

Shaking the mouse to wake up the screen, Skye searched her mind for Wally's password. She had all that kind of information in the file cabinet at home. Or at least she'd *had* it. Who knew where that folder was now?

Think! Think! Think! She pounded her forehead with the heel of her hand. As she gazed at their wedding portrait, the answer popped into her brain. She quickly typed

HoneymoonCruise2006 and she was in. Too bad the only entry on Wally's schedule for today was her ob-gyn appointment.

Shit! Now what? She considered the various icons on the home screen. Maybe he'd gotten an email and had decided to respond in person.

Inspecting the list dated today, Skye paused at the one from the medical examiner. It was the preliminary findings from Zeke Lyons's autopsy. Even though it didn't look as if Wally had opened the email from the ME, Skye thought maybe there was a way to keep messages appearing as new. Her tech skills were pretty limited.

If he had read it, there might be something in the description that Wally could have left to investigate. Someone he'd want to interview.

Skye clicked on the ME's email and skimmed the report. The only interesting information was that the half a dozen pair of distinctive, round burn marks on Zeke Lyons's chest were thought to have come from a device that had administered an electric shock. However, they didn't match any of the standard stun guns and the crime lab was still trying to figure out the kind of weapon that was used.

The electrical discharge had aggravated

an underlying arterial weakness in his brain, which led to a hemorrhagic stroke. And evidently, that type of stroke caused peripheral neuropathy, which would have made Zeke's feet feel as if they were on fire. The ME theorized that the victim's shoes were off because of that sensation.

Delusions were another byproduct of that type of stroke, which might explain the location and position of Zeke's body. He might have wandered into the bathroom and barricaded himself inside before dying.

Skye contemplated what she'd learned about the councilman's death. If she were Wally, where would she go after reading the medical examiner's summary?

After several long seconds, she shrugged. She'd want to talk to whoever might have administered the electrical shock. But she had no idea who, besides looters, would have been around in the period right before or after the storm. Did burglars carry devices that could shock people?

Shaking her head, Skye tried unsuccessfully to call Wally. While leaving yet another voicemail, Skye received a text from May stating that the motor coach had arrived and was being set up. After thanking her mom for the update, Skye buried her head in her hands and cried. There was still no sign of Wally or any clue to his whereabouts. Something had definitely happened to him and she wasn't sure what to do next.

A few minutes later, Skye scrubbed her eyes and took a deep breath. She needed to be strong and control her emotions. Shoving her fears aside, she trudged down the stairs. Her legs felt as if they were made of lead instead of flesh and bones, and she barely made it to the first floor without falling to her knees and giving up.

Finally, she smoothed her hair, straightened her spine, and went to find Thea. It was time to call in Sergeant Quirk and get all the officers searching for their missing chief.

"It'll be fine. You don't have to worry." Roy Quirk awkwardly patted Skye's back. "We'll locate Chief Boyd. It's probably just some kind of mix-up because of the confusion with the tornado aftermath. He'll show up safe and sound and we'll all laugh at ourselves for being so upset."

From the corner of her eye, Skye studied the sergeant. Roy was in his midthirties, and except for his lack of hair, he still looked like the football player he'd been in high school. He had a muscular build, no discernible neck, and tree-trunk-like thighs.

Skye and the sergeant had gotten off to a rocky start when they'd first met. Skye hadn't been hired as an official consultant yet, and although Wally had been open to her help in solving cases, Quirk hadn't thought a female civilian should be sticking her nose into police business. However, unlike the previous time when Wally hadn't been around during an investigation, now Roy seemed more than happy to consult with her and include her in the process. Which was a darn good thing. Otherwise, the sergeant might find himself singing soprano instead of bass.

"I've issued a bulletin to all police departments in Illinois to be on the lookout for Chief Boyd and/or his vehicle." Roy repeated what he'd already told her several times. "And if the chief doesn't turn up within the next few hours, the state police have agreed to launch an aerial search of the region."

"That's good." Skye sniffed, refusing to cry. "I read about this officer that was found using location equipment in his police cruiser. Can't we tap into Wally's car?"

"If Mayor Leofanti had approved our request for new vehicles we could." Quirk scowled. "But he didn't and our current cruisers don't have that technology. I have put a request in to the county crime lab to attempt to track the chief's cell."

"But?" Skye tilted her head. Roy was holding something back.

"But, if the device is off or the SIM card has been removed, that won't work," Quirk admitted. "And since the chief's phone keeps going directly to voicemail, there's a good chance it isn't on."

"So we're stuck with the old-fashioned method?" Skye paced the length of the interrogation/coffee room. "Besides our people searching, what else can we do?"

"That's the thing." Quirk's tone was reluctant. "I can't pull our guys away from clearing the buildings demolished by the tornadoes."

"The hell you can't!" Skye snapped, skidding to a stop in front of Roy and leaning past her huge belly so they were nose to nose. "Get volunteers on the houses. Wally's officers should be the ones looking for him."

"I promise you that every officer, firefighter, and paramedic in the area is keeping their eyes peeled for any sign of the chief." Roy retreated a few feet and held up his palm. "Every five minutes, Thea tries his radio and Lonny tries his cell."

"Okay." Skye strangled the word. "But there has to be something more we can do."

"If the chief's vehicle is located and he isn't in it, I will pull our guys from clearing houses and we'll do a grid search. I've reached out to an organization in Wisconsin that will bring in bloodhounds once we have a general area for the dogs to explore."

"Uh-huh." Skye swallowed, trying to hold back her tears. "I guess I should call Wally's father and let him know what's happening. I don't want him finding out from the media that his son is missing."

"You do that." Quirk stepped toward the door. "Can I get someone here for you?"

"Mom will be here for her shift soon," Skye said, attempting to paste a brave smile on her face. "I'm fine and I don't want to take anyone away from helping people who really need it."

"Is your cell charged?" Roy paused halfway into the hallway.

"I plugged it in while I was searching Wally's office." Skye exhaled. "As much as I want to panic, I'm trying to keep it together for my babies."

"Babies?" Quirk's eyebrows rose.

"I mean this baby." Skye patted her belly. "And our kitty, Bingo."

"Of course." Roy's expression let Skye know that he questioned her sanity. "If you think of anyplace the chief might be, let me know."

Skye nodded and Quirk closed the door behind him as he left. Skye blew out a breath. She needed to be more careful. That had been a close one. She had to warn her mother again not tell anyone about the twins. Wally had the right to be the first to hear that news.

After getting a bottle of water from the coffee room fridge — if she didn't stay hydrated, the Braxton-Hicks contractions were more likely to start up — Skye took out her cell and dialed Wally's father.

The phone barely rang before Carson answered. "Did the motor coach arrive?"

"It did." Skye decided to ease into the bad news. "They're in the process of setting it up right now."

"What do you think of it?" Carson asked. "I hope it's big enough."

"I'm sure it will be wonderful," Skye assured him. "I haven't seen it yet, but Mom's on site supervising and she says it's amazing."

"Good. Good." Carson's voice oozed satisfaction. "How did your doctor's appointment go? Is my adorable grandchild behaving and on schedule?"

"So far." Skye battled the urge to tell him

about the twins. "Dr. Johnson seemed pleased."

"I checked her out," Carson said. "She's been named the best ob-gyn in Illinois five years running. She's very well thought of in her field."

Skye rolled her eyes. Of course Carson had looked into her doctor. She wasn't just carrying his grandchild; she was carrying what he hoped would be the next president of CB International.

"I like Dr. J," Skye said firmly. "And that's what really counts."

"How're things in Scumble River? From the news, it looks like a significant portion of the town has been devastated." Carson seemed settled in for a long chat. "Is there anything that I can do to help out? Say the word and I'll get whatever the community needs."

"Thanks, Dad." Skye smiled. "Once the dust settles a little, I'll let you know what folks need. At this moment, people are still too shell-shocked to have figured out much beyond their immediate necessities. And those seem to be under control."

"How's my son doing with all this?" Carson asked. "I imagine seeing *his* town in ruins is hard on him. I'm glad you're with him."

"Actually . . ." Skye fought back the urge to cry. "That's why I'm calling."

"Oh." Carson's tone was cautious. "Is there a problem with Wally?"

"We don't know." Skye decided the best way to tell her father-in-law was to rip off the bandage. "No one has seen or heard from him since this morning at eleven o'clock. He's not answering his radio or cell phone, and he didn't tell the dispatcher where he was heading."

"What's being done?" Carson demanded. "I hope they aren't making you wait twenty-four hours to declare him a missing person."

"No." Skye had been afraid of that herself. "When an on-duty officer goes missing, those restrictions aren't an issue."

"In that case, what's happening?" Carson sounded strained.

Skye outlined what was in place, then added, "I've been racking my brain as to where Wally could be. Yesterday, after the tornadoes, he discovered that someone had been murdered. I'm thinking that his disappearance has something to do with that case."

"Is there a list of suspects?" Carson asked. "Could Wally have gone to interview one of them and been ambushed? Has Quirk checked on that?"

"As far as I know, there aren't any suspects yet. Mr. Lyons's life seems too boring to inspire a passionate murder."

"Those quiet ones can fool you."

"Maybe. But I think the working theory is that he was killed by looters." Skye moved the water bottle on the table and drew her fingers through the condensation left behind. "The preliminary medical examiner's report only came in a few hours ago and I'm not even sure Wally saw it."

"Oh." Carson paused, then asked, "Did you read the ME's report?"

"Uh-huh." Skye blew out a frustrated breath. "I need to think about it some more. My first impression was that it didn't really point to anyone."

"So if Wally didn't go to interrogate a suspect, what else might he do to investigate a murder?" Carson asked. "Would he take another look at the crime scene or go talk to the medical examiner?"

"The dispatcher checked with the ME, and if his cruiser was at the crime scene, someone would have seen it," Skye explained. "My father is arranging for me to borrow my uncle's car, and once I have wheels, I plan on driving down every road in the city limits."

"Not alone! What if Wally was grabbed by

a bad guy and that creep gets you, too?" Carson roared. "Someone needs to go with you. Preferably someone armed."

"Everyone is busy." Skye slumped in defeat. "Uncle Charlie has lots of displaced people at the motor court. All my relatives and friends are either clearing their own property of debris or helping their own families. There's just no one for me to ask."

"Listen to me, sweetheart, you go get settled in the motor coach," Carson ordered. "I'm hopping on the company plane. You hold off until I get to you, and then you and I will find my boy." Skye could hear him giving orders to someone on his end, then he came back on the line. "Hang in there. I'll be with you by ten tonight."

"If I wait until then, we'll lose the light," Skye argued. "I can't just sit around and do nothing while Wally may be in trouble."

"You aren't," Carson soothed. "Your first priority is to take care of your baby. And while you're getting into some fresh clothes and resting, you let that amazing brain of yours go to work."

"Well . . ." Skye sighed. Carson was right. She owed her babies the best she could do for them. And as it was, she was too tired to think straight. A shower, a different outfit, and a nap might be just what she needed to kick-start her brain and figure something out. "Okay. I'll do what you suggest. But if you aren't here by ten and I can't find anyone else, I'm going out on my own."

"I'll be there and the dark won't stop us. I'm having my Hummer loaded on the plane as we speak. It has the most powerful searchlight made attached to the roof." Carson paused, then said, "And I'm licensed to carry. Anyone who messes with me or mine will be real, real sorry, darlin'."

"Got it." Skye wiped at her eyes. When Carson had called her darlin', he'd sounded just like his son. "See you soon, Dad."

Disconnecting, Skye took a deep breath. She could do this. She could be as strong as she needed to be to find Wally and take care of her babies.

Skye called Frannie, who agreed to keep Bingo for a couple more days. Hanging up, Skye sent a text to May, asking her to come get her, then headed outside to wait for her mother to arrive.

As she passed the multiple whiteboards listing people trying to connect, find possessions, and locate pets, Skye saw an elderly woman leaning against the board, crying. She started to walk by, but even with all her own troubles, she just couldn't do it.

Stopping, she said, "Is there anything I

can do to help? Anyone I can call?"

"No." The woman dug a hanky from her pocket and wiped her eyes. "My daughter and son-in-law are on their way here from Maryland." Her breath hitched. "It's just when the tornado took my house, it took everything I had of my husband. He died last year and all our pictures and souvenirs from our trips are gone. There's nothing left. So I came to see if anything had been found. But there's nothing."

Skye swallowed the lump in her throat. What could she say? She couldn't assure her that her things would be recovered.

Instead, she held out her arms to the elderly woman and murmured, "How about a hug to tide you over until your daughter gets here?"

The woman nodded and moved into Skye's embrace. A few seconds later, she straightened her spine and said, "Thank you. I'll be fine. The tornado may have taken my things, but certainly not my memories."

Skye gave her a final squeeze and waved goodbye. The community had lost a lot when the tornadoes ripped through Scumble River. But country folks were tough and resilient. The town would come back stronger than ever. And so would Wally.

CHAPTER 11

"You have plenty of courage, I am sure. All you need is confidence in yourself. There is no living thing that is not afraid when it faces danger. The True courage is in facing danger when you are afraid, and that kind of courage you have in plenty."

— The Wizard

Wally had been trying to get his hands free from the duct-tape restraints since Tin had left him alone, but he hadn't made much progress. The tape wasn't that tight around his wrists, but it was so damn sticky it seemed more like superglue than regular adhesive was holding the ends together.

The swollen tissue of his right eye made it difficult to see anything on that side of his body and his entire face felt like one giant bruise. At least he wasn't gagged and Tin hadn't punched him in the nose. With a broken nose or a rag stuffed in his mouth, breathing could be a problem.

As it was, Wally's mind felt fuzzy and he wasn't sure how long it had been since his capture. It seemed like forever, but his sense of time was distorted and he might have dozed off for a while.

Initially, the only sounds he heard were the occasional creaks of someone walking across the floor above him. But fifteen or twenty minutes ago, several motorcycles and what sounded like a large pickup truck had roared past the house. He assumed they were heading to the machine shed he had attempted to check out earlier.

The way the light was changing as it seeped around the edges of the cardboard-covered basement windows suggested it was now late afternoon or early evening. Wally's best guess was he'd been held prisoner for at least five hours, and that worried him.

Even sixty minutes was a long stretch for an officer to be out of touch. Especially the chief. By now, someone at the police department should have figured out Wally was missing and come to find him.

He figured his captors would have hidden the squad car, but Dante knew Wally's last location. Surely, when his staff started looking for him, the mayor would tell Quirk where he had been heading.

Of course, it was entirely possible that Dante wasn't even aware of Wally's absence. Hizzoner might very well already be home enjoying a drink before sitting down to eat supper with his wife. It wasn't as if Quirk would think to seek out the mayor. The Scumble River officers tended to keep their distance from the slimy politician.

Shit! No one was coming to his rescue. Wally's stomach knotted, then he lifted his chin. *Fine!* He was not dying in this dank basement. He'd figure a way out of here himself.

No way in hell was he leaving Skye a widow. Reid would move in on her before Wally's body was in the ground. And that smarmy bastard wasn't ever sharing Skye's bed again, or raising Wally's child.

Tightening his jaw, Wally renewed his efforts on the tape manacling his wrists. He dug his fingernails into the smooth outer surface. If he could just find an edge, he could peel it apart. And once his hands were free, he'd escape. Either through one of the windows, if he could fit through the small opening, or by kicking down the door to the kitchen.

Wally began to take a careful inventory of the basement's contents for a weapon. The concrete walls were cracked and a single were right here to take advantage as soon as the tornadoes went through. We got all kinds of valuable shit from those empty houses and the twister did all the work for us. Lots of 'em was opened up like a can of sardines."

So they'd done a little looting, too. Why wasn't Wally surprised?

"You remember that guy with the German shepherd?" one of the bikers asked. "Can you believe" — the voice trailed off, and Wally heard footsteps walking away then coming back — "old lady — ?"

"Enough reminiscing." Veep cut him off. "It'll take us a few days to move to a new clubhouse. What're we going to do with the heat in the basement?"

"Kill him," someone suggested, his voice rasping like a knife against a whetstone. "Lots of land around to dump the body."

"That's one option." Tin's tone was casual. "But 5–0 won't look for us too hard if all we're doing is ripping people off. We kill a cop and they never give up. And I got a pillowcase over his head right away, so he ain't seen none of our faces."

"He saw mine," Boo-Boo whined.

"Only for a few seconds and you don't have a record, so all he's going to be able to do is describe you." Tin laughed snidely. "It

bare bulb hung from the ceiling rafters. In addition to the punching bag Tin had beaten on when he'd spared Wally any further pounding, there was an old metal workbench, its surface bare of tools.

Several busted-up chairs that matched the one Wally occupied were leaning against a farmhouse table missing one leg. And directly in front of him stood a stained, 1950s-era refrigerator minus its door. Other than an ancient furnace and water heater huddled near the back, the rest of the space was empty.

No. Wait. Resting against a wall in a dim corner to Wally's left was a rusted shovel that would make a jim-dandy bludgeon. Now all he had to do was get his hands free.

As he returned to picking at the tape around his wrists, raised voices interrupted his efforts. Wally froze, then, wanting to hear better, he scooted his chair to the bottom of the stairs.

The aroma of hamburgers and onions frying drifted down the steps, and his stomach growled, reminding him that he hadn't had anything to eat since breakfast with Skye and Charlie. The gang must be sitting down to dinner in the kitchen. Were they arguing, or was that their normal mealtime conversational tone?

Wally could identify Boo-Boo and Tin's voices, but he hadn't heard anyone else speak. Now, if he'd counted correctly, there were ten men in the house.

If Wally had to guess, the loudest and most frequent voice most likely belonged to the leader of the motorcycle gang, the guy Tin had called Veep. Commanding a bunch of criminals wasn't for the soft-spoken, and this guy was dominating the discussion. Although Tin was a close second.

Wally hadn't heard Boo-Boo say much, but someone ordered him to speak and he stuttered, "Uh . . . this bull came to the door and I . . . uh . . . I thought he was raiding the place so I pulled my nine and . . ."

"And now we have 5–0 in the basement," one of the other men finished.

"Boo-Boo." Veep's tone was sharp edged. "You and I will have a powwow about this later. Right now, we need to decide what to do with the cop."

"We been talking about packing up and moving on, and I been looking around. There's a place across the state line that we can have as soon as we hand over the rent," Tin said. "You gotta think that if the guy who owns this place had someone checking on it, he'll keep sending people until he finds out what we got going on. It might be

a good time to find another spot ri
the picking."

"Satan's Posse don't run away wh
gets rough," someone sneered.

"Remember, when we established
offshoot of the club, Prez told us we
supposed to work smart rather than h
He ordered more stealth and less swagg
Tin's tone was mild. "Does it really m
you the toughest bastard in town if you
through a pile of shit for the prize rath
than stroll a few feet downstream to pick
the gold just sitting there?"

"Tin's got a good point." Veep's voice me
lowed. "The storm screwed up our nice little gig here. They got the town tied dow
so tight, it'll be a long time until we can ge
back to business, and even then it will be a lot harder to rip off houses with all the media attention."

Ah. Wally nodded to himself. So these were the guys behind all the recent burglaries in the area. The sheriff had been sure there was some kind of organized ring involved in the thefts. Reports of a motorcycle gang using drugs and prostitutes to recruit kids put the bikers on the top of the suspect list, but no one had been able to locate their hideout.

"Hey," another member said, "at least we

ain't as if there aren't a million nineteen-year-olds that don't look exactly like you."

"Why you so interested in keeping the fuzz alive?" a suspicious voice hissed like a wasp hovering near a lighted window.

Tin drawled, "Because we can make some bank on the guy."

"How?" Veep's tone was interested. "Who'd pay to get him back?"

"His old man," Tin answered. "I did a little internet research this afternoon. At first, it seemed as if the guy wasn't nothing more than a small-town cop. But then when I was reading his wedding announcement, his father's name sort of tickled something in the way back of my mind, so I looked daddy-o up."

"And?" Veep asked impatiently. "Who is his old man, and how much will he pay?"

"An article on the old dude said he was a Texas oil millionaire, but I suspect he's probably more like a billionaire." Tin spoke in the gratified tone of a satisfied customer. "His name is Carson Boyd. He's the sole owner and CEO of CB International, which is a family business."

Well, shit! On the one hand, Wally was glad the gang had a reason to keep him alive. On the other, if an outlaw biker could figure out his father's worth, so could any teenager in Scumble River. Which meant it was time to clue in the townspeople as to Wally's real family background before it came out in an inappropriate way. He'd have to ask Skye the best approach to revealing that information.

"Son of a bitch!" Veep thundered. "What in the hell is this guy doing working a shitty-ass job in the middle of Podunk, Illinois?"

"Good question," Tin said, his tone brisk. "But a better one is: How much is he worth?"

Despite Veep being the leader, Tin seemed to be the brains of the outfit. Maybe that's why he'd gone easy when he'd roughed up Wally. Maybe he'd already been thinking of ransoming him off to the highest bidder.

But something still didn't sit right about the guy. Tin's demeanor with Wally was just a shade different from when he was with the gang. Even his language patterns seemed different. Was he a well-educated man who was hiding that from his fellow gang members, or was there something more going on with him?

Before Wally could decide, the kitchen door slammed opened and he hurriedly scooted his chair to its original position and pretended to doze. In an instant, boots thundered down the staircase.

"Wake up, sleepyhead." A slap across the face forced his eyelids open, then Tin tied a bandana over Wally's eyes and whispered, "Veep's coming down to have a few words with you. Don't screw up."

A few seconds later, a hand grabbed Wally's chin and a voice like gravel rumbled, "So you got yourself a rich daddy?"

Wally ignored Veep's question and Tin growled, "Answer the man."

Wally wasn't sure why, but he took Tin's advice and said, "Yeah. I guess my father's done all right for himself."

"Why you working a crap job here in Butt-crack, Illinois, instead of living the good life with your daddy in Texas?" Veep dug his ragged nails into Wally's cheeks. "You on the outs with him?"

"No." Wally gritted his teeth. "Dad and I are good. I just wasn't the type to be able to sit behind a desk and go to meetings all day."

Wally wanted to refuse to cooperate, but being macho wouldn't get him out of this situation alive. And he'd rather swallow his pride and see his baby born than go to his grave for mouthing off.

"What do you think? You figure your old man will come up with a cool mil to get you back safe and sound?" Veep asked.

"That's a lot of money," Wally said. "His assets might not be that liquid."

"Maybe some motivation will liquefy them." Veep cackled. "Nothing like seeing your flesh and blood's flesh and blood to help open a wallet."

From the feel of cold metal against his neck, Wally assumed the man had a knife next to his ear.

"Let's not permanently damage the merchandise just yet," Tin cautioned.

"Here's the thing," Wally said, deciding his best chance at making it back to Skye and his baby alive was to cooperate. "It will take my father four or five business days to get a million dollars in cash. And I'm guessing you guys would like to get your money and make tracks as fast as possible." When Veep snarled a yes, Wally continued. "Dad keeps two hundred and fifty thousand in his safe. You could literally have it in your hands by tomorrow night."

Tin and Veep were silent, then Veep said, "A quarter mil it is. How we going to do this, Tin? You got a number to call?"

"All I got is the company's listing," Tin said. "But that won't get to Old Man Boyd directly, which is what we want." He snatched a handful of Wally's hair. "What's your father's private number?"

"I don't know it by heart." Wally shrugged. Hoping someone was trying to track his cell, and if Tin turned it on, they could draw a bead on his location, he suggested, "It's in the contacts on my phone."

"Well, isn't it lucky I have your cell right here in my pocket," Tin said. "Got it!" He paused, then added, "You know, if we use the cop's phone to call, his father will definitely pick up. Especially if they've figured out he's missing. The guy will be anxious to talk to his son."

"Smart." Veep's voice held a chilling smile.

As predicted, his call was answered in one ring.

Evidently, Tin had put the phone on speaker, because Wally heard his dad yell, "Wally!" Then ask, "Where the hell are you? You got your pretty, little wife all in a tizzy and that isn't good in her condition."

"Glad to hear you're worried about your son," Tin crooned.

"Who the hell are you, and what have you done with my boy?" Carson snapped.

"Wally is snug as a bug in a rug," Tin answered. "That's a Texas expression, right?"

"Are you out of your mind?" Carson thundered, then ordered, "Put my son on the line immediately. Do you have any idea who I am?"

"Actually, I do." Tin's voice was cold. "Which is the only reason your baby boy isn't dead."

"I . . ." Carson sputtered. "You . . ." Then, his tone defeated, he asked, "What do you want?"

"Now that's better." Tin chuckled smugly, then said, "If you put two hundred and fifty thousand in unmarked bills in a suitcase and leave it . . ." He paused, obviously muting the phone, then directed his questions to Wally. "We need a spot in town that we can get to without going through a bunch of cops stopping us to check IDs."

Wally's mind raced. All roads into and out of Scumble River were barricaded. What was on the edge of town before the roadblocks?

Finally, Wally remembered the breakfast conversation and said, "The old Hutton dairy farm by I-55." He hesitated, then added, "But it will only work if the exchange is made in the next couple of days, because they might use it as a school after that."

"Okay." Tin instructed Carson, "Leave the money in the trash bin on the northeast corner of the Hutton dairy farm."

"How do you know there's a garbage can there?" Veep whispered.

"I don't," Tin whispered back. "Tomorrow, a couple of hours before the drop, we send Boo-Boo to the farm to put one in that corner. Since he got us into this mess, he can wait there until the cash shows up." Raising his voice, Tin said, "Carson, my man, have the dough there by midnight tomorrow or your son dies."

"Wait," Carson begged. "How do I know my boy's still alive?"

Tin smacked Wally on the arm and ordered, "Say hi to your daddy, but don't try nothing stupid."

Wally nodded and said, "Hey, Dad. I'm okay. How's Skye doing?"

"She's fine and I'm on my way to be with her, so don't worry."

"Where are you?"

"On the company plane heading toward O'Hare. Good thing I'm not flying commercial or I wouldn't have been able to have my cell phone on and I would have missed your call." Carson's voice hitched. "I'll have your cousin get the money together and fly out with it tomorrow."

"Thanks, Dad." An idea flickered through Wally's head. He was surprised Tin hadn't removed the phone yet, but before he did, Wally hurriedly said, "Tell Skye I love her and she should go to her uncle Dante. He can help her. She should go talk to him."

"Enough!" Veep roared.

Tin quickly said, "Daddy-O, we'll be expecting you personally with the Bennies by midnight tomorrow."

"Fine. But at eleven fifty-five, you need to call me and have Wally on the line to prove that he's still alive."

"We can do that. But once you hear his voice, you need to immediately put the cash in the trash can and walk away. Don't be stupid and involve the cops. Don't make us do something we don't want to do. Don't make your son's wife a widow."

Chapter 12

> "I think you are wrong to want a heart. It makes most people unhappy. If you only knew it, you are in luck not to have a heart."
>
> — The Wizard

At a few minutes to four, May was finally forced to leave Skye alone and headed off to work her shift at the police station. Enjoying the silence, Skye stood in the luxurious motor coach, marveling at Carson's ability to snap his fingers and have something like this RV appear in the middle of rural Illinois. The man who had delivered and set up the coach had bragged that it was nearly forty-five feet long, had a ninety-one-gallon freshwater tank, and slept five. There should be plenty of room for the twins and even an additional overnight guest.

Exploring her temporary new home, Skye was impressed at the features. Prior to now, the one and only time she'd been in an RV was when she was ten years old and her brother, Vince, was fourteen. Their parents had rented some sort of shell that was installed in the bed of Jed's pickup. When the family had tried using this hybrid creation to camp in the Colorado mountains, they'd ended up freezing.

Skye chuckled. Maintaining a comfortable temperature in her new motor home sure wouldn't be a problem. They may not need heat, but in addition to a furnace, it had an air-conditioning unit, thirty-two- and fifty-five-inch LED Smart HDTVs with a Blu-Ray DVD player, an electric fireplace, and a master bedroom with a king-size bed and en suite bathroom.

Then there was the additional bathroom, the stacked washer and dryer, and a full-size refrigerator, which May had stuffed with food. Skye's mom had also packed the cabinets with tasty treats. Evidently, she didn't want her soon-to-be-born grandbabies to go hungry.

Skye's bags from her shopping trip to Target, Walmart, and JC Penney were lined up neatly on the bed, and she decided to put everything away before she washed up. She hummed as she stowed household goods and toiletries in their proper places, but when she found the sack with Wally's clothes, tears slid down her cheeks. Would he ever have a chance to wear the jeans and shirts she'd bought him?

Feeling like the rattling lid on a pot of boiling water, Skye perched on the edge of the mattress and tried to steady her emotions. She couldn't afford to have a meltdown now. Wally was depending on her to keep a level head and be an asset in finding him rather than a liability. And her babies were depending on her to carry them to term rather than letting stress throw her into premature labor.

What was it she always told the kids she counseled about handling stressful situations? Something about leaning into the curves life throws at you instead of just falling off the bike. She needed to take her own advice.

After taking a shower in the surprisingly spacious bathroom, Skye changed into a pair of knit capris and a maternity T-shirt. For the first time in almost twenty-four hours, she felt comfortable. Now if only Wally were here to share it with her.

Checking her newly purchased Timex, she saw that Carson would still be in the air. There were at least a couple of hours until she could reasonably expect him to arrive in Scumble River. Longer if traffic on I-55 was bad.

Skye's stomach growled and she felt a kick. One of the babies was reminding her that it was eight p.m. and she hadn't had anything since her lunch at Olive Garden. Wondering if Wally was hungry, and feeling guilty, Skye forced herself to eat a serving of the chicken-and-spinach pasta casserole May had somehow found time to whip up.

With the dishes washed and put away, Skye stood in the open door and gazed across the backyard at what remained of her home. Explaining that it would give Skye and Wally some privacy when they hired a crew to clear out the rubble and rebuild, May had directed the guy to set up the motor coach as far as possible from the destroyed house.

Through the late twilight, Skye saw, as Wally had predicted, that two of the walls had collapsed and she could now look directly into the kitchen and sunroom. Pieces of their lives were strewn on the floor and across the lawn. She fought the visceral urge to pick through the debris to try to reclaim some of their previous existence.

Intellectually, she understood that things could be replaced, but emotionally, she wanted the pictures and mementos. She wanted the baby afghan her Grandma Cora had made for her. She wanted her sorority pin and chapter songbook. But most of all, she wanted her husband.

How had things gone to hell so fast? Slumping against the doorframe, Skye wrapped her arms around her stomach and let her tears flow.

Several minutes later, she wiped her eyes with the bottom of her shirt and went inside. Her cell phone vibrated and she snatched it from her pants pocket. There was a text from Carson. He'd landed at O'Hare and he would be in Scumble River in an hour.

As soon as her father-in-law showed up, Skye intended to start searching the country roads around town. Because Wally's officers would have been on the lookout for him in the tornado-damaged areas, she and Carson would scour the outlying regions.

Knowing it was going to be another late night, Skye removed the spread and stretched out on the bed to rest until her father-in-law arrived. As she chewed a couple of antacid tablets to relieve the almost constant heartburn caused by her pregnancy hormones, she considered Carson's question about the Lyons homicide. Was the councilman's murder connected to

Wally's disappearance? If there was any chance it was, she should try to figure out what Wally might have been investigating when he went missing.

Skye closed her eyes and tried to visualize the ME's report. Why hadn't she printed out a copy? All she could recall was the unusual cause of death and that he had been killed in the period right before the storm to right after it.

Hmm . . . When Mrs. Lyons had been demanding that May send someone to look for her husband, she'd mentioned a heart problem. But according to the autopsy, Zeke died from an arterial weakness in his brain.

Had the killer known about the councilman's condition and given him a jolt, hoping his heart would give out? Was the location of the marks from the electrical shock a coincidence? Someone would have had to get mighty close to the man to zap him in the middle of his chest.

The more Skye thought about it, the less she was convinced that Zeke Lyons had been a victim of looters. The whole scenario suggested someone who knew him and whom he trusted. As with so many cases, motive would be the key. Who would want the councilman dead?

As Skye dozed off, she dreamed of tornadoes and houses falling from the clouds. She was surrounded by Munchkins in the middle of an endless poppy field. Suddenly, flying monkeys were attacking and the Cowardly Lion lay dead at her ruby-slippered feet.

The sound of pounding woke her and she tried to sit up but couldn't quite manage the maneuver. Rolling to the edge of the mattress, she scooted her butt over until she could get her legs under her, then awkwardly lumbered to her feet.

"Are you all right, darlin'?" Carson's voice was muffled, but his Texas twang was distinctive. "Skye, sugar, I'm getting worried."

"Everything is fine," she called out. "I'll be right there."

Hurrying through the length of the RV, Skye flung open the door. It was beginning to rain again and lightning crackled behind Carson as he pulled her into a hug. Kissing his cheek, she moved back and gestured him inside. He put his suitcase and briefcase near the leather sofa and gazed around the motor home.

"Not bad." He nodded toward the couch. "I take it this unfolds?"

"Got me, Dad." Skye shrugged. "Since the setup guy claimed we're able to sleep five in this thing, I would hope so. Or the king bed could get mighty crowded."

Her father-in-law was a distinguished-looking, older version of his son, with a trimmer but still muscular build, and more silver streaks in his dark hair. Seeing Wally's warm, brown eyes and strong jaw on Carson made Skye blink back tears.

He obviously noticed and grasped her arm. Taking a seat on the sofa, Carson tugged her down beside him. "I have some news. It's not the best, but in a way it's good." He paused, then asked, "Ready?"

"Definitely," Skye said, her heat thumping so hard she could barely hear over it.

Carson took her hands. "Wally is alive and seems to be relatively unharmed."

"How do you know that?" Skye barely stopped herself from screaming. "What does that mean?"

"Two and a half hours ago, I received a phone call," Carson explained. "It was from Wally's cell, but another man was on the line."

"A doctor?" Skye asked. Fear clogged her throat and she squeaked, "But Quirk said he checked all the hospitals."

"Not a doctor." Carson's lips thinned. "Wally is being held for ransom."

"But . . ." Skye started to ask why someone would take a police chief hostage, then realized that whoever had her husband had called his father, not her. Obviously, the kidnapper knew about Wally's wealthy family.

As Skye processed the information, Carson remained silent.

Finally, the realization of what he'd said about the timeline dawned on her and she demanded, "Why did you wait? Why didn't you call me right away?"

"I thought this was a conversation better held in person." Carson frowned when Skye jerked her fingers from his and struggled to her feet.

"At least I would have known he was alive." Skye glared at her father-in-law.

"Sorry, my dear." Carson's face reddened. "I forget how tough you are."

"Did you notify Sergeant Quirk?" Skye snapped, waving away his apology, still angry at her father-in-law's actions.

"No. And we're not going to tell him. The kidnappers said no police." Carson ran his fingers through his salt-and-pepper hair. "Truthfully, I doubt the Scumble River PD would be able to do much, considering their current situation."

"You *are* paying the ransom, right?" Skye asked. "Please tell me you don't buy that 'we can't negotiate with criminals' crap?"

"Of course not." Carson rose and put an arm around her. "As soon as I hung up, I contacted Quentin to bring out the money. Once the storm lets up, the company plane will head back to Texas to get him. He'll be here by tomorrow afternoon. The ransom drop-off is scheduled for midnight, so he has plenty of time to get us the cash. Tuck Tucker, the head of CB International security, and several of his men are accompanying Quentin. They'll have eyes on the kidnapper when I make the drop."

Quentin Boyd was Wally's first cousin and second in command at CB International — a position Carson had wanted Wally to take. Although Quentin's father had died when Quentin was a teenager, and Quentin had lived with Wally and his parents, the two men had never been close. But things had been better between them once Carson had accepted that Wally was not taking over the company.

"Did you speak to Wally?" Skye asked. When Carson nodded, she gripped his shoulder. "How did he sound? Did he say he was okay?"

"He said he's fine." Carson patted her hand. "And to tell you that he loves you."

"I know." Skye's voice cracked. "He makes

sure of that every single day."

"He's a good man." Carson stared at Skye. "And an even better one with you."

"And I'm a better woman with him." Skye took a deep breath and straightened her spine. "Do you want anything to eat or drink before we hit the road? The bathroom is over there if you need it."

"No thanks," Carson said. "When you fly via private plane, all of that and more is provided."

"Right." Skye briefly recalled the luxurious flight from Illinois to Florida's port for her honeymoon cruise. "Then let's get going."

"You still want to drive around?" Carson wrinkled his brow. "Now that we know Wally's been kidnapped, it's a lot less likely that we'll find any sign of him. Whoever has him will have hidden his car."

"Probably," Skye agreed. "But are you willing to take the chance that the kidnapper might be stupid, but we didn't bother to look?"

"Hell no!" Carson thundered. "Grab your handbag and let's go."

"Ready." Skye put her purse strap over her shoulder and walked to the door.

Carson had parked his specially modified SUV next to the car that Skye's Uncle Wiley had loaned her. Thanks to Jed, the Grand Am had been waiting in the driveway when May drove her home from the police station. The old Pontiac looked like a Hot Wheels toy next to Carson's humongous vehicle.

After helping Skye into his Hummer, Carson asked, "Where to?"

"We can eliminate the areas to the north and east," Skye said thoughtfully. "Those regions were heavily damaged by the tornadoes and emergency workers would have spotted Wally's cruiser if he were there."

"Which direction is the old Hutton dairy farm?" Carson asked.

"West. Near the I-55 exit." Skye felt a flicker of something up her spine. "Why?"

"That farm is where the kidnappers ordered me to make the ransom drop." Carson fired up the engine, turned on the windshield wipers, and threw the SUV into reverse. "Maybe they picked that place because it was close to where Wally is being kept."

"Oh, my, gosh." A tiny spark of hope warmed Skye's heart. "At breakfast, we talked about the school possibly using the Hutton farm for classes. Maybe Wally went there to look it over."

"Good thinking." Carson backed out of

the driveway. "Show me the way."

Skye gave her father-in-law directions, then held on tight as he pressed down the accelerator and they sped into the stormy darkness. As they drove, she observed that the ginormous Hummer was equipped with giant searchlights and even a heavy-duty grill guard.

Noticing all the extras, Skye teased, "Where did you get this thing? It looks like it was designed for the zombie apocalypse."

"This beauty is an H1 Alpha." Carson smiled fondly. "This model had a very limited production of one year. The chassis is made of high-strength steel and it has a Duramax diesel engine with a five-speed Allison transmission." He patted the instrument panel. "It has run-flat tires and a sixteen-inch ground clearance."

"Which explains why you had to boost me into the passenger seat," Skye murmured, still squicked out over his hands on her rear end.

"Yep. This sweetheart could pret' near float down the Scumble River."

"If the rain keeps up, we might get to test out that capability," Skye murmured.

Skye guided Carson south on Kinsman and then west on Maryland. Once they passed Up A Lazy River Motor Court and

Great Expectations, the hair salon her brother owned, the scenery became rural.

There was an occasional house along the way, but they were separated by acres of corn and soybeans. With the crops fully mature, the residents had complete privacy. Exactly the kind of seclusion a kidnapper would prize.

As they drove past each home, Carson slowed and swept the searchlight around the property. Nothing at any of the houses aroused either Skye or her father-in-law's suspicions. Just before they reached the highway ramp, an old sign advertising the defunct dairy loomed up on their right.

As Carson swung the Hummer onto the rutted dirt road, Skye looked at the pair of decrepit wooden gates lying on the ground. They were a painful reminder that agriculture's heyday was long gone. After the huge vehicle bumped down the lane for a quarter of a mile, the buildings came into view.

The Hummer's searchlights illuminated the once-white clapboard farmhouse that was situated on the left side of the property. It was separated from the other structures by a neglected yard and a detached garage with a large, gravel parking area in front of the doors. A row of overgrown evergreen bushes completely blocked the front porch, and the grass was so tall, Skye could barely make out the rusted, windmill lawn ornament that spun madly back and forth in the wind that had kicked up again.

The entrepreneur who had hoped to turn the property into a country music theater had renovated the milking barn and a couple of outbuildings, but most of the structures remained untouched. With the exception of there being no dead body squashed under a steamroller, the place looked exactly as it had the last time Skye had seen it. There was no evidence that anyone had set foot there since the crime scene techs had cleared out nearly two years ago.

Like an overweight cat, disappointment settled on Skye's chest, and she saw a matching expression on Carson's face. The kidnapper may have chosen this spot for the ransom drop, but there was no sign that Wally or anyone else had ever been there.

Carson tapped Skye's shoulder and said, "Where shall we try next?"

Gathering her resolve, Skye instructed her father-in-law to get back on Maryland, then go south on Rosemary Street. As they drove up and down each rural road to the west and south of town, they continued to examine every driveway, lane, or dirt turnoff.

Several hours later, they admitted defeat and headed back to the motor coach. Skye fought to keep her eyes open and Carson's face was gray with fatigue. Exhaustion and frustration hung heavily in the air.

Neither had spoken for the last thirty minutes, when Skye asked, "Do you think the kidnapper will really free Wally if you give him the money?"

"If Wally hasn't seen his face, there's a good chance he'll be released."

"Do you think that the kidnapper is also Zeke Lyons's killer?"

"I think we can't ignore the possibility."

"So we have less than twenty hours to solve that murder." Skye firmed her jaw. "I'm not going to rely on Wally's abductor being an honorable criminal and letting him go."

Chapter 13

"Come along, Toto," she said. "We will go to the Emerald City and ask the Great Oz how to get back to Kansas again." She closed the door, locked it, and put the key carefully in the pocket of her dress. And so, with Toto trotting along soberly behind her, she started on her journey.

— Dorothy

When Skye and Carson got back to the motor home, she helped him turn the sofa into a bed, handed him a stack of linens from the well-supplied closet, said good night, and left him to his own devices. She wasn't sure if her mom had provided the sheets and pillows or if they'd come with the RV, but she was betting on May. Especially since her own bed was already made up and smelled like her mother's favorite fabric softener.

Changing into one of her newly purchased

nightshirts, she brushed her teeth and collapsed on the unbelievably soft mattress. When the aroma of bacon woke her from a weird dream about a talking scarecrow, Skye knew it had to be morning but wasn't sure how long she'd been dead to the world. It had been a couple of months since she'd been able to sleep for more than an hour at a time, but evidently exhaustion trumped the discomforts of being hugely pregnant.

Thankful she'd remembered to buy a watch, she checked the time. It was nearly nine o'clock.

Shoot! She'd wanted to be at the police station by eight and she wasn't even out of bed yet. Either her next shopping trip needed to include a clock radio or she had to figure out how to set the alarm on her cell phone.

After a quick shower, she pulled on a pair of navy Bermuda shorts and a white-and-navy top. She didn't bother with makeup. It was supposed to be a scorcher today, so any cosmetics she applied would just melt right off her face. The predicted heat also meant that wearing her hair in any style other than a French braid was just asking for a frizzy mess.

When Skye emerged from the bedroom, she found Carson issuing orders into his phone while he slid perfectly fried eggs onto a pair of waiting plates. Toast and bacon were already on the dishes and he waved Skye to a chair.

Finishing his call, he placed breakfast in front of Skye, grabbed a container of hot sauce from his briefcase, and joined her at the dinette table. Skye noticed that the bottle's handmade label had the words EAST TEXAS BURN printed in red.

"Is Quentin in Illinois yet?" Skye asked as she took a bite of toast.

She gazed longingly at Carson's coffee. Her ob-gyn had approved one cup a day, but she tried to save it for midmorning when she usually needed a boost. The current crises had her considering breaking the rules and having two doses of liquid energy today.

"He's still in Texas." Carson poured hot sauce over his eggs. "By the time the weather cleared up here and the plane was able to take off from O'Hare, the storm had traveled to Texas. It's supposed to blow itself out in the next couple of hours and the pilot says they can take off then. Quentin and Tuck should be in Scumble River by five thirty at the latest."

"Okay. That should be fine," Skye said, reassuring herself. "That's still more than six hours before the deadline. There's no need to worry."

"Absolutely none at all." Carson ate his eggs and bacon, then asked, "Any idea how we're going to solve the Lyons murder?"

"I've been going over the facts in my head." Skye drummed the tabletop with her fingernails. "I think our best course of action is to pursue the personal angle because I'm fairly certain that Zeke knew the person who attacked him. Someone would have had to get pretty close to him to zap him repeatedly in the chest. And there's the choice of weapon. I doubt looters carry stun guns. I'd swear Zeke's murder wasn't a matter of wrong place, wrong time."

"So we look into his life." Carson got up, fetched his laptop, and powered it up. "Good thing this motor coach has Wi-Fi."

"What are you doing?" Skye watched her father-in-law's fingers dance over the keyboard as she finished eating her breakfast.

"Digging into Zeke Lyons's background." Carson continued to stare at the screen.

"You can do that?" Skye resisted the siren song of the coffeepot, got up, took a jug of milk from the refrigerator, and poured a glass. "Are you hacking into some database?"

"Not at all." Carson grinned. "I'm using

employee screening software."

"And it can be applied to anyone?"

"Yep." Carson typed additional information into the laptop.

Skye leaned forward and peered over her father-in-law's shoulder. "What did you find out about Zeke?"

"That he's a dull, dull man." Carson wrinkled his brow. "He's fifty-two and has worked as an accountant at Grandma Sal's Fine Foods since he graduated from Illinois College. Until this previous spring, he lived in the same apartment in Brooklyn for almost thirty years. In June of last year, he bought a house in Scumble River. A few days later, he married Billie Gulch."

"Does it mention he was recently elected to our city council?"

"Uh-huh." Carson squinted at the computer screen and muttered, "Bingo."

"What?" Skye couldn't see what had excited her father-in-law.

"On their first anniversary, which was two months ago, a half-million-dollar life insurance policy was purchased on Zeke Lyons. His wife is the sole beneficiary."

"Yikes! That's not a good sign." Skye drained her milk glass, brought it to the kitchen counter, and after squirting dish detergent into the sink, turned on the hot water. "I need to talk to Roy and see what he's done about the murder."

"Without Wally here, will the sergeant share information with you?" Carson closed his laptop and put it back into his briefcase.

"I think so." Skye cleared the table and put the plates in the sink. "Now that I am officially employed by the department as a psych consultant, I'm usually asked to work on any serious case that's difficult to solve."

"I'm ready to leave whenever you are," Carson said, picking up his briefcase.

"Let me grab my purse." Skye dried her hands. "The dishes can soak."

As Carson drove them to the station, Skye realized it was odd she hadn't gotten any calls or messages since last night. She checked her cell and found it had been set to vibrate.

Glancing at her father-in-law's fake-innocent expression, she suspected he had pilfered it from her purse and silenced it. *Heck!* He was even more protective than her mother.

The thought of the two of them working together to "safeguard" her made Skye shudder. She was hanging on to her sanity by her fingernails, and if Carson and May teamed up to take care of her, that might be the nudge that shoved her over the edge.

Turning back to her phone, Skye listened to a voicemail from both the home and automobile insurance adjusters, stating that they'd appraised the property damage and would like to meet with her to go over their report. Skye sent both guys a text, putting them off for the next couple of days.

Next, she played the voicemails from her brother and sister-in-law. May had told them about Wally's disappearance and they offered to help. Vince said he was available to search and Loretta wanted to come and be with Skye. She called both and assured them that if she needed them, she would let them know.

There were also numerous messages from her Alpha Sigma Alpha sorority sisters around the country asking if she and Wally were okay. Their concern made her smile. Good friends were like the stars up above — they may not always be visible, but they are always there.

Skye sent a group message, assuring everyone that she and Wally had survived the tornado and she would give them more details once the dust had settled and she had the time. There was no need to worry them with Wally's abduction. They couldn't do anything to help, and Skye couldn't cope with more phone calls.

After a quick text to Dorothy Snyder, her part-time cleaning lady, to inform her that she wouldn't be needed for the foreseeable future but her salary would continue to be paid, Skye took a deep breath and faced the several voicemails from May.

Skye shuddered. Horror movies didn't scare Skye, but five missed calls from her mother did. She quickly texted May that she was fine and spending the day with Wally's dad, hoping that would satisfy her mom and save her from May's hysteria when they finally came face-to-face.

Knowing what she did about Wally's circumstances, Skye played Roy's message last. She felt guilty about not telling the sergeant that his chief had been kidnapped, and even guiltier when Roy reported that while Wally's cell had been briefly powered on, it wasn't in service long enough to track. Skye figured the techs picked up the signal when the phone was used by the kidnapper to contact Carson.

Roy also said the state police's aerial search hadn't turned up anything, but the Scumble River officers would be finished clearing the tornado-damaged houses by noon and would begin a grid search for the chief.

Skye assured herself that none of what had

been done or would be done was wasted man-hours. If the police found Wally before the ransom was paid, whatever efforts Roy put in place would have been well worth it.

When Carson parked the Hummer in the PD's lot, Skye managed to get out of the vehicle without her father-in-law's assistance and hurried into the garage as fast as her pregnancy-swollen body would allow. As she unlocked the door to the station and went inside, Carson caught up to her. No one was in the rear, so she and her father-in-law walked to the front to ask Thea to find Roy for her.

Thea told her the sergeant was using the chief's office and Skye clenched her hands into fists. Intellectually, she understood he was now in charge and needed the space and privacy, but emotionally, it still felt like he was pushing Wally aside and usurping his position.

Carson remained quiet as they climbed the stairs. Skye knew he was used to being in control and this situation had to be as hard on him as it was on her. However, she didn't have the energy to soothe him, so she just gave him an encouraging smile before knocking lightly on the half-closed door.

Without waiting for the sergeant to respond, she poked her head inside the room and said, "Can I talk to you a minute, Roy?"

"Of course." He half stood and said, "Please sit down." Looking behind Skye, he added, "Mr. Boyd, I didn't realize you were in town, sir. Let me assure you we are doing everything in our power to find your son."

"Glad to hear it." Carson shook the sergeant's hand, then sat beside Skye in the second visitor chair.

"Sorry I didn't pick up your call, Roy." Skye shot her father-in-law a scowl. "The volume on my phone was mysteriously muted."

"No problem." The sergeant resumed his seat behind the desk. "I'm sure you needed your rest, and there wasn't any news."

"Can you bring me up to speed on what's been done so far?" Carson asked.

"We've pushed all the radio traffic to another channel to keep the system clear." Roy ticked off the items on his fingers. "Notified all state, county, and local first responders."

"I'm sure with the severity of the twister damage, most of those agencies are already maxed out regarding personnel," Carson said, raising a dark brow. "Skye tells me an ILEAS team was previously mobilized and I suspect other towns have also called for their help."

"That's correct." The sergeant scrubbed his hand over his closely shaved head. "The multiple tornadoes have drained most of their resources."

"How about the county tech team?" Skye asked. "You mentioned that Wally's cell phone was turned on briefly. Are they still monitoring it and attempting to triangulate the location?"

Roy nodded. "Absolutely. But nothing more so far."

"But you expect to begin a grid search within an hour or so," Carson stated.

"Actually, the first team is already in the field, sir." The sergeant pushed a map across the desktop and pointed to one of the highlighted sections. "Alpha squad started here about ten minutes ago."

When Skye saw that Roy was indicating the area near the Hutton dairy farm, she glanced worriedly at her father-in-law. What if the searchers interfered with the ransom drop and got Wally killed?

Carson met her eyes, then said, "I'm glad you had them start there, Sergeant. Skye was telling me that she, Wally, and her godfather had discussed that place as a possibility for the school to use for classes, so my son might have gone there to check it out."

"This morning, I remembered the chief mentioning that to me, which is why I put the first team there," Roy said.

"Good thinking." Carson smiled, then said mildly, "If we don't have some results by tomorrow, I'm bringing in my own team of investigators."

The sergeant bristled. "There's no need to do that, sir. This is an officer-in-jeopardy case and we are pulling out all the stops."

"Glad to hear it." Carson's jaw clenched. "But additional resources are always helpful." He narrowed his eyes. "It's not who finds my son. It's that he's found. Don't you agree, Quirk?"

Roy's face turned a dull red and he clenched his fists. Skye could almost see the steam coming from his ears. She was afraid her father-in-law's words had just put a match to the sergeant's notoriously short fuse.

"Roy" — Skye softened her voice — "I know between the tornadoes and Wally's disappearance, you've had your hands full. And I really appreciate all you've done." She exhaled in relief when the sergeant nodded at her and leaned back in his chair. "Which is why I was thinking perhaps I could assist you with the Lyons investigation."

"That's not necessary." Roy's expression was a little guilty and Skye guessed that he hadn't even thought about the murder.

"You'll be doing me a favor, Roy." Skye rubbed her stomach. "If I just sit around waiting to hear about Wally, I'll go crazy and stress is bad for the baby. I really need to keep my mind occupied."

"Okay." The sergeant's tone was reluctant. "But Wally would kill me if you talked to suspects alone, and I don't have anyone I can spare to go with you."

"I'll be accompanying my daughter-in-law wherever she goes," Carson stated.

"Well . . ." Quirk hesitated, obviously unsure of what he should do.

"If it makes you feel any better," Carson said, "I'm licensed to carry."

"Fine." Roy shot Skye a stern look. "But I want you to keep me apprised of your movements and promise not to take any chances."

"Believe me, Sergeant, you have my word as a Texan that nothing will happen to Skye." Carson stood. "Or my grandchild."

"Can I have the Lyons file, Roy?" Skye asked as Carson helped her to her feet.

"I saw it just a minute ago." The sergeant pawed through the piles of papers on Wally's desk, finally grabbing a thin folder. "Here it is."

"Where would be a good place for us to work?" Skye glanced around sadly. She usually camped out in Wally's office when she was at the station.

"With everyone in the field, the interrogation/coffee room isn't needed." Roy shrugged. "And it's the only place with a door."

"That'll be fine." Skye clutched the file to her chest. "Thanks."

Once Skye and Carson were settled in the interrogation/coffee room with the door closed, Skye said, "I'm really worried that the kidnapper is watching the Hutton farm and will be scared off by the search team."

"The guy who called me didn't seem like a hothead." Carson put his arm around her shoulder. "If he is observing the place, he'll wait to see what the searchers do. And since they won't find anything, they'll move on quickly and the kidnapper will just wait for the money."

"I hope you're right." Skye chewed on her thumbnail. "I feel guilty for not telling Roy that we heard from Wally and about the ransom demand." She looked at her father-in-law. "Maybe if we told him, there'd be something he could do to find Wally."

"Darlin', I know this is killing you, but the sergeant admitted that not only are his resources stretched thin, but so are the state's and the county's." Carson kissed Skye's temple. "If they knew about the kidnapping, what could they possibly do to find him that they aren't already doing? And telling Quirk could put Wally at risk."

"You're right, Dad," Skye whispered. "But I'm just so scared."

"Like you said to the sergeant, the best thing for you is to get your mind on something else." Carson flipped open the Lyons file. "Where do you think we should start?"

"Considering the recent life insurance policy, I'll go along with what Wally always says." Skye tapped the picture of Billie Lyons attached to folder. "The spouse is always the best suspect."

Chapter 14

"For my life is simply unbearable without a bit of courage."

— Cowardly Lion

Interviewing Billie Lyons would have been a whole lot easier if the woman's entire street hadn't been destroyed by the tornado. Or if Skye had been able to find a local relative, or even a close friend of the elusive Mrs. Lyons. Or if anyone could tell Skye where the heck Billie and her mother were staying.

Skye had called all of the most plugged-in Scumble River busybodies and still hadn't been able to get a lead on Widow Lyons's current location. Aunt Minnie, the queen bee of the gossip hive, had suggested checking out the shelter provided by the Methodist church.

However, when Skye phoned the number provided by her aunt, the church's volunteer coordinator hadn't had any record of either Billie or her mother ever checking in to the shelter. They also hadn't registered with the Red Cross or posted their whereabouts on the whiteboards at the police station.

With no idea where to look for Billie and having run out of tattletales to cross-examine, Skye and Carson opted for plan B: a chat with Zeke Lyons's employer, Grandma Sal's Fine Foods.

Fine Foods had been a part of Scumble River for close to forty years. Built in the late 1960s, the factory had pretty near singlehandedly saved the town from dying out — the fate of many of the neighboring agricultural-dependent communities.

The plant employed a large percentage of the area's residents and provided jobs for the next generation, who otherwise would have had to move away in order to make a living. The company had always been a good neighbor, making generous contributions to the local charities and sponsoring several sports teams.

Because the Fine Food factory was located northeast of town, between Scumble River and Brooklyn, adjacent to the railroad tracks that ran through both communities, Skye had been worried it might have been damaged in the tornadoes. But the receptionist who answered Skye's call had assured her that the closest twister had passed a mile south of the huge complex and it was business as usual at the plant.

When Skye asked to see Jared Fine, the company's CEO, she had been given an eleven thirty appointment and told that Mr. Fine would be happy to talk to her about poor Mr. Lyons. The receptionist had seemed genuinely sad about Zeke's death, which was nice to hear. The information that Carson had dug up on the man seemed to indicate that he led a fairly isolated life and Skye had feared few people would mourn his passing.

As they drove to the meeting, Skye stole a glance at her father-in-law. A few years ago, Carson had considered buying Fine Foods. He'd hoped to persuade Wally to manage the local company and, in turn, eventually lure him into taking over CB International in its entirety.

When Fine Foods became the center of a murder investigation, Carson had been forced to withdraw from negotiations. His corporation acquired only companies that had squeaky-clean public reputations and Fine Foods's image had been badly tarnished.

Skye wondered if her father-in-law had

ever regretted his decision to rescind his offer on the factory. For her part, Skye was glad Carson hadn't acquired it for his empire. Its dated facility and hulking equipment gave her the creeps.

The working factory was bad enough, filled with huge bins and sacks the size of refrigerators stacked on wooden pallets, monster-sized mixers, and endless conveyor belts. But the boneyard, where out-of-date apparatuses and broken machinery was stored, was the stuff of nightmares.

Especially since the last time she'd been in the plant, a killer had chased her through the building, intent on silencing her forever. In the dark, stalked by a madman, the place had felt like a demonic amusement park and she was the intended sacrifice.

Skye was lost in that chilling memory when Carson guided the Hummer through the gates of the Fine Factory. Returning to the place where she'd been terrorized sent a shudder down her spine. Her father-in-law shot her a concerned look and switched off the vehicle's air-conditioning.

Skye didn't want him to worry about her, so she kept silent about the real cause of her shiver. Thankfully, they didn't have to go anywhere near the area where she'd been pursued by the killer, which allowed her to regain her composure and thank Carson for adjusting the SUV's temperature.

After they parked in one of the spots marked VISITOR, they headed toward the office entrance. Although it was hot and humid, the sky was gray and the clouds were flat. It was almost as if the tornado had thrown off Illinois's usual climate pattern and the whole town had been blown to a different geographical region.

Impatient to get out of the weird weather, Skye barely waited while her father-in-law opened the building's glass door for her, then hurried up to the front desk. After giving the receptionist her name, Skye and Carson were escorted down a narrow hallway, where Jared Fine's secretary showed them into his office.

When Skye and Carson entered the room, Jared was sitting behind a huge glass-and-metal desk, staring at his computer monitor, but he immediately rose to his feet to greet them. Gesturing to the leather-and-chrome visitors' chairs, he resumed his seat and waited silently.

"Thank you for seeing us on such short notice, Mr. Fine." Skye eased into the low, sling-like chair, hoping she'd be able to get back out of it. "I believe you've met my father-in-law, Carson Boyd."

"Of course." Jared's blue eyes widened. "Has the conglomerate you work for reconsidered acquiring Fine Foods, Mr. Boyd?"

"No. Sorry. I'm just here on escort duty." Carson crossed his legs. "With the twister and all, my son is tied up." He shot a look at Skye. "My sole purpose is to make sure that my daughter-in-law and grandbaby are safe."

"Oh." Jared shoved his hands through his curly, gray-blond hair, disappointment flashing like a neon sign across his face.

"But I have been keeping an eye on your company and you've made some exceptionally shrewd business decisions." Carson smiled. "For instance, moving your corporate offices out of Chicago and taking advantage of the property you already own here in Scumble River was a huge savings. And continuing your expansion in the southern states was extremely smart."

"Thank you." Jared's pudgy fingers drummed on the desktop. "We *are* doing much better than when you were considering purchasing us."

"As I mentioned to your secretary," Skye interjected, "I'm here as the Scumble River police psychological consultant. As a member of the department, I'm looking into Zeke Lyons's murder. I understand he worked for you for many years."

"Yes." Jared pursed his lips. "Zeke was a valued part of the Fine Food family."

"Did he bring any concerns regarding the company's books to your attention?" Skye asked.

"He wouldn't have come to me about that." Jared wrinkled his brow.

"Why is that?" Skye asked. "I'm assuming that after being with you for thirty years, he was head of the accounting department."

"Not precisely." Jared cleared his throat. "Zeke was never in our Chicago offices and has always worked out of this location. He preferred to remain in the trenches. He wasn't the type who sought a leadership position."

"Why wouldn't he want a promotion?" Skye asked, taking a legal pad from her tote bag.

"Well . . . uh . . . the thing is," Jared stuttered, "I guess I don't know why."

"Had he ever been offered advancement?" Skye tilted her head.

"Not in so many words," Jared hedged. "But he never indicated a desire for one either. He wasn't a man who liked change."

"In that case" — Skye tapped her pen on her notepad — "I'm a bit shocked that he would decide to marry so late in life. Marriage is a big change. Adjusting to a spouse can be quite a stressor."

Carson let out a chuckle and Skye nudged his calf with her foot.

"Absolutely." Jared scratched his jaw. "We were all astonished when he passed out the invitations to the wedding."

"But?" Skye sensed there was more to the story than Jared had mentioned.

"But when one of his colleagues expressed his surprise, Zeke told us that he'd loved Billie for years and years." Jared shook his head as if amazed. "He stated that the day she finally said yes to his proposal was the happiest of his life."

"Interesting." Skye jotted down a reminder to revisit this subject when she finally located the elusive Mrs. Lyons. "You mentioned Zeke's coworkers. Were there any who didn't get along with him?"

"Not that I ever heard." Jared laced his fingers over his belly. "Zeke pretty much kept to himself. He didn't interact much with anyone."

"How about during his breaks?" Skye probed. "Who did he sit with at lunch?"

"I can ask his supervisor," Jared offered. "However, every time I saw him, he had his head buried in a book." The CEO paused, then said, "Wait. Occasionally, he and one of the secretaries talked about their dogs."

"May I speak to her?" Skye requested. "I promise not to keep her too long."

"Sorry." Jared shrugged. "She moved away about six months ago."

"Then I'd like to talk to Mr. Lyons's supervisor." Skye returned her legal pad to her purse and when Jared didn't respond, she added, "If I could do it now, it would save me a return trip."

"Certainly." Jared leaned forward and pushed a button on the telephone. When his secretary appeared a few seconds later, he rose and said, "Please show our guests to the accounting offices and tell Mr. Bandar he has my permission to speak freely to them."

"Thank you." Skye struggled to rise from the low-slung chair, finally having to accept her father-in-law's assistance to get to her feet.

She shook Jared's hand and Carson did the same as he said, "We appreciate your cooperation." He hesitated, then added, "I really do think it was for the best that your family didn't sell the company. I'm glad it's doing well."

"That's very kind of you." Jared resumed his seat and turned his attention back to the computer monitor he'd been gazing at when they arrived.

His secretary led them down a narrow corridor to an outside exit, then across a small concrete apron. She ushered them through a door leading into what had been a warehouse last time Skye was at the factory. Apparently, after closing the Chicago corporate headquarters, the space had been repurposed to hold, among other departments, the accounting offices.

Jared's secretary walked past half a dozen gray-fabric-covered workstations before pausing outside one that was slightly larger than the others. This cubicle had a gold nameplate with ABE BANDAR engraved in a fancy font, as well as a frosted panel fastened over the top of its frame.

Skye had never seen a workstation with a door before and mentioned that to the secretary, who said, "When we moved out here from Chicago, Mr. Bandar complained about losing his private office and said a cubicle was just a padded cell without a door." The secretary chuckled and pointed to the screen. "A few days later, Mr. Fine had this contraption installed."

The sheet of molded plastic was mounted on two wheels and the secretary knocked lightly on the flimsy surface before sliding it out of the way. The man inside looked up from his computer monitor and frowned.

Jared's secretary gestured to Skye and Carson and said, "Abe, this is Skye Denison-Boyd and Carson Boyd from the Scumble River Police Department. Mr. Fine would like you to fully answer their questions."

Skye thanked the secretary, who after making sure they didn't need anything further, nodded and left.

Abe Bandar leaped to his feet and said, "Please sit down, Mrs. Boyd." He gestured to the only chair other than his own, then looked at Carson and asked, "Shall I have a chair brought for you as well?"

"I'll stand." Carson leaned against the wall. "We won't be long."

Resuming his seat, Abe asked, "How can I assist the police department?"

"As you probably have already heard, after the tornadoes, Zeke Lyons was found dead," Skye said.

"Yes. It was quite a shock." Abe gestured to the partition behind his desk. "Zeke and I have shared a cubicle wall since I was relocated to this facility."

"What you may not know is that he was murdered," Skye continued.

"Oh my." Abe's dusky complexion turned gray and he asked, "By looters?"

"Possibly." Skye took her legal pad from her purse. "But the evidence suggests otherwise. The method seems more personal."

"But who would do such a thing?" Abe asked. "Zeke really wasn't the type to inspire much in the way of passionate feelings. Neither positive nor negative ones."

"Did he have any concerns regarding Fine Foods?" Skye asked. "Perhaps something he found in the accounts that didn't quite balance?"

Abe shook his head wildly. "No! Never! There haven't been any problems with our books. And if there were, Zeke would have certainly brought it to my attention immediately. That's my job."

"Any issues with any of his colleagues?" Skye asked, figuring Zeke's supervisor would know more about the man's interpersonal relationships with his coworkers than the company CEO.

"Zeke kept to himself." Abe shrugged. "He was an introvert."

Abe leaned forward and Skye observed his shoes barely touched the floor. She'd noticed that he was shorter than her own five foot seven, but hadn't realized he was that tiny.

"So you hadn't been aware of anything

unusual with Zeke?" Skye asked.

"Well . . ." Abe rubbed his bald head. "He did mention regretting that he'd agreed to serve on the Scumble River city council. Evidently, his mother-in-law had pulled some strings and insisted. She wasn't happy with his lack of social status in the community."

"Why didn't he want to be on the council?" Skye made a note on her pad, then looked at Abe.

"The mayor was proving, uh . . . uh, difficult," Abe said carefully.

"In what way?" Skye asked, glad that Zeke's supervisor wasn't from Scumble River and didn't seem to know that Dante was her uncle.

"His Honor was pressuring him to vote the party line," Abe said.

"On any matter in particular?" Skye wrote DANTE on her pad with a big question mark.

"Zeke mentioned that he had some concerns regarding several minor issues." Abe held up his hand before Skye could open her mouth. "And no, I don't know any particulars about those issues."

"Was there any other city council business that he was worried about?"

"There was a vote coming up about something Zeke said he wasn't at liberty to discuss." Abe laced his fingers over his belly and played with the chain of his pocket watch. "But Zeke did say that in good conscience, he couldn't go along with the mayor."

"That's very useful information." Skye underlined her uncle's name, intending to question him about the matter as soon as she left the factory.

"I'm afraid that's about all I know." Abe's tone was apologetic.

"You've been very helpful." Skye started to rise, then when she heard a voice speaking to someone in the next cubicle, she sat back down.

The comment Jared had made about Zeke loving Billie for years and years and that she had *finally* accepted his proposal had been bothering Skye. Suddenly, it occurred to her that maybe Abe could shed some light on the matter. Zeke may not have confided in his supervisor, but as the man had pointed out earlier, they did share a cubicle wall. There was a chance he'd overhead something.

Clearing her throat, Skye said, "I understand that Zeke was recently married."

"Yes." Abe looked at her quizzically. "I think it was about a year ago or maybe a little more."

Pretending ignorance, Skye asked, "How long did Zeke and Billie date?"

Abe smiled. "Zeke had been courting Billie as long as I've known him."

Skye raised her brows. "Wow. Any idea why he didn't ask her to marry him sooner?"

"He did. I believe he had proposed every Valentine's Day for the past twenty years." Abe shook his head. "We were all shocked when she said yes."

"Did Zeke tell you how, after all that time, he persuaded her to marry him?"

"All Zeke said was that Billie finally realized that life was passing her by."

"I wonder what changed her mind," Skye murmured.

Chapter 15

"But I thought all witches were wicked."
— Dorothy

Night had been long, miserable, and extremely frustrating for Wally. After supper, while the men upstairs had guzzled beer and whooped it up, he'd forced himself to consider what would happen once his father paid the ransom demand. Almost none of the possible scenarios were comforting.

It hadn't taken a mind reader to figure out that the majority of the gang members hated the police. Keeping an officer alive had obviously rubbed most of the bikers the wrong way. Odds were slim that they would just let him go once they had the money.

Despite Tin Man's argument that the bikers were better off not adding "cop killer" to their résumés, Wally hadn't been willing to take that chance. He'd continued to work on the tape around his wrists and had been making some progress when the basement door had squeaked open.

Tin had assured Wally that he was the only one with a key to the lock, but the footsteps stumbling down the stairs seemed a lot lighter than his. Immediately, Wally had slumped over and pretended to be asleep. Tin had removed the blindfold after Veep had left and the last thing Wally had wanted was to see any of the gang members' faces.

A hand had smacked his cheek, forcing Wally to open his eyes, and Boo-Boo had stood in front of him, glaring. The teenager could barely remain upright and had been unmistakably plastered. Wally had increased his efforts to loosen the duct tape. This might be his chance to escape. If he could get his hands free, he should be able to overpower the wasted adolescent and grab his weapon.

"It's all your fault." Boo-Boo poked Wally in the chest. "You made me look like a loser and now the guys might not vote me into the club."

"Everyone makes mistakes," Wally soothed. Drunks were often irrational. "I take it you're on probation?" When Boo-Boo nodded, Wally continued. "Then I'm sure they'll cut you some slack."

"I'm tired of everyone treating me like someone left the bag of idiots open and I escaped," Boo-Boo slurred.

"I bet when you come back here carrying a cool quarter million, they'll all be impressed." Wally was glad some of Skye's counseling skills had rubbed off on him. "And they wouldn't have that moola without you taking me hostage."

"Yeah." Boo-Boo puffed up his chest. "None of them ever brought in that kind of bread." He frowned. "Your old man better not screw it up."

"He won't," Wally assured the guy, as he worked loose another corner of the tape. "I'm his only son. Dad will definitely pay up."

"Must be nice." Boo-Boo scowled, his rage clearly beginning to ramp up again. "My old man wouldn't piss on me if I was on fire."

"How about your mother?" Wally asked trying to calm him back down.

"She died when I was fifteen. She was killed in an accident coming to pick me up from an after-school detention." Boo-Boo blinked and Wally thought he might have seen a tear. "My old man blamed me for her death. Dad crawled into a bottle and never came out."

"That's a shame." Wally picked at the one last strip of tape keeping his wrists together. "Wasn't there anyone who you could go to? Grandparents or maybe your teachers? My wife's a school psychologist and she helps kids in that situation all the time."

"Not in the city schools." Boo-Boo swayed. "In my neighborhood, no one's interested. You just drop out and take care of yourself."

"It isn't too late, man," Wally said. "You can get your GED and get out of this life before you end up in prison or d—"

"Shut the hell up!" Boo-Boo cut him off with a punch to the gut. "You're just tryin' to confuse me." Another blow knocked the wind out of Wally. "The club is my family now and I'd never give that up."

"Okay, man." Wally fought for air. "Just giving you some alternatives if things don't work out the way you want them to here."

"I'm only in the shit house because of you!" Boo-Boo shouted.

He drew back his fist to throw another punch, but Wally's hands were finally free and he blocked it, then grabbed the front of Boo-Boo's T-shirt and hauled him closer, reaching for the gun tucked into the waistband of the punk's low-riding jeans.

Boo-Boo was yelling obscenities and clawing at Wally's face, but Wally ignored both the noise and pain. His fingertips had been scraping the butt of the weapon when he heard a set of boots thundering down the steps and Tin's voice shouting at Boo-Boo.

Before Wally was able to grab Boo-Boo's gun, Tin hauled the drunken bozo out of Wally's reach. Wally watched as Tin pushed the guy toward the staircase, then prodded him up each of the steps.

A door slammed close and Wally heard Tin mutter, "Time to sleep it off, dipshit."

Wally was busy trying to free his feet when Tin reappeared and tsked. "I thought you were smarter than that, Chief."

Pointing his weapon at Wally's chest, Tin dug a fistful of zip ties from his back pocket and fastened Wally's wrists behind his back. He paused, then used the ties to secure his ankles to the legs of the chair. Once he was done, Tin leaned against the workbench and rubbed his jaw.

"What I can't figure out is how that dumbass got the door open." Tin scratched his head. "He had to have picked the lock, but I'd have sworn he was too tanked up to manage it."

"He was definitely three sheets to the wind," Wally said, trying to figure out Tin's game. "A few more seconds and I'd have had his weapon."

"Yeah. Don't do that again." Tin rolled his eyes. "When I leave here, I'm putting a padlock on the door. If anyone but me comes down these stairs, you need to scream and keep screaming, not fight them or go for their gun." He gave Wally a hard stare. "I'm doing my best here to keep you alive. Trying to escape isn't your best play."

"Why would you want to keep me alive when I've seen your face?"

"Let's just say that you identifying me is the least of my worries."

Wally raised a skeptical brow. "Seriously?" Recalling what he'd previously overheard about the gang looting after the tornadoes, he asked, "Is it because one of your guys already committed murder while they were ransacking the deserted houses after the storm?"

"Shit no!" Tin scowled, then grinned. "But they might have seen something that could point your investigation in the right direction."

"And what is that?"

"That's on a need-to-know basis and you don't currently need to know."

"Currently?" Wally zeroed in on the word. "So maybe I will later?"

Tin shrugged. "Maybe. Right now, what I

need for you to do is relax and not worry about any of this shit. You behave yourself and by this time tomorrow, you'll be holding your pretty wife in your arms." He gazed unblinkingly at Wally. "You feel me, bro?" After Wally nodded his understanding, Tin added, "I'll be back with some food later."

After Tin disappeared, Wally pondered what he'd learned. Had the gang seen the murderer? Wouldn't that be a kick in the pants? The only witnesses were career criminals. The jury would love that.

A few minutes later, Wally heard a drill whine to life. After a while, there was the sound of a padlock clicking closed. Tin had been serious when he'd said he'd keep Boo-Boo from returning.

Sighing, Wally began to work on the zip ties. He'd managed to keep his hands side by side instead of wrist to wrist, so he had a little wiggle room. As the plastic cut into his flesh, he gritted his teeth and kept trying.

Wally had made some progress when, true to his word, once the sounds of the drunken revelry had been silenced for a while, Tin reappeared with a couple of sandwiches and a bottle of water.

Keeping a gun pointed at Wally, Tin freed him from the chair. After allowing him to eat, drink, and avail himself of an old bucket in the back corner of the basement, Tin used a fresh set of zip ties on Wally, then tucked his weapon into his shoulder holster and parked his ass on the workbench.

He lowered his voice and said, "Is there any chance your father won't come through with the money?"

"Unless his plane crashed, he'll deliver the ransom as instructed," Wally answered. "And if something happens to him, Skye will get the cash and bring it." Wally's heart warmed. "My wife is an angel."

"You're lucky. My old lady is still alive," Tin joked.

"You're married?" Wally examined the gang member. For the millionth time, he wondered what he was missing. Why was Tin being so nice to him? Why had he taken off the blindfold? Why was he willing to reveal his face? He certainly didn't act worried about the exposure.

"Not anymore." Tin's eyes dulled.

"Sorry, man."

"Anyway." Tin shook his head and continued. "Tomorrow night" — he paused, then chuckled — "or, I guess since it's way past midnight, tonight, as soon as Boo-Boo comes back with the cash and everyone else is on the road, I'll come down here and leave a knife just out of your reach. It'll take you a while to grab it and cut the zip ties, but it's doable. Your squad car is in the machine shed. I'll put the keys in the wheel well and the rest of your shit in the trunk. Then you can get home to your angel."

"Thanks, man." Wally's tone was sincere. "I appreciate the briefing." He again wondered at the guy's behavior and motivation.

"Your father wouldn't be stupid enough to involve the cops, would he?" Tin pushed himself off the workbench and crouched so he was eye to eye with Wally. "As you just witnessed up close and personal, Boo-Boo isn't the sharpest tool in the chest, and if something unplanned happens, that boy will panic and someone will surely get hurt."

"Dad won't bring in the police." Wally's lips quirked upward. "He's way too Texas for that." Wally stared at Tin. "But if he pays and I don't get home safe and sound, he'll hunt you until his dying breath. And he has enough juice to call in a lot of favors." Wally didn't blink. "He'd have the Rangers here in a heartbeat, and the Texas Rangers always get their man. Remember Bonnie and Clyde."

"In other words, a deal is a deal?" Tin grinned. "I can dig that."

With that declaration, the gang member bounded up the stairs, and between catnaps,

Wally worked on freeing himself from the zip ties around his wrists. Unfortunately, all of his previous progress had been lost when Tin had put on the new set after Wally had eaten.

He must have finally fallen into a deep sleep because Wally was jerked awake the next morning when someone started hammering on the door between the kitchen and basement. The pummeling turned into kicking, and then whoever was trying to get to him howled his frustration and threw something heavy at the door.

Wally's pulse raced and he prayed the old wooden door would remain intact until Tin discovered what was going on. Judging from the loud voices, the bikers had begun to emerge from whatever shithole they'd crawled into after the party, so he hoped Tin would be up, too.

The hangovers must have been intense, because Wally had recognized Veep's voice when he'd yelled, "Squirrel. Get away from the damn door. Everyone else shut your pie holes until I tell you to open 'em." There was a pause, then he'd ordered, "Boo-Boo, make the coffee."

After the commotion, the ensuing silence had been soothing, and Wally had rolled his neck and squinted at the sun peeking around the cardboard window coverings. From the amount of light, it had to be midmorning.

Last night had been the first time Wally had slept away from Skye since they'd gotten married. And even if he'd been in a feather bed, he wouldn't have liked it. He'd ached to hold her in his arms again.

Sighing, he'd gone back to work on the zip ties. They were tighter than before, but the pointed end was longer than on the previous set. He'd just managed to get it between his fingers and into the locking slot when he'd heard Veep give Tin permission to speak.

"All of you!" Tin shouted. "Take a seat and get some java and food down you. Everything in this house and in the machine shed needs to be loaded in the trailers by five o'clock." Tin's voice hardened. "I ain't tolerating any excuses or slackers. You all got me?"

There were grunts and an occasional, "yeah, man," then the sound of chairs scraping on old linoleum as Veep ordered, "Squirrel, since you're so wide-awake and bushy-tailed, you cook."

As the smell of coffee and frying bacon had drifted down the stairs and Wally continued to work the pointed end of the zip tie in the tab, his stomach growled. All he'd had in the past twenty-four hours had been two peanut butter and jelly sandwiches.

Granted, beyond getting the snot beaten out of him — twice — he hadn't done much to burn calories, but he'd still been starving. Would Tin bring him any more food? Probably not. He'd noticed that the gang member did stuff like that only when no one else was around.

After the bikers had finished their breakfast, Wally had heard them moving around upstairs. He'd assumed they were packing up their possessions and hauling everything outside.

They'd been at it a couple of hours or more, and Wally thought it was around one or two in the afternoon, when he realized that the upstairs was now silent.

Wally listened intently. They must have finished with the house and moved on to loading the stolen goods stored in the machine shed. This was his chance to escape.

Working feverishly on the zip ties, he managed to loosen them, but not enough to free his hands. He needed something sharp to cut through them.

Wally scooted his chair toward the workstable and turned his back to the bench. Wally had noticed that the metal edges were jagged and now that he didn't need to worry about being quiet, he laid his wrists across the edge and sawed at the plastic. The ties cut into his flesh and he could feel blood dripping down his arms, but he continued.

One way or the other, he was getting out of here. There was no way he was trusting his life to an outlaw biker. Even one that seemed as decent as Tin.

Chapter 16

"That's all right," said the Stork, who was flying along beside them. "I always like to help anyone in trouble. But I must go now, for my babies are waiting in the nest for me. I hope you will find the Emerald City and that Oz will help you."

When Skye and Carson left the Fine Foods factory, she suddenly felt woozy. Clutching her father-in-law's arm, she managed to get to the Hummer without passing out, but Carson insisted they return to the motor home where she could eat some lunch and lie down.

After a bowl of soup and a power nap, Skye felt much better, and she was determined to get back to the Lyons murder investigation. It felt as if she were playing hide-and-seek with Billie, a game she'd always hated to lose.

Fed and rested, Skye and Carson drove to

the police station. Impatient to resume working on the case, Skye marched in ahead of her father-in-law. She rushed through the lobby, then using her key to let them into the back of the station, she headed to the dispatcher's office.

It was nearly three o'clock, which meant May shouldn't have been on duty yet, but Skye wasn't surprised to find her mother already behind the desk. In fact, Skye had counted on it, knowing she'd better check in with her mom before she did anything else.

May was on the phone, but when Skye paused in the office doorway, May motioned for her to come inside. Holding up a finger indicating she'd be free to talk in a minute, she turned her attention back to her telephone conversation.

As Skye waited, she glanced at her father-in-law. She had been astonished at how quiet he'd been during the interviews with Jared Fine and Abe Bandar. Actually, she couldn't recall him saying a single word when she was questioning the head accountant. And now, without fussing at her to hurry or offering suggestions, he took out his phone and leaned against the opposite wall.

Carson was more like his son than Wally

realized. It appeared that the only time her father-in-law took charge was if he felt Skye was endangering herself or the baby. Carson was a lot easier to be with than she'd expected, and for that she was exceedingly grateful.

"Where have you two been?" May demanded as she placed the receiver back in the base unit. "You weren't home at noon when I stopped by the motor coach, and you haven't been answering your cell. Is there any news about Wally?"

"I haven't heard anything since Roy briefed me this morning." Skye shoved down the desire to blurt out that Wally had been kidnapped. Her chest tightened as she was reminded that right now his only hope was the ransom. "Didn't the sergeant bring you up to date when you took over the dispatcher's desk from Thea?"

"No. Thea wasn't feeling well and asked me to come in early." May wrinkled her brow and confided, "You know she's got the diabetes and this stress makes it act up." Skye's mom shook her head, then said, "Anyway, a few minutes after I got here, Roy was called out to settle a dispute, so I didn't get a chance to talk to him."

What in the world would anyone argue about so soon after a third of the town was destroyed? Hard as it was to believe with all that had happened since the tornadoes had touched down, it had been less than forty-eight hours since the twisters had blown through town.

Refocusing, Skye asked, "What kind of dispute?"

"A semitruck landed nose first on the roof of some house and the owner took exception at the folks stopping to take pictures." May cocked her head. "I believe a rifle was involved and a couple of the tires on the looky-loo's vehicle were flattened by a stray bullet or two."

"I see." Skye blinked at the image.

May repeated her original question. "So what's going on and why haven't you been answering your phone?"

Skye passed on what Sergeant Quirk had reported to her about the search for Wally. After that, she explained that she and Carson thought it was possible Zeke Lyons's murder was connected to Wally's disappearance and relayed to her mother what they had accomplished in their search for the killer.

She felt guilty that she couldn't share the information about Wally's kidnapping with May, but her husband's safety was more important than keeping her mother in the loop. Suddenly, it hit her again that Wally was being held by a criminal who could easily decide to kill him. Her heart hurt at the thought of what he was likely going through and what might very well happen to him.

Sighing, Skye blinked back a tear. She didn't have time for a breakdown. The only thing she could do for her husband was figure out who murdered Zeke Lyons and pray that person would lead them to Wally's location.

Before Skye could turn to go, May put an arm around her and said, "They'll find him and he'll be fine." Skye nodded and her mother added, "I started a novena to St. Anthony last night." Carson raised a brow and May explained, "He's the patron saint of missing people."

"Thanks, Mom." Skye cleared her throat. "How are you and Dad doing? Are you still staying with Aunt Minnie? How are Vince, Loretta, and the baby?"

"Your brother and his family are all fine, but their road is still blocked." May frowned. "Jed bought a generator at Farm and Fleet in Kankakee, so we're back at home." She sighed. "It's pretty small, but we can run the pump and a few lights. He won't let me put on the air-conditioning though, and the satellite is still out, so no TV."

"The heat and humidity are pretty bad today, and tomorrow is supposed to be worse." Skye wrinkled her brow. "Maybe you and Dad ought to stay with Aunt Minnie again. Since her daughters' houses are okay and they both have generators, she has plenty of room. You and she can visit so you don't get so bored without television."

"Jed won't go because of the darn dog." May pouted. "The pen was destroyed and he's got that beast living in our utility room. I couldn't possibly ask Minnie to put up with that dirty creature."

Although Skye's aunt wasn't as animal-phobic as May, Jed's pooch wasn't house-broken. And Skye's dad used the pinball dog training method. He let Chocolate run wild, then every once in a while, when he got annoyed, he would hit the poor thing on the rear with a rolled up newspaper. Skye had given her dad several books on positive reinforcement and behavior management, but Jed just thanked her, then stacked them next to his chair without reading them.

"I suppose expecting Aunt Minnie to put up with such a rowdy dog would be pushing the boundaries of hospitality and sibling affection," Skye murmured.

"If Jed would just board Chocolate until we get the pen rebuilt," May grumbled. "Linc Quillen's offering to lodge all animals displaced by the tornadoes free of charge at his veterinary clinic."

"Linc is a sweet guy to help out like that," Skye said.

Which reminded her, she needed to give Frannie a generous check for pet sitting Bingo. Thank goodness she'd been willing to take care of the cat until Skye's life calmed down. But Frannie and Justin would be heading back to college on Monday, so she had only a few more days to get herself together before taking back responsibility for her kitty's well-being.

Although Skye hadn't thought about it before, there were a lot of Scumble River pets that would have to adjust to new places when the displaced families moved into temporary lodgings.

Maybe that was why Billie Lyons was proving so difficult to locate. Wally had said Animal Control would keep Zeke's German shepherd until the crime scene techs had a chance to process him for forensic evidence, but they might have finished with the dog and released him to Billie.

Had she had to go somewhere away from the area in order to accommodate her husband's pet? Billie might have even had to go as far as Joliet or Kankakee to find a place that allowed animals. Or maybe she'd boarded the dog at Linc's clinic and he'd have a way to contact the elusive widow.

Making a mental note to follow those leads, Skye continued to talk with her mother, checking on the status of other family members and friends. It appeared that everyone had checked in and, considering the situation, were doing as well as could be expected.

Finally, Skye wrapped up the conversation and asked, "Do you know if Uncle Dante is in his office or not? I need to talk to him about Zeke Lyons's responsibilities on the city council."

"Oh. Didn't you hear?" May wrinkled her nose. "Dante is under the weather. He's been home sick since late yesterday afternoon. According to Olive, it was coming out of both ends and he was camped in the bathroom all night and most of the morning."

"Maybe I could stop by his house."

"Absolutely not!" May screeched. "There's no way you can get anywhere near him and expose the babies to his germs."

"Then if he's feeling a little better, perhaps I could talk to him on the phone."

"Possibly." May shrugged. "But you'll need to wait awhile before you call him. Olive told me that Dante took a sleeping pill and will be out cold until suppertime. She was darned relieved. That man hasn't given her a moment's peace for the last twenty-four hours."

"Well, heck!" Skye stamped her foot. "With him sleeping off his meds, that means we *have* to find Billie Lyons. She's the only one left I can think of who might have a motive to kill Zeke."

"Shit! I forgot —" Carson glanced at May and gave her a strained smile. "I think I might have forgotten to shut off the water in the bathroom at home." He turned to Skye and said, "I need to make a phone call to my housekeeper and make sure she looks into that."

"Okay." Skye shot her father-in-law a puzzled look. "Let's go back to the break room so I can sit while you do that. My ankles are swollen and my feet are killing me." Carson nodded his agreement and Skye kissed her mother's cheek, then said, "See you later, Mom."

Once they were out of May's hearing, Skye asked, "What did you really forget?"

Carson waited until they were behind the closed door of the interrogation room before he answered, "It slipped my mind until I heard you mention your uncle, but Wally told me to tell you that you should go to Dante. He can help you. And you should go talk to him."

"That's odd." Skye's eyes widened. "Wally knows that the last person around here who would want to help me is my uncle. He's not too fond of Wally or me." She tapped her chin. "It must be a clue. Could Uncle Dante be a code word for some location?" She chewed her thumbnail, then straightened. "Maybe Wally is being held where Dante wanted to build the incinerator. I don't recall any buildings on that land, but I haven't been out that way in ages, so who knows."

"Do you have Sergeant Quirk's cell number?" Carson asked. When Skye nodded, he said, "Good. We don't want this to go out over the radio. Call him and ask him to send officers to that area. Tell him you just remembered that Wally said he might go out to that site. I'm not thrilled with sending the police out there, but my security team hasn't arrived yet and you and I can't go there by ourselves."

"Why would Wally want to check on that place?" Skye dug out her phone and pulled up her contact list.

"If he asks, say you don't know why." Carson was intent on his own phone. "It was a casual comment, which is why you didn't remember it until now."

Although deception was probably a prerequisite for her father-in-law's profession, Skye was impressed with the ease in which Carson lied. It would be tough to be married to someone like that. How would you ever be able to trust him?

After Skye spoke to Roy, who assured her that the area had already been cleared, she tuned in on her father-in-law's phone conversation with Quentin. Evidently, the company plane was finally in the air, heading back to Illinois.

"You and the security team are sharing a cabin at the Up A Lazy River." Carson listened, then scowled. "Yeah. I said sharing. He's putting in a couple of rollaway beds and there are two queens, so you figure out the sleeping arrangements among yourselves. You're lucky Charlie had a room he'd kept available or you'd be sleeping on the floor of the motor coach."

Skye could hear Quentin speaking, but she couldn't make out his words.

"Just get your butt down here with the money," Carson growled. "If you're too much of a candy-ass to rough it at the motor court, after you cover me at the ransom drop, you can drive back to O'Hare and fly home." He paused. "Although, I'd think you would want to stick around and see if your cousin makes it back alive."

Skye's throat tightened. Evidently, Carson wasn't as confident about Wally's safe return as he had been telling her. She stared at her father-in-law and struggled to stem her always-on-the-brink-of tears.

Carson patted her hand and concluded his call. "Text me when you guys get to Skye and Wally's place. We'll meet you there to go over the strategy."

"We need to find Billie," Skye said after her father-in-law disconnected.

"Any ideas?"

"Although the volunteer coordinator didn't have any record of Billie or her mother, I think we should go out to the Methodist church." Skye struggled to her feet. "In all the chaos, they very well may not have registered, and they could still be there."

"Lead the way."

Carson and Skye returned to the Hummer, and after she fastened her seat belt, she said, "Before we head to the church, can we drive through the affected areas? I've been so busy with my own concerns that I haven't seen a lot of the worst-hit parts of town."

"Will they allow us through?"

"With my police ID, yes."

Carson nodded, and as he drove north from the police station, he asked, "Did Mrs. Lyons's mother live with her and her husband?"

"I don't know. I assumed so, since they came into the police station together and it seemed that they had been evacuated from the same neighborhood." Skye scrunched her forehead. "Are you thinking they may be staying at the mother's house?"

"It crossed my mind."

"I'll call my aunt Minnie and find out if she knows where Mrs. Gulch lives." Skye sighed. "If she doesn't know, can your handy-dandy computer software find out?"

"If your aunt can give us the woman's first name, absolutely."

"I'm on it."

After leaving a voicemail for Minnie requesting Mrs. Gulch's address and first name, Skye stared out the SUV's side window. This afternoon, with the house checks complete and ComEd's assurance that the downed electrical wires were no longer live, for the first time since the storm, the residents and volunteers were being allowed back into the devastated zones.

Officers in uniforms representing the various nearby Illinois municipalities and counties were stationed at the crossroads. They stopped each vehicle and inspected the occupant's identifications before permitting them to pass the barricades.

As promised, Skye's police ID got their Hummer through, and while her father-in-law maneuvered down the streets still strewn with rubble, she put her hand over her mouth and stared at the utter destruction. Entire blocks were completely leveled. Debris was everywhere. Buildings had collapsed and trees looked as if a giant chainsaw had slashed off their tops. It was heart-rending to see people attempting to find their treasured possessions among all the wreckage.

Although Skye had heard how much damage had been done to the neighborhoods, seeing it firsthand was a thousand times more horrible than she had imagined. Considering the damage to her own house and garage, she should have been prepared. But the sheer annihilation was overwhelming. It would take years for the town to recover.

Turning east, Carson glanced at Skye, both concern and sympathy in his gaze. She tried to speak, but she couldn't squeeze a word through the lump lodged in her throat. She swallowed several times before giving up and shaking her head at him.

Skye pushed down her emotional reaction to the devastation, dug in her purse, and pulled out the small memo pad she used as a to-do list for her school psych duties. She wrote a note reminding herself that once she found out for sure when school would be back in session, she needed to contact the special education cooperative to set up counseling for the kids and consultations with their parents.

The students were going to need help processing their emotions in order to heal, and Skye and the intern couldn't cope with the magnitude of the required services all by themselves. There would be children who had lost everything, others who experienced some property damage, and the remainder who, while not directly affected, had observed the horrifying aftermath of the storm.

If, as the superintendent was promising, classes resumed on Monday, it was likely that parents would still be handling their own feelings and wouldn't have had the time or energy to deal with their children's questions and fears. Which meant the school staff would need to be prepared to deal with both the children's and adults' issues that would arise.

When Carson turned onto Elm, Skye glanced up from her notes and chuckled. Her father-in-law raised a brow at her giggles and she pointed to the house. Spray-painted on the side of a partially collapsed home were the words NIGHTMARE ON ELM STREET. Evidently, the residents still had a sense of humor. She admired the family's cheeky attitude.

Carson grinned, then asked, "Seen enough, darlin'? Ready to go over to the church?"

"Definitely." Skye grew serious. "I want to get this done before Quentin and your security guys get here. Their ETA is now six, right?" When her father-in-law nodded, she asked, "Was Quentin giving you a hard time about bringing the money for the ransom?"

"Nah. He's just not used to roughing it."

"I could stay in Charlie's guest room and Quentin could take the motor coach," Skye offered. "It's about as luxurious as a five-star hotel."

"Absolutely not!" Carson thundered. "It'll do that boy good to see how regular folks live. I spoiled him after my brother died. It's probably too late to fix my actions, but it's time to try."

"You did what you thought was best at the time," Skye soothed.

"Wally ended up playing second fiddle." Carson sighed. "And it pushed him away."

"Not anymore," Skye reassured him. "You two are on the right track now."

"I hope that I can make up for the way I treated him back then."

"You already have." Skye patted his thigh. "By being here with me. I'm not sure I could have handled everything on my own. Wally will appreciate it as much as I do. Thanks, Dad."

"You're my daughter just as if you'd been born to me. Of course I'm here." Carson squeezed her hand. "Now. What did your mother mean when she said you couldn't expose your *babies* to your uncle's germs?"

"Nothing!" Skye yelped.

"Don't try to kid a kidder." Carson raised a brow. "Spill."

Hell! Skye had been relieved when Carson hadn't seemed to notice her mother's slip. Now what was she going to do?

Chapter 17

"Yes," answered the tin man, "I did. I've been groaning for more than a year, and no one has ever heard me before or come to help me."

After several stuttered excuses that Carson refused to believe, Skye finally said, "I'll explain everything after Wally gets home." She tucked an errant strand of hair behind her ear, then looked her father-in-law in the eye. "Until then, I have nothing to say."

Carson's voice was sympathetic. "I take it my son doesn't know yet."

"No." Skye barely got the word out. She had vowed not to cry anymore, but apparently her hormones hadn't gotten the message.

"I understand." Carson drove in silence for a few minutes, then, as they neared the city outskirts, he asked, "Have you heard anything about when the power might be restored?"

Skye shrugged. "Not really. The ComEd guy told Mom at least another couple of days."

Carson frowned. "That seems excessive."

"My guess is that so much of their service area was hit, they're as overwhelmed as everyone else."

"I suppose," Carson muttered. "It just grinds my spurs that things aren't being accomplished faster and there's nothing I can do to hasten the process."

"I bet you're not the only one," Skye commiserated, thinking of her godfather, another alpha male who liked to be in charge.

After a few more grumbles of dissatisfaction, Carson changed the subject and said, "When you talked to Jared Fine and Abe Bandar, the conversation was fairly straightforward. If we do find Billie Lyons, how are you going to approach her?"

"I pretty much use the same techniques to question suspects as I do in sessions with the kids." Skye tilted her head, thinking about her counseling process. "I try to get them to tell me how they feel about the situation and reflect those feelings back to them."

"Does that work?" Carson slowed as the Methodist church appeared on his right.

As Skye's father-in-law turned into the circular drive, she gazed at the enormous building. It wasn't even a year old, and the pristine red brick had almost a divine glow in the bright sunshine.

Responding to Carson's question, Skye answered, "My interview method works most of the time. And if it doesn't, I try something else. Considering that a big part of my job is to get information out of uncooperative teenagers, most adults don't stand a chance."

"Good to know." Carson's tone was cautious, then he narrowed his eyes. "Any chance you'd come to work for me? CB International could use you."

"Nah." Skye grinned. "I use my mad skills only for good, not evil."

"Are you saying that my company is evil?" Carson sounded hurt.

"Of course not, Dad," Skye quickly reassured him. "But I suspect there isn't any business, other than maybe a nonprofit one, that is always completely kind."

"Humph." Carson pursed his lips, then changed the subject again. "This lot is packed. It could take a while to find a parking spot."

"Especially one big enough for this beast of a vehicle," Skye teased.

Carson circled the lot until someone left, then hastily nabbed the opening. He helped Skye down from the Hummer and they walked quickly across the hot asphalt. The afternoon temperatures had risen into the high eighties and the humidity made every breath miserable.

Blessedly cool air greeted Skye and Carson as they pushed through the double, etched-glass doors. Skye had heard that several families from neighboring towns had donated their generators and propane supply to keep the facility's electricity running and that food and clothing donations were pouring into the shelter as well.

Skye took a few steps inside and paused to get her bearings. To her immediate right were the open doors of the sanctuary. People sitting in the pews were listening to the minister speaking from the altar.

"All of us have been touched by the horrible storm that swept through our community." The young man bowed his head and, in a resonant voice, said, "When our lives are going well, it's easy to praise God." He tented his fingers. "And when we run into difficulties, it's natural to seek God." He lifted his eyes to the congregation. "Now, we need not only to trust God to see us through our troubles, but also to remember to thank Him for every moment we have."

Skye nodded her agreement and made the sign of the cross. She imagined that similar scenes were being played out in many of the area churches. Which reminded her, she wanted to ask Carson to stop at St. Francis on their way home and light a candle . . . or twelve . . . for Wally's safe return.

But for now, her goal was to find Billie Lyons. Turning away from the sanctuary, Skye was stunned at the piles of clothes, food, toiletries, and other miscellanea crowding the lobby separating the sanctuary and the church hall. It was clear that while the volunteers had attempted to organize the donations, the massive amount of people in need, as well as the mountains of contributions, had swamped their best intentions.

A beleaguered woman sat behind a long folding table, her finger in one ear as she held her cell phone next to the other. Another woman wandered through the stacks of contributions with a clipboard, evidently trying to take an inventory, while a pack of children raced back and forth among the carton maze, screaming and giggling as they played tag. Although their shouts contributed to the general bedlam of the situation, it was good to hear the kids laughing and having fun.

When the woman on the phone disconnected, Skye said, "My father-in-law and I are trying to locate Billie Lyons. I called earlier and was told she wasn't registered, but would it be okay if we looked around?"

"Be my guest." The woman waved toward the church hall to Skye's left. "The night of the tornadoes, we tried to get everyone's information when they arrived. But there were so many folks with no other place to go, eventually we were just overwhelmed and let them go in without filling out the paperwork."

"I can imagine." Skye shook her head. "How wonderful that your congregation was prepared and able to open up the church to give them shelter so quickly."

"When Pastor Braden came to us, he encouraged us to organize a disaster recovery team." The volunteer smiled. "He got us all mobilized."

"A man of foresight. I like that in a minister," Carson murmured, then asked, "What is the one thing you need most right now?"

"Baby formula, bottles, baby food, diapers, and wipes," the woman reeled off without even pausing to think. Then added,

"Portable cribs and car seats."

"Will someone be here to accept delivery?" Carson waited for the woman to nod. When she did, he took his cell from his pocket, glanced at Skye, and said, "I'm putting my PA on it. I'll be right back."

Once Carson stepped outside, the woman looked at Skye and asked, "Is he for real?"

"Yep." Skye beamed. "He'll have everything on your list here by morning."

"Wow." The woman's eyes widened. "You're married to the chief of police right? Wally Boyd?"

"I am." Skye half expected the woman to mention Wally's disappearance, but evidently the tornadoes had screwed up Scumble River's grapevine, because the volunteer didn't say a word about him being missing.

"And you said that guy was your father-in-law?" the woman asked.

"Uh-huh." Skye winced. With Carson around, it really wasn't going to be possible to keep the Boyd family's affluence a secret much longer. They'd have to come up with a plan to manage the information.

"So your father-in-law has some serious money?" The woman's gaze was speculative.

"Not him personally," Skye said quickly. "But he works for a very generous company.

He's probably contacting their HR department."

"Right." The woman's interest waned. "We're now a tax deduction."

"Yep. You know how big business likes their write-offs," Skye agreed. "So, I'm just going to go see if I can find Billie Lyons. Okay?"

"Sure." The woman sighed and picked up her phone. "Back to wrangling volunteers."

As Skye stepped away from the table, her cell dinged. With Wally missing, she'd turned the volume to high so she wouldn't miss any calls or messages. Of course, that meant that May could reach her, too. Crossing her fingers, she checked to see who was contacting her.

Instead of news that Wally had been found, it was a text from Trixie. Yesterday afternoon, after hearing about Wally's disappearance from Charlie, who got the scoop from May, Trixie had called to ask if she could do anything for Skye. But Trixie and Owen had their own tornado-related problems and Skye had reassured her friend that everything that could be done was being done.

Trixie's text was just checking to see if anything had changed and another offer of assistance. Skye quickly replied that there was no news and she didn't need any help at the present.

She'd gotten similar calls from her brother and sister-in-law, and others on May's phone tree. But everyone had their own troubles and there really wasn't anything anyone could do to find Wally.

Tucking her cell into the outside pocket of her purse for easy access, Skye entered the church hall. Cots were arranged into family groups with cardboard cartons positioned between the clusters in an attempt to give the occupants a semblance of privacy.

Now that the neighborhoods had been reopened, most of the people staying in the shelter were probably at their homes, searching for any undamaged possessions, leaving the large auditorium nearly deserted. If Roy hadn't mentioned that the crime scene techs had cordoned off the Lyons house until they had time to process it, Skye would have wondered if Billie was at her home, looking for salvageable belongings like the other survivors.

Hearing noise from the hall's kitchen, Skye inhaled, smelling oregano, garlic, and tomatoes cooking. It had to be spaghetti: an old church-supper standby that was low cost, could feed a crowd, and was relatively easy to throw together.

Skye's stomach growled at the appetizing odor and she noticed a table along the rear wall holding a massive urn and several trays of various mouthwatering pastries. The pot had to have contained at least a hundred cups of coffee and a giant box of tea bags was sitting next to a smaller container sporting a sign that read HOT WATER.

As Skye walked to the table and examined the goodies, she was 99 percent sure the muffins, scones, and Danishes were from Orlando Erwin, the baker and co-owner of Tales and Treats. She hoped the food was an indication that the combination bookstore and café hadn't been damaged by the storm.

Orlando's wife was definitely the type to have a generator ready for any emergency. And Skye smiled at the thought of folks able to take a break from the destruction at the café.

Resisting the tasty temptations, Skye made her way through the improvised aisles, searching for Billie Lyons. Having seen the murder victim's wife and mother-in-law when the two women had been asking May to find Zeke the night of the tornado, Skye was certain she'd be able to recognize the pair.

She worked her way from the back to the

front, intent on getting a look at each person present. White tent cards with the names of the absent occupants were placed on many of the empty cots, and when Skye reached the entrance, her shoulders drooped. There had been no sign of Billie.

"Excuse me." A tiny elderly gentleman dressed in a navy, three-piece, pin-striped suit tapped Skye's arm. "Are you looking for someone?"

"I am." Skye smiled at him and held out her hand. "I'm Skye Denison-Boyd. I work for the Scumble River Police Department, and we're trying to locate Billie Lyons. Do you know if she is, or was, here?"

"Bartolommeo Capuchini, at your service." He glanced at Skye's large baby belly and waved her toward a folding chair next to a cot. "Perhaps it would be best if you got off your feet while we talk."

"Thank you." Skye sat down. "It is hard to stand for too long."

"Please allow me to fetch you a cup of tea and a pastry." Bartolommeo bowed slightly. "The lemon-blueberry scones are outstanding."

Before Skye could decline, the sweet, little man hurried off. *Oh, well.* One of Orlando's treats would hit the spot around now. It was 4:39, and who knew when she'd get a chance to eat supper?

While Skye waited for Bartolommeo to return, she kept her eye on the auditorium's entrance. A steady stream of people was trickling into the church hall. The families displaced by the tornadoes were doubtlessly returning for a hot meal after spending the day combing their destroyed houses, looking for any bits and pieces of their lives that had survived the destruction. Come rain, or sleet, or gloom of twister, Scumble Riverites preferred to dine at five o'clock sharp.

Most of the folks coming into the shelter were dirty and sweaty, and Skye glanced around the room. She doubted that there were showers available anywhere in the facility. The poor people would likely have to make due with sponge baths in one of the church's restrooms.

Skye suddenly felt guilty for the comfort of the motor home that her father-in-law had provided. Although Carson was already doing a lot, perhaps he would be willing to bring in a portable shower trailer like the one she had seen on the news after a disaster had hit another community.

After all, her father-in-law was a generous man and truly wanted to help out his son's adopted community. As soon as he got back from making his phone call about the baby supplies, Skye vowed to ask him if arranging for bathing accommodations for the shelter would be possible.

Carson still hadn't appeared when Bartolommeo returned, carrying a tray containing two cups, sugar and creamer packets, plastic utensils, paper napkins, and a plate of goodies. He rested his burden on the cardboard box next to his cot. The carton had been covered with a piece of gingham cloth, and a vase holding a single yellow gladiolus was placed in the very center.

Bartolommeo perched on the edge of the cot and proceeded to transfer the tray's contents to the makeshift table, folding the napkins and arranging the plastic silverware as if they were about to have a party.

When he was satisfied, he asked, "How do you take your tea, my dear?"

"Just as it is will be fine." Skye accepted the cup and took a sip.

"May I tempt you with one of Mr. Erwin's delectable masterpieces?" Bartolommeo's hand hovered over the dish of pastries.

"A scone would be lovely." For a moment, Skye felt as if the tornado had blown her into Oz and Bartolommeo was actually one of the Munchkins.

"Excellent choice." Bartolommeo twinkled at her. "I'll join you."

Once he finished serving her, Skye prodded, "Were you going to tell me about Billie Lyons? I'm afraid I'm a bit pressed for time."

"Ah, the charming Billie." Bartolommeo sipped his tea. "Where to begin?"

"Has she been staying here at the shelter?" Skye wondered if the man truly had any information to share or was just lonely.

"She and her unpleasant mother spent last night here." Bartolommeo broke off a corner of his scone and popped it into his mouth.

"Do you know if they're planning to come back tonight?" Skye asked.

"Does anyone know for sure where they'll lay their heads anymore?"

"No. I guess not." Skye shoved down her impatience. As in counseling, there was rarely any way to make someone disclose information before they were good and ready to talk about it. "But what's your best guess?"

"I sorely doubt it." Bartolommeo chewed thoughtfully. "Billie got a call about picking up Zeke's dog, and she was determined to find a place that allowed pets. Her mother tried to talk her into having the animal euthanized, but Billie's grown a backbone since she got married, and she refused."

"You sound like you know Billie pretty well," Skye murmured encouragingly.

"I've lived next door to her mother for the past forty years," Bartolommeo said slowly, then asked, "How much do you know about Billie Lyons?"

"Only that her home was destroyed and her husband killed." Skye wasn't sure if it was common knowledge yet that Zeke had been murdered, so she had kept her answer vague enough that his death could be attributed to the tornado. "What can you tell me about her?"

"Sweet Billie was one of those women unequipped for the modern world." Bartolommeo sighed. "For a long time, she reminded me of that song 'Delta Dawn.' "

"In what way?" Skye took a sip of tea, trying to remember the lyrics.

"She was always a pretty, little thing, but for one reason or another, she never married." Bartolommeo scowled. "And she always appeared a little lost."

Hmm. Skye frowned. That wasn't how Billie had seemed when she was trying to get May to have the police search for her husband.

"I heard she and Zeke dated for many years," Skye said. "Do you have any idea why they didn't get married until recently?"

"Oh. I have better than an idea." Bartolommeo tsked. "Her mother didn't want to lose her daughter to some man, so every time it looked as if Billie might accept Zeke's proposal, Myra would develop some mysterious illness. Or fall and get hurt. Or come up with a million reasons why Billie couldn't leave her."

"How did Billie finally get married?" Skye asked, glad her own mother wasn't anywhere near as controlling as Billie's mom. May hadn't initially liked her daughter's choice of groom, but she was all for her marriage and the swift production of grandchildren.

"Billie had a health scare of her own and that seemed to put some steel in her spine." Bartolommeo raised an eyebrow. "The whole neighborhood heard old lady Gulch screaming when Billie came home wearing a wedding band."

Skye chuckled, then asked, "So Billie and Zeke were happily married?"

"Oh. My. Yes."

"Is there any scenario where you could see Billie killing Zeke?"

"None." Bartolommeo polished off his scone and wiped his fingers on his napkin. "They were so much in love that it almost hurt to watch them together."

Chapter 18

"Don't mind Mr. Joker," said the Princess to Dorothy. "He is considerably cracked in his head, and that makes him foolish."

Skye hugged her father-in-law. When he'd joined her at Bartolommeo's tea party and she'd told him about the lack of bathing facilities, he had immediately agreed to arrange for a portable shower trailer to arrive before bedtime. The folks staying at the shelter could go to sleep clean and refreshed for the first time in two days.

As she and Carson made their way back to the Hummer, Skye's cell rang. She hurriedly grabbed it from her purse's outer pocket and swiped the screen.

Her heart leaped when she saw it was Roy, but when she put the phone on speaker and answered it, the sergeant immediately said, "This isn't about the chief. Sorry, there's nothing new."

"Oh." She blew out a disappointed breath. She'd hoped Wally had been found.

"I . . . uh . . . hate to bother you, but . . ." Roy stuttered to a stop.

"Just spill it, Roy," Skye said impatiently. "What can I do for you?"

"It's Earl Doozier and his kin." Roy's tone spoke volumes. "Things are getting out of hand with them, and I need your help to stop it."

Earl Doozier was the patriarch of a loosely related group known as the Red Raggers. The Red Raggers were hard to explain to anyone who hadn't grown up in Scumble River and Skye saw the questioning look in her father-in-law's eyes. She mouthed the word *later* and turned her thoughts back to Earl and his relatives.

The Doozier clan was the reason mothers warned their children not to go into certain parts of town. They had the dubious distinction of being the most criticized family in the local newspaper's "Shout Out" column. But only because those complaints were allowed to be anonymous, because unless someone had a death wish, they would never sign their names and purposely get on the wrong side of the Red Raggers. In a nutshell, the Red Raggers didn't live by the rules.

Throughout her years working as the school district's psychologist, Skye had formed a special relationship with the Dooziers. She protected them from the bureaucracy, and they protected her from her own gullibility. Still, she didn't like to press her luck. Earl's wife, Glenda, hated her and someday the Red Ragger queen would ignore her husband's objections. And when that happened, Skye would be the one in Glenda's gunsights.

"I'm really sorry, Roy, but don't think I can help you," Skye hedged. "You know with the baby and Wally missing and the murder and the tornado . . . It's just too much."

"Yeah. I understand," the sergeant said slowly. "But the thing is: I'm pretty sure that the chief wouldn't want anything to mar the town's reputation. And Earl just gave an interview to the media, claiming his family was either starting a self-defense class to help folks protect themselves from looters or they're doing a fund-raiser to get money for all the poor homeless people living in the streets."

"Which is it?" Skye asked, knowing she was about to cave in and help out.

"I couldn't really tell." Roy's voice held pure frustration. "You know Earl doesn't ever talk in any kind of straight line. For all I know, he plans on teaching people to shoot the looters and rob them, then contribute the money to the tornado victims."

"Fine." Skye pressed her lips together. There was still time before Quentin and the security guys were due to arrive. "I'll stop by Earl's on my way home." She firmed her tone. "But after that, I'm off duty for the day. Unless you have news about my husband, don't call again. Because you won't like my response."

Disconnecting before the sergeant could respond, she turned to her father-in-law, rolled her eyes, and said, "Ready for an adventure?"

"Lead the way." Carson grinned and helped Skye into the Hummer.

As they drove toward Red Ragger territory, Skye attempted to clarify why she was the one handling the current crisis rather than Roy.

"After seven years of working with the endless supply of Doozier offspring in the schools, I have a better relationship with the unconventional family than any of the other law enforcement employees in Scumble River and Stanley County." Skye rested her hands on her baby bump. "And by that, I mean when we pull into their driveway, they are less likely to shoot first and ask questions later, than if a squad car showed up at their place."

"Fu— I mean fudge!" Carson looked guiltily at Skye, then asked, "How much less likely?" He raised his eyebrows, fingered the gun at his hip, and frowned. "I knew I shouldn't have let Quentin talk me out of ordering you a maternity bulletproof vest."

"Is that even a thing?" Skye asked, thinking that if such a garment existed, Wally surely would have gotten her one. Not waiting for her father-in-law to answer, she continued to prepare him for what he might encounter. "I'm 99 percent sure there will be no shooting. Because of my rapport with the Red Raggers, I often act as a goodwill ambassador between the cops and the crackpots. But the Dooziers are a breed unto themselves, so there are no guarantees."

Carson had had a brief taste of Earl's family at Wally and Skye's wedding reception, but a Doozier in his or her natural habitat was a whole other animal. One that most people thought was long extinct. Like a dodo bird.

"Tell me more about these people," Carson ordered, keeping his eyes on the road. "Why is Sergeant Quirk so leery of them?"

"The clan lives by their wits," Skye started, then cautioned, "which should not be mistaken for smarts. They have their own set of rules, but those rules aren't the same as society's laws."

"And they get away with it?" Carson asked. "You all need to bring in the Texas Rangers to clear them out of their hidey-holes."

"Most of the time, they're fairly harmless." Skye shrugged. "And I'm working on changing the next generation. Think of them as local color."

"Wally allows you to deal with these 'fairly harmless' people?"

"Allows?" Skye narrowed her eyes. "I'm not his child or his dog."

"Now don't go squatting on your spurs." Carson patted her knee. "I just can't see my son being happy with his wife walking into a dangerous situation."

"He may not be thrilled, but he understands that I'm a good psychologist and that I'm often the best person for the situation."

"Hmm." Carson's lips formed a straight line. "You remind me a lot of my wife. She always thought she could save the world. She's been gone for well over twenty years and I still miss her every day."

"I'm sorry you lost her so young." Skye

squeezed his arm. "And I'm flattered you think that I'm like her."

As Carson and Skye neared the Red Ragger colony, it dawned on her that the Dooziers had been in the tornadoes' pathway, too. Although, with the already dilapidated condition of the homes in their area, it would be hard to tell if they'd been hit by a twister or not.

After carefully guiding the massive Hummer over a narrow plank bridge, Carson paused at the crossroad and said, "So if I turn left, we'll drive past summer cottages and retirement homes; however, if we go right, we enter the heart of Red Ragger country?"

"Yep." Skye smiled. "And never the twain shall meet. For the first couple of years, the Chicago people and the Red Raggers tested each other like a kid with a new stepparent. Eventually, they just ignored one another. Then, a while back, shots were exchanged and the peace treaty was breached, but it turned out to be paintballs rather than bullets and the agreement was renegotiated without bloodshed." She grimaced. "Although I ended up painted orange."

"Oookay." Carson paused, then asked, "I don't suppose Wally took pictures."

"We wouldn't be having this baby if he

had." Skye stared at her father-in-law. "Because his equipment to reproduce wouldn't be in working order."

"I love a feisty woman." Carson grinned and took the left on Cattail Path. "No wonder Wally adores you."

As they drove down the road, Skye saw a series of hand-painted placards.

If UR sceered. Don't be afeared. Grab a gun. And have some fun.

She shook her head. The Burma-Shave sign people were probably rolling in their graves.

A few seconds later, Skye and Carson arrived at the Dooziers. Earl and Glenda's lot was shaped roughly like a scalene triangle, with the longest side resting along the riverbank and the shortest adjacent to the road. From the street, Carson and Skye could see only the front of the house, and with that limited vantage point, the sole evidence of anything unusual was the large piece of cardboard taped between two wooden boards stuck in the yard.

Bright-red lettering invited people to:

Come on back. Put your money toward a good cause while you learn to defend

yourself from the wild gangs invading
Scumble River.

Well, shoot! No wonder Roy had been confused.

Still, Skye was impressed that unlike the signs leading here, this one had every word correct. Earl must have had his daughter Bambi make it. She was the only one of his brood who was doing well enough in school to manage perfect spelling.

Carson parked in the empty driveway and helped Skye down from the Hummer. It was hard to tell for sure, but if Skye had to bet, she'd wager that none of the recent tornadoes were to blame for the condition of the Dooziers' property. Although the ground in front of the run-down shack was uneven and covered with weeds, discarded toys, and rocks, it always looked like that. As for the skeletons of rusted-out pickups and the husks of ancient appliances adding to the obstacle course, they had been there as long as Skye could remember.

Once she and Carson had gingerly picked their way to the fenced-off backyard, they found another sign on the gate that read:

Stun Guns for sale. Lessons extra.
Money will go to needy Scumble River

families.
Guns $40 Lesson $10

"Didn't you say that Zeke Lyons was killed with a stun gun?" Carson asked.

"Of some sort," Skye muttered, distracted, then realized what her father-in-law was implying and added, "But I'm sure this is a coincidence. The Dooziers would just use a shotgun if they wanted him dead."

Carson's expression was skeptical. "If you say so. Are stun guns legal in Illinois?"

"You need a Firearm Owner's Identification card for one," Skye answered. "I had to get my FOID card before I could get one."

Carson pursed his lips. "So how can this Doozier guy be selling them?"

"More than the legality of the sales, the question that really concerns me is how he got a supply to sell so fast." Skye peered anxiously over the chain-link fence, squinting in the sunlight.

Several feet back, near where the yard merged into the wooded area, a folding table with crooked legs had what looked like a pyramid of disposable cameras piled in the center. Sitting with his cowboy-clad feet propped up on the table's surface was a skinny, densely tattooed man wearing a pair of filthy running shorts, a torn tank top, and a huge cowboy hat that he had pulled low over his eyes. Empty beer cans and snack food wrappers were strewn next to his lawn chair.

Skye blinked, then leaned toward Carson and lowered her voice. "What's with all the cameras? Do you think Earl is providing a photo opportunity? He snaps your picture as you zap someone with a stun gun?"

"Nope." Carson's expression was almost admiring. "I'll bet you that the cameras *are* the stun guns." He shook his head. "I read a how-to article in one of the survivalist magazines. A disposable camera is pretty easy to convert. All you need are a few simple tools, some electrical wire, metal screws, and bonding glue."

"Seriously?"

"Uh-huh. You shoot it by rotating the film-advance knob."

"Terrific. Who knew Earl could follow directions?" Skye wrinkled her forehead. The ME had reported that the marks on Zeke's chest didn't match any known devices. Maybe because the gadget wasn't one that had been professionally manufactured. She was still sure the Dooziers hadn't killed Zeke, but how about one of their customers? "We need to confiscate those homemade stun guns. There is no way on earth that those things are safe."

"Do you have a plan?" Carson asked, glancing uneasily at Earl.

"Nope." Skye followed her father-in-law's gaze. It was never a good idea to startle a Doozier. Was he sleeping or passed out? Did it matter?

The gate was unlocked, and as she stepped over the metal threshold, she noisily cleared her throat and said, "Earl, are you awake?"

An earsplitting snore was the Doozier's only reply.

"Earl?" Skye inched closer and raised her voice. "Wake up, Earl."

Carson stuck to Skye's side, one hand resting on the butt of his gun and the other gripping her elbow. Clearly, he intended to thrust her behind him if Earl made any kind of threatening move.

Although Earl never stirred, the dogs penned nearby barked and bared their teeth at Skye and Carson. Trying to break free, the hounds jumped against the steel mesh of their cage, bouncing off the fencing like water on a hot pan.

Giving the furious animals a wide berth, Skye crept toward Earl, stopped just out of stun gun range, and shouted, "Earl!"

The Doozier jumped and his chair went over backward, collapsing around him in a tangle of plastic webbing and bent aluminum. As he fought to free himself, his cowboy hat slid farther down his face, totally obscuring his view.

Although blinded by the hat, he leaped to his feet and waved a camera around. "Get back. I'll shoot iffen you're here tryin' to rob me."

"It's Skye, Earl." She took a step closer, but then quickly moved downwind. His body odor was at an all-time high and her stomach made its displeasure known. Earl must have used the tornado as an excuse to delay bathing even longer than usual. "Chief Boyd's father and I are here to talk to you about your fund-raiser."

Earl finally pried off his cowboy hat and scowled. "Miz Skye, you shouldn't be walking around here in your condition." He glanced at her stomach. "I can't believe you're still knocked up. Aren't you pret' near ready to pop out that kid?"

"It'll be a while yet." She sighed, then said, "Sorry for waking you, Earl."

"That's okay, Miz Skye." His wide smile revealed several blackened stumps and missing teeth. "Nice to meetcha, Mr. Boyd." He loped toward Carson.

As the men shook hands, Skye noticed her father-in-law's nose twitching and his eyes watering. She hid her smile. Doubtlessly, Earl smelled worse than the cow patties scattered throughout the pastures of Carson's ranch.

Once the formalities were over, Earl asked, "What can I do you for?"

"Sergeant Quirk saw your television interview and was confused as to the details of your fund-raiser." She gestured toward the contents of the table. "Are you aware of the legalities in owning a stun gun? People need to have a FOID card." She frowned. "And I'm not even entirely sure it's legal to sell them here."

"We is in a state of emergency." Earl put his hand over his heart. "The anus is on all of us to do our part. I'm willin' to put myself at risk of arrest to help protect my neighbors."

Carson's brows crawled up to his hairline. "Anus?"

"Onus," Skye translated, then turned to Earl and asked, "How did you get ahold of this many disposable cameras so fast?" Skye counted under her breath. "You've got what, forty? Fifty?"

"Every mornin' is the dawn of a new error." Earl hooked his thumbs in the elastic waistband of his nylon shorts. "I been plannin' for an emergency for a long time."

"Are those things safe?" Skye gave up preaching about the law. "Did you test them?"

"Of course." Earl stared at the ground. "And they worked fine."

"Oh?" Skye didn't trust him for a second. "Tell me about it."

"You promise not to say nothin' to Glenda?" Earl looked over his shoulder.

"You have my word," Skye vowed. It wasn't as if she and Earl's wife got together for tea . . . or even a nice cocktail at the bowling alley.

"Good." Earl's grin was sheepish. "I told her I didn't know nothin' about the burn spot on the front of the microwave and she's madder than a wet hen about it since she just bought the thing."

"Go on." Skye shuddered, thinking of Glenda's reaction if she found out.

"Anyways, after that, I had Junior read me the directions again and I made a few tweaks."

"Right." Skye rolled her eyes. "If at first you don't succeed —"

"Put in new batteries." Earl scratched his crotch. "Anyways, I figured I needed to try it out on something live." He tugged at his greasy, brown ponytail. "You know, something that was breedin'."

"What?" Skye clutched her belly, then with a huge sigh of relief realized he meant breathing.

"Anyways, I grabbed —"

"You didn't use one of the kids?" Skye's mind raced, thinking she'd have to call the Department of Children and Family Services if he'd shock one of his offspring. And wouldn't that be a real mess?

"Nah." The sunshine highlighted the cereal-bowl-sized bald spot on Earl's head. "Now days, they all run too fast for me to catch 'em."

"So who did you try it on?" Skye and Carson exchanged a worried glance.

"I considered one of the dogs," Earl admitted, reaching into a cooler and coming out with a dripping can of beer. "But they didn't do anything to deserve bein' zapped, so I didn't."

"That was real fair of you." Skye inhaled sharply, relieved she wouldn't have to call the ASPCA either.

"Glenda said I ought to try it on MeMa." Earl scratched his nose. "My sweet ums ain't ever forgiven her for try'n' to talk me outta gettin' hitched. The day of the weddin', MeMa told me I should just live with her for the rest of my life and forgit about gettin' married."

The infamous MeMa was the clan matriarch and Earl's grandmother, or maybe great-grandmother; Skye had never quite untangled the Dooziers' twisted family tree.

"Did you consider it?" Carson asked.

"Nah." Earl burped. "Glenda might not a been the best-lookin' girl at the party, but likes I always says: beauty is only a light switch away." He glanced uneasily over his shoulder. "But that's just between the three of us."

Skye opened her mouth to respond, then paused. There was something about what Earl had been saying about MeMa that nudged an idea deep in her brain.

When it failed to emerge, she said, "So you never did test it on a human."

"I didn't say that." A hangdog expression stole over Earl's face. "Accordin' to the directions, a one-second burst would just shock and confuse ya, so I —"

"You decided to use it on yourself," Skye guessed. "What happened?"

"I'm pret' damn sure the Incredible Hulk grabbed me by the nape of the neck and slammed me into the wall. Again and again." Earl popped the top on his beer and chugged it. "I woke up drenched in piss and I couldn't find my balls for a couple hours after that. My face was numb, I was drooling worsen the hound dog, plus my hair was smokin'." He finished his beer and tossed the can on the ground. "And the recliner that I was sittin' on is still missing."

Carson, who had been silent, stepped forward, and said, "Earl, you see why you can't sell those things."

"I already sold a couple." Earl expression was stubborn.

"Who to?" Skye asked excitedly. Maybe one of Earl's customers was Zeke's killer.

"How would I know?" Earl sneered. "Does you think I take credit cards?"

"Were they from around here? What did they look like?" Skye asked, hoping she'd recognize the person from Earl's description.

"One was a fat, white dude and the other was a skinny, black woman." Earl sucked his teeth. "I ain't ever seen either of 'em before."

"Shoot!" Skye's shoulders slumped. So much for a clue to the murder. It wasn't as if Scumble River had a police artist. Maybe they could get one to come in from the state police.

Carson gave her a brief hug, then turned to Earl and said, "Well, you can't sell the rest of those stun guns. They aren't safe."

"But I invested a lot of money in them,"

Earl whined.

"How much?" Carson asked.

Before Skye could stop him, he reached for his wallet. Then as he pulled his billfold from his pocket, she heard a high-pitched cackle that reminded her of someone who had been sucking on helium balloons. She didn't have to turn around to know that Glenda Doozier had appeared out of nowhere like the Wicked Witch flying in on her broomstick.

From her bright-yellow, stiletto-clad feet to her bottle-blond hair, she was the embodiment of an ideal Red Ragger woman, but all Skye could think of was — how much had Glenda heard? And how much was this mess going to end up costing Carson?

Earl rushed over to his wife. "Baby doll, look who's here, Miz Skye and Chief Boyd's daddy."

Glenda ignored Skye, turned to Carson, and poked him with her inch-long, fire-engine red, fake fingernail. "We spent four hundert dollars on the cameras alone. Plus all the extra doodads and our time and labor, we couldn't take less than a thousand for 'em."

"I'll give you two hundred." Carson rubbed the spot on his shoulder where she had jabbed him. "Cash money right now."

"You ain't cheatin' us out of our earnings." Glenda crossed her arms, shoving her considerable bosom nearly out of the neon-green tank top she wore.

Skye stepped out of fingernail range. "I thought you were donating the profits."

Glenda rounded on Skye. "You, you know-it-all, stuck-up Goody Two-Shoes, stay outta this or that baby will be an orphan before it's even born."

Huh? Skye had no idea what Glenda meant, but she zipped her lip.

"Now, Mrs. Doozier." Carson stepped between the women. "There's no need to get upset."

"Yer right." Glenda narrowed her rabbit-like eyes. "Cause you're either payin' our price or we'll go with our original plan."

"I'll give you two hundred and fifty." Carson's tone was firm. "Or we'll let the police settle the matter. I'm sure they'd be interested in your illegal gun selling and fraudulent fundraising operation."

Skye recoiled, then hastily scooted behind Carson. Telling Glenda something she didn't want to hear was dangerous. Threatening to bring in the cops was suicidal.

When Glenda didn't immediately respond, Carson crossed his arms and warned, "And the amount goes down every second I have to wait."

As quick as a squirrel shimmying up the pole of a bird feeder, Glenda launched herself at Carson. As he dove to one side, Skye turned to run. But it was too late. Glenda was already in midair, heading straight toward her.

Chapter 19

> "Don't you suppose we could rescue them?" asked the girl anxiously. "We can try," answered the Lion.

"I am so sorry. I had no idea that you had stepped behind me." Carson glanced anxiously at Skye as he tossed a large cardboard box containing the disposable-camera stun guns into the back of the Hummer. "You know I would never put you in danger."

"Of course I do." Skye allowed him to open her door and help her into the passenger seat, then rubbed her baby bump and said, "And even if I wasn't sure of that, which I am, I'm absolutely positive that you wouldn't jeopardize your grandchild."

"I never would have jumped out of the way if I knew you were there," Carson continued as if Skye hadn't spoken. "I only moved aside because in Texas, we don't hit women. Even one like Glenda Doozier."

"I know." Skye patted his arm. "You've proven you're always there for your family, so I'm sure you'd take a flying Glenda for me."

"Anytime, sugar." Carson's voice was hoarse as he walked around to the driver's side. "For a minute there, before Earl tackled his crazy wife, I was ready to draw my gun and blow her away."

"It was a little surreal to see him make such a split-second interception." Skye scrubbed her eyes with her fist. "If he can move like that, Earl should be playing for the Chicago Bears."

"Nah, that boy has too much yardage between the goalposts to make the team." Carson winked at her before starting the engine.

"True."

"You sure you're okay?" Carson asked worriedly as he reversed out of the Dooziers' driveway. "Even if that dang fool woman didn't plow into you, you did stumble around a lick."

"Except for a little damage to my vanity, I'm fine," Skye assured him.

"It's a good thing" — Carson gripped the SUV's steering wheel — "or I'd be using her for target practice and her husband would be in jail."

"You sound just like your son." Skye chuckled. "Do you remember me telling you about my experience as an Oompa-Loompa?" When her father-in-law nodded, she continued. "The reason I ended up orange was because Wally jumped out of the way when Glenda tried to shoot him with a paint gun. Like you today, he didn't know I was behind him then either."

"We're going to have to put a bell around your neck," Carson teased.

"Or let me handle the Dooziers without your or Wally's 'help.' " Skye smiled at the look of indignation on her father-in-law's face, then glanced over her shoulder at the box of disposable cameras in the back of the Hummer. "What are you going to do with forty-seven homemade stun guns that may or may not work?"

"Well, I suppose I could rewire them and use them to take pictures of my grandbaby," Carson suggested with a twinkle. "Or, I could dump them all in your burn barrel and we could have a bonfire." At Skye's appalled expression, he grinned. "But we probably should turn them into the police for proper disposal."

"And to be tested to see if one like them was used in Zeke Lyons's murder," Skye said, then added, "Besides, there will be enough snapshots of this baby without ones from the Doozier Photography Studio. And who knows what kind of hazard cremating them might create."

"Testing and proper disposal it is."

"Phew." Skye wiped a pretend drop of sweat from her forehead.

After a quick stop at the Catholic church to a light a candle for Wally's safe return, Carson and Skye headed home. As her father-in-law drove the short distance between St. Francis and her house, Skye imagined Father Burns's face when he opened up the candle donation box and found the hundred-dollar bill Carson had slipped into the slot while Skye had been praying.

Glancing affectionately at her generous father-in-law and his seemingly bottomless wallet, she smiled when he turned the SUV onto Brooks Road. It would be good to get home. Even if right now, home was an RV.

As Carson pulled into Skye's driveway, her eyes widened and she stammered, "How . . . Who . . . What . . ."

"Did I forget to mention that I hired a crew to come in to tarp the house, clear up the downed trees from your property, and haul away the damaged cars?" Carson asked innocently.

"Yes. Yes, you did." She frowned and said, "You really have to stop doing stuff like that. What if the insurance people didn't want us to touch it? Now the company might not reimburse us."

"I checked with both adjusters and they said we could start the cleanup." Carson beamed. "I got their contact info from your cell while you were talking to that old guy at the church shelter."

"I had my phone in my purse and my purse with me that whole time." Skye scowled and her father-in-law raised his brows as if to say *Your point?* "Okay. I don't know how you're doing it, but you really have to stop swiping my cell." She wrinkled her brow and asked, "How did you figure out my password to unlock the screen?"

"Sugar, 1234 is not a password." Carson snickered. "And if you change it, don't use your birthday or Wally's or the baby's."

She wrinkled her brow, trying to think of a password she could remember. If she didn't have something simple, she'd forever be looking it up. Maybe she'd use her weight. If she got any bigger with the twins, it would probably be a four-digit number soon.

"Fine," Skye huffed, hoping Carson realized that when a woman said *fine,* she didn't really mean it as *okay,* but rather that she was ending the argument and he needed to stop talking.

Clearly, her father-in-law didn't get the hint, because he continued. "With the tarps covering the exposed first floor, any of your possessions that are recoverable are protected from the weather. That way, you can wait to deal with it all when you have more time."

"Thanks." Skye gritted her teeth and reminded herself that he meant well.

Heck! If it weren't for her pregnancy hormones, she probably would have been grateful rather than irritated by his methods.

Carson pulled the Hummer up next to the motor home and turned off the engine, then checked his phone and frowned. "Quentin and the security team hit some bad traffic and won't be here until six fifteen."

"I need to call Dante." Skye glanced at her watch. "But he won't talk to me now because it's after five and before seven." When Carson shot her a puzzled glance, she elaborated. "He doesn't take calls during dinner or the news. And his favorite program comes on at eight, so he won't let Aunt Olive answer the phone then. That leaves me only between seven and eight."

"Are you serious?" Carson took off his

seat belt, then walked around the Hummer to help Skye get out of the vehicle. "How about the electrical outage? And is the television even back on?"

"Dante has a generator, and if the satellite isn't working, he has an old-fashioned antenna." Skye shrugged. "He probably made Aunt Olive get up on the roof to adjust it. Dante is in love with the machinations of reality television and never misses an episode of one of his beloved shows."

"Your uncle is a man of many interests." Carson's tone was sardonic as he opened the motor home's door for Skye and waved her inside.

"Getting Dante to talk about Zeke and the city council will be tricky," Skye warned, walking over to the kitchen counter and plugging her cell into its charger.

"Why is that?" Carson tilted his head. "He's your blood kin. Dante should be eager to provide you with any helpful information."

"It's complicated." Skye turned to the fridge, grabbed two bottles of water, and handed her father-in-law one of them. "You know about all the crap Dante has tried with Wally and the police department?"

"Wally's mentioned some of the issues," Carson answered, uncapping the Dasani and taking a long drink. "But surely with Wally's life in danger, Dante will call a truce in his petty vendetta."

"Unfortunately, my uncle won't see the connection between finding Wally and fessing up to whatever he's got going on in the city council." Skye finished her water. "My uncle thrives on pettiness. He has taken spiteful to a new level and gives a new meaning to the word 'feud.' He makes Snow White's stepmother seem sweet."

"Worse comes to worst, I'll buy his cooperation." Carson's hands fisted. "He seems motivated by the almighty dollar, so I'll feed his greed."

"Let's pray it doesn't come to that. In my experience as a psychologist, rewarding bad behavior just leads to even worse behavior. And the idea of an even-worse-behaved Dante is terrifying." Tossing the empty bottle in the recycle bin under the sink, Skye headed toward the master bath. "I better make a pit stop before Quentin and your guys get here."

As she used the facilities, she realized she hadn't had to pee since just before she left the police station, which probably meant she was dehydrated. And that was a problem because she didn't have time for muscle cramps or another round of Braxton-Hicks contractions.

While she washed her hands, she vowed to drink another bottle of water immediately, and a couple more before bedtime. Hearing the motor coach's outer door open and men's voices, she quickly straightened her hair, swiped on some lip gloss, and rushed out to greet Quentin and the security guys.

When Quentin swung her into a tight hug, she blinked back tears. He could pass as Wally's younger brother and his presence just reinforced his cousin's absence.

While she was busy investigating Zeke Lyons's murder, she could forget that Wally had been kidnapped. Or at least pushed it to the back of her mind. But now the fact that he was gone couldn't be ignored.

Without any warning, fear and worry slammed into her chest, robbing her of her next breath. Forcing herself to inhale, she wiped the moisture from her cheeks and stepped away from Quentin.

Turning to the huge man standing next to Wally's cousin, she held out her hand. "Hi. You must be Mr. Tucker. I'm Carson's daughter-in-law, Skye. Thank you for coming so quickly to help get my husband back safely."

"Call me Tuck." The enormous man with

the dark buzz cut gently took her hand. "Mr. Boyd has always treated me and my team right. I'd be here even if he weren't my boss." He squeezed her fingers. "If Wally is still alive, I promise you that I'll get him home to you in one piece."

Skye resolutely ignored the "if he's still alive" part and said, "I'd appreciate it. The baby and I need him whole, not in several parts." When Tuck nodded his understanding, she asked, "Where is the rest of your team?"

"Familiarizing themselves with the area," Tuck said.

Skye nodded and gestured at the couch and chairs in the living room. "Why don't you all have a seat? I'd like to hear exactly how this is going to work."

The men refused her offer of food or drink and made themselves comfortable. While they settled in, Skye grabbed a bottle of water for herself and perched on the edge of a kitchen chair she'd dragged from the table.

Once everyone was seated, Quentin put a metal briefcase on the coffee table and opened the lid. Inside were stacks of twenties, fifties, and hundreds.

Carson pointed at the ransom. "We have a list of the serial numbers and this case has a tracking device installed in the hinges."

"I'm guessing the itemized numbers and GPS-enabled briefcase isn't something you threw together in a few hours." Skye raised her brows. "This is something you've had prepared for quite a while."

"Correct." Quentin narrowed his eyes. "Wally is right. You aren't just a pretty face." When Skye didn't react, he explained, "Dealing in foreign countries is a little different than in the U.S. Occasionally, we've had to provide 'bonuses' to ensure our employees' safety."

"Lovely." Skye recalled her conversation with Quentin during the night before her wedding. They'd been discussing why Quentin didn't want Wally to take Carson's offer of a job at CB International.

Quentin had said that Wally was too honest. He'd called his cousin a Dudley Do-Right and claimed that Wally couldn't see, and didn't believe, that there were a lot of shades of gray in the world.

Skye had asked him why being honest would be a problem, and Quentin had said it would threaten the Boyd empire. She hadn't been able to understand why a company couldn't just do the right thing, but Quentin had explained that sometimes corporations had to use any means necessary to keep the business in the black and beat the competition.

At that moment, Skye had realized that because Wally would never be comfortable cutting those kinds of corners and just plain wouldn't do it, corporate life would destroy him. And although she'd never wanted Wally to take a job in his father's company, before then, she would have accompanied him to Texas if he'd decided to do so. But understanding what it would do to Wally, she'd vowed to fight him if he ever considered making that move.

While Skye had been taking a stroll down memory lane, Tuck had placed a long, camo duffel bag next to the briefcase. Now she watched him unzip it and pull the sides apart. The sinister black gun inside looked an awful lot like one she'd seen in *Shooter,* an action movie she and Wally had gone to see last spring.

Clearing her throat, she asked, "Is that a sniper rifle in that bag?"

"Two." Tuck opened another compartment and the first gun's twin was revealed.

Skye gazed at the duffel's numerous pockets. She was pretty darn sure they contained enough ammunition to take down a small country. Obviously, in Carson's part of Texas, security had a whole different meaning than Skye's limited experience in Illinois.

"What do you plan to do with the rifles?" she asked, pretty sure she knew the answer.

Tuck caressed the gun's barrel and his brown eyes darkened until they were nearly black. "I plan on shooting anyone who needs to die."

Glancing at her father-in-law, Skye said, "I'd like some specifics, please."

"We're prepared for two different scenarios. In one, the kidnappers have Wally with them when they come to get the money. In that case, Quentin, who has been training with Tuck's men for the past couple of years, will be set up somewhere with a clear view of the ransom drop site. If there's a way to do it while ensuring Wally's safety, Quentin will take out any of the kidnappers who are present."

"He'll kill them?" Skye squeaked. Could Quentin really kill someone in cold blood?

"If necessary to save my cousin, hell yeah," Quentin said, his tone completely unruffled. "A lot depends on what the situation looks like at the time. Are they armed? What are their positions relative to Wally? Can I get them all before they can do anything to him?"

"Why Quentin and not one of the security

men?" Skye asked.

"Because next to Tuck, who's needed elsewhere, I'm the best shot." Quentin stared at Skye. "Do you have a problem with that?"

She sucked in a breath and shook her head. She didn't like it. But Wally's life in exchange for a criminal's? There was no contest.

"Good for you, darlin'." Carson got up and stood with his hands on her shoulders. He inhaled sharply and continued. "However, it's much more likely they'll have Wally stashed somewhere else, which is where Tuck and his team come in. They'll follow whoever picks up the money."

"After the kidnappers have the ransom, shouldn't we wait to see if they release Wally before we do anything else?" Skye could barely speak.

"We can't take the chance. Once they have the money and count it, they have no incentive to free Wally or keep him alive." Carson shoved his fingers through his hair. "And depending on where they have him, the tracker in the briefcase might not work. Which would mean we'd have no idea how to find Wally or the bad guys."

"What if the kidnappers see Tuck or his men and execute Wally?" Skye's pulse was racing and she tried to calm down. She could almost feel her blood pressure rising. This couldn't be good for the babies.

"They won't." Tuck voice was utterly sure. "My team and I did two tours in Afghanistan and two more in Iraq. We never once were spotted and we never ever missed our target. The scumbags holding Wally will be incapacitated without harming your husband." He paused and stared into her eyes. "Mr. Boyd wouldn't risk his only son if he wasn't absolutely certain of our ability to bring this mission to a successful conclusion. Successful being Wally coming home alive."

"Right. Of course." Skye was still nervous and didn't completely believe Tuck's assurances. But she didn't really have any choice. "So does that mean you're making the drop, Dad?"

"Yes. That was what the kidnapper demanded." Carson shrugged. "They have doubtlessly seen my picture online, so I have no choice. After I get the call and hear Wally's voice, I'll put the briefcase in the trash can."

"I'm coming with you," Skye said. When all three men started to yell at her, she added, "I'll wait in the car, but if you ever want to see your grandchild, Dad, you won't try to leave me behind."

Chapter 20

> "See what you have done! In a minute I shall melt away!"
>
> — Wicked Witch of the West

Skye waited for Carson, Quentin, and Tuck to calm down. They each presented an argument as to why she shouldn't accompany them to drop off the ransom, then she crossed her arms and refused to budge on her decision. Finally, after wresting several concessions from her, the men gave up and agreed she could go along.

Once that was settled, the three guys left to reconnoiter the drop-off site. They wanted to map out the property's access points and find the best spot for the sniper station.

Skye closed the door behind them and blew out a sigh of relief. She needed some time to herself. She'd been surrounded by people since Carson's arrival and she wanted a few moments to think about everything that had happened, as well as to plan her future actions.

Not really hungry, but knowing she should eat, Skye heated up a can of tomato soup and made a toasted cheese sandwich. She had to call Dante soon, but the conversation would go better if she was centered.

As she ate her supper and drank another bottle of water, Skye thought about Tuck's plans. She had to admit that she was glad she hadn't given in to her guilt and told Roy about Wally's kidnapping. Unlike her father-in-law, there was no way in the world the Scumble River Police Department would be able to bring in a top ex-military extraction team. Not to mention have access to the type of equipment Tuck had described.

Skye's head spun with thoughts of flash-bang grenades that emit high-intensity light to temporarily blind and disorient the enemy, thermal imaging devices to see in the dark, and even a Doppler radar gadget that picked up breathing and movement within a house. Sad to say, Tuck's security team was much better trained and equipped to rescue Wally than his own officers.

Finishing her meal, Skye put her dishes in the sink, took her cell from the charger, and grabbed the notepad and pen from her purse. After arranging everything on the table, she sat down and called Dante. She'd put off this conversation as long as possible. It was time to grow a backbone and interrogate her uncle.

Olive answered on the first ring and Skye quickly said, "Hi, it's Skye, Aunt Olive. I was so glad to hear you weren't hit by the tornado, but sad to hear about Uncle Dante's illness. How's he doing?"

As much as Skye wanted to, she couldn't avoid the pleasantries and get right down to business. If she did, the instant she disconnected, Olive would on the phone complaining to May. And Skye was not in the mood for a call from her mother reminding her to be polite.

"He's doing much better." Olive's voice had a definite edge. "Almost back to normal."

"That's great." Skye couldn't tell from her aunt's tone whether Olive thought Dante's quick recovery was a good thing or not.

"I was so sorry when May told me about your beautiful house," Olive said. "You've spent so much time and money rehabbing it."

"At least none of us were injured." Skye was truly tired of saying this, but it was the only acceptable answer in the circumstances.

"I took a ride past this afternoon," Olive said. "Is it at all salvageable?"

"No." Skye's voice hitched. "According to the insurance company, it's a complete teardown. And they totaled out both cars, too."

"It was sure nice of your father-in-law's company to bring in a motor home for you." Olive's tone was probing. "And so quickly."

"Yes, it was." Skye thought fast. "Luckily, the motor coach was being used at a jobsite in Chicago that had just finished up."

"How fortunate." Olive's voice was cynical. "And your dad's brother is lending you a vehicle. So many aren't as blessed. But as always, my dear, you seem to have landed on your feet."

"Yep." Skye clenched her jaw. "That's me. I must have been a cat in another reincarnation. I just hope I haven't used up my nine lives."

Olive chuckled politely, then said, "As long as you don't become complacent."

"Oh, I don't expect everything to be just handed to me," Skye snapped. "People are free to put their offerings down anywhere."

There was a moment of shocked silence, then Olive gave a forced chuckle and said, "Well, if there's anything I can do to help you, just let me know and consider it done."

"Thanks so much." Skye said, then added sweetly, "If it's not too much trouble, I do need to speak to Uncle Dante."

"Of course, dear." Olive hesitated, then warned, "With his illness and the town in such a state from the tornado, he's a tad cranky."

"Understandable." Skye rolled her eyes. When wasn't her uncle grouchy? "I promise not to keep him long. I know his favorite show is coming on television soon and I wouldn't want him to miss it."

"Right. I almost forgot." Olive's haste was evident. "Let me get him for you."

Skye tapped her pen on her notepad as she waited for her uncle to pick up.

"What do you want?" Dante's scowl came through the line loud and clear.

"Hello to you, too, dear Uncle," Skye said sweetly. "I'm so relieved to hear that your upset tummy is better and you're out of the bathroom."

"Yeah, yeah, yeah," Dante grumbled. "Olive's going to need to bring in a fumigation crew to deal with that place." He snorted. "Now, what do you want?"

"I spoke to one of Zeke Lyons's colleagues today." Skye decided to cut to the chase. "He mentioned that Zeke had been concerned that you were urging him to go along with a city council matter that he didn't feel he could vote for in good conscience."

"So?" Dante belched.

"What was the issue on which you two disagreed?" Skye asked.

"None of your beeswax," Dante sneered. "And before you go accusing me of murdering him over it, I really didn't need his vote. I just thought it would be nice to have a unanimous front."

"Oh, come on, Dante," Skye wheedled. "Surely nothing is that clandestine."

"You'll find out when every other Scumble Riverite is informed."

Skye pursed her lips, thinking. "Does it have anything to do with the budget freeze?"

"I'm not saying," Dante grunted. "If you have nothing else you need from me, I want to hit the can before my program comes on."

"I can always ask Kathryn Steele to have one of her reporters look into it," Skye said. "You know the *Star*'s owner and I are friends."

"Son of a —" Dante cut himself off and said, "Considering you and your husband's positions in the community, you both are mighty fond of blackmail."

"What are you talking about?" Skye wasn't

aware of Wally coercing her uncle about anything.

"Don't try to make me believe that he hasn't told you about forcing me to allow him to replace that druggy cop he fired," Dante thundered.

"No, he hasn't," Skye said. "When did this whole thing come about?"

"The day after the tornado," Dante growled. "Your precious husband refused to do his job unless I signed a paper letting him hire someone."

"What did you ask him to do?" Skye's pulse raced. Was this why Wally had wanted her to talk to Dante? Had her uncle sent him somewhere dangerous?

"All he had to do was drive out to my friend Hollister Brooks's rental property, check it for damage, and let Hollister know if it was okay," Dante huffed. "I assume the chief did so, since I received a thank-you text from Hollister, but it would have been nice if your husband had done me the courtesy of letting me know himself."

"What's the property's address?" Skye demanded, barely able to breathe.

"Why do you want to know that?" Dante's tone was suspicious.

"Because Wally's been missing since you sent him there." Skye barely restrained herself from screaming at her uncle's paranoia.

"What do you mean he's missing?" Dante screeched. "The chief of police vanishes and I'm not informed? I'll have Quirk's badge."

"You will do no such thing." Skye wished she could reach through the phone lines and slap her uncle. "Roy is doing a wonderful job juggling the problems from the tornadoes, Wally's disappearance, and Zeke Lyons's death." Skye inhaled and enunciated every word. "Now. What. Is. The. Address?"

"You think I have it memorized?" Dante snorted. "It's on my desk at city hall. Since I'm feeling better, I plan on going in to work in the morning. I'll call you with it when I get to my office tomorrow."

"Wrong!" Skye gave into her need to yell at her uncle. "Either you go and get me that address immediately or I swear to God, I will come to your house, haul you from your recliner, tie you to my back bumper, and drag you through town." She gulped in air. "Are we clear?"

"Geeze Louise," Dante complained. "You don't have to be so damn dramatic."

"Are. We. Clear?" Skye asked again. Maybe she should just call her father-in-law and ask him to have Tuck pay her uncle a visit.

"Yeah. Yeah. Yeah." Dante paused and she could hear him hollering at Olive to find his car keys. "Give me fifteen minutes."

"Starting now." Skye got up and set the timer on the microwave. "After that, I'm coming after you. And uncle or not, I will hurt you."

Skye disconnected, then quickly dialed Carson and said, "I'm pretty sure I know where the kidnappers are holding Wally."

After she explained what she'd learned from Dante, Carson said, "Tuck and I are heading back to your place right now. We'll leave Quentin and the beta team at the dairy farm to keep an eye on things there. As soon as you text me the address from your uncle, alpha team will proceed to those coordinates."

"I should have it ASAP." Skye got to her feet and started toward the bedroom.

As she walked, she glanced at her watch. It was 7:27. Her uncle had six minutes left to call before she sicced her father-in-law on him. Carson wouldn't have any problem ordering Tuck to "persuade" Dante to cooperate. And she wouldn't have any problem letting him.

Skye hurriedly changed into maternity

jeans, a dark T-shirt, and sneakers. She twisted her hair into a messy bun on the top of her head and briefly considered grabbing one of Earl's stun guns, then shook her head. *No.* Tuck would doubtlessly have something better for her to use.

As she sat back down at the kitchen table, her cell rang, and when she answered, Dante said, "Fifty-one fifty-seven Harvester Road." After a short pause, he added, "Let me know if Wally's okay." Then apparently realizing what he'd said, Skye's uncle barked, "But not during my show."

Dante disconnected and Skye tapped her fingernail on her chin. Her uncle's concern about Wally had lasted less than a minute. Which, in a way was comforting. If Hizzoner ever turned into a decent person for any length of time, she'd have to start looking for other signs of Armageddon, too.

Shoving aside thoughts of her uncle, Skye stared at the tiny piece of paper in front of her. The address looked so innocuous. She'd half expected it to be on Devil Lane. Was this where Wally was being held? Even if it wasn't his exact location, at least now they finally had a place to start searching.

Wally jolted awake. The motorcycle gang was in the kitchen and they were arguing again. He'd briefly dozed off after his last failed attempt to get away. It seemed as if every time he had almost gotten his wrist free of their bindings, Tin would appear. It was odd that the guy never commented on the fact that the zip ties were damaged.

Instead, he'd cut off Wally's restraints, given him food and water, put on a fresh set of zip ties, and said, "Hang in there, bro. You'll be out of here and home with your pretty wife in a few hours."

After Tin's supper visit, Wally had figured he'd be left alone for the rest of the night and renewed his efforts to get his hands free. The last time Tin had been in the basement, he'd spotted blood on the jagged edge of the workbench and turned it over. Now, Wally looked around for another way to slice through the plastic.

As he scrutinized every detail of the basement for the hundredth time, he heard a voice like a dentist drill whine, "Once we have the cash, we should kill him."

"Not a good idea, Jackal." Tin's tone was casual, but Wally thought he detected a nervous flicker. "There's no good reason to bring down that kind of heat on us. We just leave the dude tied up, ride into the sunset, and we keep a nice low profile."

"We bury his worthless carcass six foot

deep in one of the fields," Jackal argued. "No one will ever connect that pig to us."

Several voices joined in, agreeing with the plan to kill and plant Wally.

Shit! Wally had almost allowed himself to believe Tin when he'd said he'd be released unharmed. But this Jackal asshole was stirring the pot. What if Tin was overruled or one of the gang came back after Tin had left and finished off Wally without his knowledge?

"Cops kill us all the time without anyone doin' anything about it," Jackal snarled.

"Yeth. Jackal'th right." Squirrel's distinctive lisp helped Wally identify him. "The motherth shot down my old man in cold blood."

"My brother's in a wheelchair because of the pigs," a deep voice boomed.

"And a lot of our club members are in the joint because of them."

Gritting his teeth, Wally remembered reprimanding Quirk when he'd overheard the sergeant jeering at Martinez when she arrived for her shift riding behind a guy on a motorcycle. "What's the difference between a Harley and a Hoover?" Without pausing, Quirk had answered his own question. "The location of the dirtbag."

At the time, Wally had stepped in and put

a stop to Quirk's disparaging jokes. Wouldn't it be ironic if Wally died at the hands of a biker?

"Listen up!" Veep had obviously had enough of the insubordinate behavior and shouted above the gang members' grumbling. "We are sticking to the plan. All of you need to be ready to saddle up and ride by ten o'clock tonight. Boo-Boo will go over to babysit the ransom drop and we'll head to the new place. I want all of us, and all our stuff, out of here and everyone having a beer at the new clubhouse by the time Boo-Boo comes back with the cash."

When there were a few muttered protests about Boo-Boo's tendency to screw up things, Tin said, "I'll hang back until Boo-Boo gets here, then we'll join you and celebrate our newfound wealth."

"What if the cop's old man doesn't show?" Jackal challenged.

"If 5–0's father ponies up the cash, we leave him alive," Tin answered. "If the ransom is a single dollar short or the cops show up or anything feels at all hinky, I'll shoot him, dump his body, and ride."

Hell! Wally closed his eyes. Was Tin just saying that for the benefit of the other gang members, or had he been stringing Wally along the whole time with his buddy-buddy act? Maybe his humane treatment had been nothing more than a performance to make controlling Wally easier.

Wally knew his dad would pay. But would he follow the instructions not to bring in any law enforcement? Probably. But there was no way in hell that Carson wouldn't have mobilized the company's elite security squad. What if the team was spotted?

Wally glanced at the cardboard-covered windows. Judging from the diminishing light, he figured it was closing in on eight o'clock. He had four hours before the ransom was paid. And if he didn't plan to just sit here and wait to be executed, he needed to get his damn hands free. Maybe he could use the old shovel to cut through the zip ties.

Either that or he'd have to get his wrists so bloody he could slip the ties off.

Chapter 21

When, at last, he walked into Dorothy's room and thanked her for rescuing him, he was so pleased that he wept tears of joy, and Dorothy had to wipe every tear carefully from his face with her apron, so his joints would not be rusted.

— Tin Woodsman

Skye kept a wary eye on her infuriated father-in-law, worried that he was going to have a coronary. His face was a particularly alarming shade of purple, and while Tuck organized Wally's rescue, Carson paced the length of the motor home, muttering curses and threats.

As he completed another trip up and down the center of the motor coach, Skye heard him plotting Dante's demise. She wasn't sure if Carson truly meant her uncle harm, or if this was just his way of handling stress.

However, once they had Wally back safe and sound, she needed to have a chat with her father-in-law and persuade him not to have Hizzoner assassinated. As much as she wanted Dante out of the mayor's office, killing him probably wasn't the solution. That is, as long as Wally made it home unharmed.

Which was what Tuck was busy arranging right now. Once Dante had provided her with the address and she'd passed it on to Carson, the security chief had sent two members of his team to investigate. At the moment, he was on his cell with them and his one-word responses were driving Skye crazy.

Walking over to the huge man camped out on her sofa, she poked his shoulder. "Put the phone on speaker."

He frowned, but after a glance at Carson, who nodded, he complied and said, "Boss and OB would like to hear your report. Start over."

"OB?" Skye asked, glancing at her father-in-law with a raised brow.

"Other boss." Carson smirked, then pointed at Skye and said, "You."

She nodded. *Damn straight!*

"The house is occupied by what appears to be a motorcycle gang. The RANGE-R picked up breathing and movement of ten tangos inside the house," a detached voice recounted. "Eight bikes are parked out front, along with two large panel trucks that have trailers attached holding one motorcycle each. Best guess: the tangos are getting ready to haul ass out of here."

Tucker glanced up at Skye's gasp, then asked, "Any sign of the chief?"

"There's a Scumble River Police Department squad car hidden in a machine shed on the property. That building's only window is blocked with cardboard, but Weasel picked the lock on the door and did a quick recon." The voice paused. "It looks as if the gang still has some stuff to pack. Maybe another hour or two of loading."

"Any tangos visible?" Tuck asked, his eyebrows meeting over his nose.

"Negative. RANGE-R shows them all in what we believe is the kitchen."

"And the chief?" Tuck asked. "Any indication of his location?"

"Most likely he's being held in the basement," the anonymous voice continued. "There's someone breathing there, but no detectable movement."

Skye inhaled sharply. Breathing was good. It meant Wally was alive. Suddenly lightheaded, she sat down at the kitchen table. Not wanting either Carson or Tuck to realize she was dizzy, she casually unscrewed the top of a bottle of water and took a long drink.

"Maintain surveillance and contact me immediately with any changes. In the meantime, keep one in the chamber and be ready to rock and roll," Tuck ordered. "Beta Leader and his team will remain at ransom drop site. Mr. Boyd and I will join you in a few minutes. Stay frosty."

"I'm going, too." Skye stood, and as both Carson and Tuck voiced their objections, she said, "I can either go with you or drive myself. It's not as if I don't know the address. Let's not waste time arguing because, one way or another, I will be there."

Complaining about her stubbornness, the men gathered up Tuck's equipment, then escorted Skye to the Hummer. Her father-in-law helped her climb into the backseat, assisted her with the seat belt, then got behind the wheel and roared out of the driveway, gravel flying behind the SUV.

"What's the plan?" Carson asked, glancing at Tuck as he made a sharp turn at the corner.

"From alpha's team recon, your son's kidnappers are a small motorcycle gang." Tuck turned toward Carson and Skye studied his calm expression. "The gang appears to be in the process of retreating from the area. Because the ransom drop is set for midnight, I figure that all or some will stick around until that time."

"When will we rescue Wally?" Skye asked, frowning at Tuck's recap.

"My men and I will be in position to make our move when the moment is right." Tuck put an arm over the seat back and looked at Skye. "As long as no one enters the basement, we'll wait until the house empties. Either when the gang leaves to pick up the ransom or they decamp for good."

"And if they head to the basement?" Skye asked, narrowing her eyes.

"Then we scoop him up immediately." Tuck reached back and patted Skye's hand. "I guarantee you that this is the safest way to extract Wally."

Skye nodded and said, "Okay. As I promised, I'll wait in the car, but I want some kind of weapon in case there's a problem."

"Absolutely," Tuck said, then asked, "What type of gun do you normally shoot?"

"Uh." Skye bit her lip. Wally had been going to teach her, but then she got pregnant. "Actually, I don't. Do you have anything easy to aim?"

"You can always be sure of hitting the target if you shoot first and call whatever you hit the target." Tuck snickered at his own joke.

Carson broke into his security chief's laughter. "Darlin', the level of difficulty isn't the issue. It's the risk."

"Right." Skye's cheeks reddened. She knew it was reckless, demanding to be present when she was pregnant, but it wasn't in her to just sit at home and wait for her husband to be rescued.

"I've got some pepper spray that I can give you," Tuck said as Carson turned the Hummer onto a dark dirt road. "But the best thing you can do is stay in the vehicle with the doors locked."

"Of course. You're right." Skye noticed that the only thing on either side of the road were cornfields and asked, "Where are you going to park?"

"Alpha Leader indicated that there is an abandoned old barn across from the house," Tuck answered. "We'll have a clear view with maximum concealment. And because this Hummer has been fitted with bulletproof metal and glass, optimal safety for you."

"Yep." Carson patted the dashboard. "When I ordered this baby, I made sure she could withstand any terrorist attacks or kidnapping attempts."

"Wow." Skye hadn't thought about it, but considering his wealth and visibility, Wally's father would be a prime target for abduction and assassination. "I'm sure glad you brought it along."

"Slow down and shut off the headlights," Tuck ordered, and when Carson complied, he instructed, "There. On your left. Back into the barn."

As Carson maneuvered the huge SUV into the ancient barn, Skye hoped there weren't any nails lying around. Then again, she remembered that her father-in-law had mentioned the Hummer had run-flat tires.

As soon as they were in place, Tuck swiped his phone and said, "We're in position, Alpha Leader. Any movement on your end?"

"Tangos now exiting the house." A pause. "The final count is eight."

Skye leaned forward and could just make out several figures scurrying toward the machine shed. The halogen light attached to the building provided a spotlight for their actions. Either they had a generator or the electricity was on in this part of the city limits.

"What's the location of the remaining two bikers?" Tuck asked.

"One's in the kitchen," Alpha Leader reported. "The other is upstairs."

"Roger that." Tuck disconnected and immediately punched another number. "Beta Leader, do you have any activity at the drop site?"

"Negative," Quentin answered. "I'm in position with a view of the trash can and the rest of the team is set up around the perimeter."

"Maintain until you hear otherwise." Tucker disconnected, grabbed a pair of binoculars, and gazed straight ahead. "Everybody chill."

It occurred to Skye that she had no idea how many men Tucker had brought from Texas. At first, she'd thought it was three or four, but now she revised her estimate upward to double that number. How on earth were they all planning to sleep in one of Charlie's tiny cabins?

When Carson lifted his own pair of binoculars to watch the activity across the road, Skye tapped Tuck's shoulder and asked, "Do you have a pair of night vision binoculars I could use?"

"There's one next to you." He nodded to her left. "That stuff is either backups or things we won't be needing. Help yourself."

"Thanks."

Skye quickly located the binoculars, then started sifting through the piles of equipment strewn on the seat beside her. She found the pepper spray that Tuck had offered her, as well as several pairs of leather gloves, a whistle, eye protectors, earplugs, combination locks, a wrist compass, flashlights, batteries, nylon rope, fishing line, and one unrecognizable object.

Tapping Tuck's shoulder again, she held up a little black tube with an odd kind of clip fastened to it and asked, "What's this?"

"A laser sight." The security chief's tone was affectionate. "It emits a beam with a hundred-yard visibility in daylight and up to a mile at night. We use it for rapid target acquisition. I like this one because it has a tactical pressure pad. You just press here and it's on. You can drive home shot after shot with hair-splitting accuracy."

After he showed her how to use it, Skye asked, "Don't you need this for tonight's mission?"

"That's a backup." Tuck shrugged. "I have a couple more in my bag."

She nodded, tossed it back on the pile next to her, and focused her binoculars on the house across the road. Men were loading stuff from the machine shed onto the trailers and lights blazed in every window. Skye could almost feel Wally behind those walls.

For the next hour, Skye, Carson, and Tuck stared at the Brooks property. At a few minutes to ten, Tuck's cell pinged and he immediately swiped the screen.

"Tangos are on the move," alpha leader reported. "Heading toward their bikes."

"Taking my position on the barn roof." Tuck quickly grabbed his sniper bag, and as he slipped out of the vehicle, he ordered, "You two stay put."

Carson snarled his frustration and Skye said, "I'm going to move into the front so I can see better."

"Only if you can climb between the seats," Carson declared, hitting the door locks. "I don't think you should get out of the Hummer."

"Fine," Skye huffed, getting to her feet. "But you're going to have to give me a hand."

Skye put one knee on the center console, then, wishing she had some body oil, she carefully shifted her belly through the opening. It was a tight fit, and just as she thought she had made it, her progress halted with half of her in the back and half in the front.

"Help." She held out her arm to Carson, who grasped her biceps and tugged.

For a long minute, Skye thought she was permanently stuck, but with a *pop,* she broke free. Sliding into the passenger seat, she quickly reached back for the binoculars. It hadn't been a graceful transition and the babies were kicking up a fuss, but she could now see the front yard and house much better.

Running a soothing hand over her stomach, she crooned to the twins. Carson reached over and ran a delicate finger over what was clearly a tiny foot outlined against Skye's T-shirt.

Skye lifted her gaze to the windshield and reported, "Seven guys are on their bikes, and two just climbed into the trucks. That only leaves one of the men inside."

Carson hastily raised his binoculars up to his eyes and both he and Skye watched as the motorcycles started with a roar, formed a line, and pulled out of the driveway. Six went east, with the trucks close behind them, and one lone bike headed west — the direction of the Hutton dairy farm.

Skye's heart sped up. This was their chance. Surely, Tuck's men could take the single gang member remaining inside the house.

Evidently, the team agreed with her evaluation, because a few seconds later, one of the security guys kicked in a window and tossed something through the broken glass.

Instantly, there was a blinding flash and four men dressed completely in black broke down the front door.

They rushed inside and Skye held her breath, waiting for the security team to come out with her husband. As she stared at the house, willing Wally to walk out safe and sound, she heard the roar of a motorcycle approaching. She hesitated, but it would be too much of a coincidence for the motorcycle not to be connected with the gang.

"Dad," Skye said. "Do you hear that? One of the bikers is coming back."

"Son of a —" Carson broke off. "Wait. The sound is fading." He blew out a sigh of relief. "Whoever it was must have turned onto a side road."

Skye and Carson sat silently. Finally, four black-clothed figures emerged from the house's gaping front entrance. One had a grip on the handcuffed wrists of a biker and two were supporting Wally as he limped down the steps.

"Let me out," Skye demanded, trying to open the Hummer's door.

"Just wait a second." Carson frowned. "Tuck hasn't given the all clear."

"I need to go to him," Skye pleaded. "He looks hurt. He can hardly walk and he's holding his stomach. Why in the hell are they stopping? They need to get him over here and call an ambulance."

"Let me go check." Carson stared at Skye. "You have to give me your word that you'll stay in the car and I'll promise to bring Wally to you."

"Okay." Skye figured it was faster than trying to argue. "But go now."

Skye watched her father-in-law jog across the road. A nanosecond later, she heard Tuck climb down from the barn's roof. She saw him sprint over to the farmhouse and join the party huddled in the front yard.

What was going on? Skye frowned and eyed the door handle. Carson hadn't locked it when he left. She chewed her lip, then shook her head. A promise was a promise. She'd sit tight. At least for a few more minutes.

Scanning the area, she noticed a shadow moving along one side of the house. Seizing the binoculars, she saw a huge figure stealthily approaching Wally, who was standing off by himself as Carson and the security team focused on the handcuffed biker.

Skye's chest tightened. Was she going to lose Wally after all?

How could she let Tuck and his team know someone was sneaking up on Wally? If she tapped the horn, the bad guy might start shooting. And right now, she doubted any of them would answer their phones. What could she use to alert them? Too bad she didn't have a way to signal them.

Wait a minute! Awkwardly wedging herself up on one hip, she turned and pawed through the pile of discarded equipment on the backseat. Snatching the laser sight, she prayed she could recall Tuck's instructions for its use. Easing the Hummer's door open, she stood behind it and aimed the device around the edge. Once she had Tuck in her sights, she pushed the pressure pad.

A green dot appeared on the security chief's chest. When one of his men noticed and yelled for everyone to get down, Skye moved the dot toward the bad guy.

Instantly, every weapon was trained on the biker standing beside the house. The bad guy pointed his gun at Wally's back and everyone froze.

"Throw down your weapon," Tuck shouted. When the bad guy didn't immediately obey, he added, "See that green dot on your chest? If you don't surrender in the next three seconds, my sniper will take you out."

The biker wavered for an instant, then threw his gun on the ground, put his hands up, and dropped to his knees.

Tucker followed the laser beam to where Skye stood and flashed her a thumbs-up. While the security team secured the second biker, Tuck and Carson guided Wally toward the Hummer.

Skye met them in front of the vehicle, threw her arms around him, and asked, "Are you okay? Why are you limping?" She stroked his cheek. "Oh, your poor bruised face."

"I'm limping because I was tied up so long the circulation in my legs was cut off. The bruises will heal. And now that you're in my arms, I'm fantastic." Wally cradled Skye's chin and kissed her as if he never meant to stop.

Chapter 22

"There is no place like home."

— Dorothy

Skye sat in the back of the Hummer wrapped in Wally's arms. Carson and Tuck were in the front seat and a part of her heard the security chief confirming that the guy sent to pick up the ransom at the dairy farm was in custody. But the majority of her attention was on her husband. She'd given him a quick rundown of what had happened since his capture and was now trying to convince him to go to the ER.

Wally smoothed her hair out of her eyes. "Sugar, I'm truly fine, and I need to be at the police station when the bikers are processed." He wiped the tears from her cheeks with his thumbs. "That guy called Tin protected me and took care of me. I have to make sure none of my officers become overly zealous and that he's treated okay."

"I understand." Skye sniffed and caressed the scruff on his jaw. Wally was so rarely anything but clean-shaven, he almost looked like a completely different person. "But I'm worried about you." She glanced at her father-in-law, who had turned in his seat and was gazing at his son as if he was the most precious person on earth. "What do you think, Dad?"

"One of Tuck's men was a combat medic in Iraq. If Wally agrees to go to the motor coach, grab a shower and some clean clothes, and let Crow look him over, I'll go along with no ER right now."

"Agreed." Wally squeezed his father's shoulder and said, "I can never thank you enough for everything you've done to take care of Skye and rescue me. I'm so sorry for all the years we haven't been close."

"That was more my fault than yours." Carson covered Wally's hand with both of his own. "And although I can't promise to ever stop wishing you'd move back to Texas and take your rightful place at the helm of CB International, I can promise to stop bugging you about it."

"Maybe I'll start bugging you to retire and move to Illinois." Wally winked at his dad and turned to Skye. He lifted her chin and asked, "Are we good?" When she nodded, he looked at Tucker and said, "Can you call Sergeant Quirk and fill him in on the past few hours? Tell him to meet us at the station and expect three prisoners, all of whom should be held separately until we get there." He paused, then added, "And no one is to touch them."

As they drove home, Skye couldn't stop caressing Wally. It was hard to believe that it had been less than a day and a half since he'd gone missing.

Heck! It was hard to believe it had been only two days since the tornado. So much had happened in such a short time, it felt as if a week or maybe a month had passed.

When they returned to the motor coach, a man Skye hadn't met was waiting. Tuck introduced the guy as Crow, and Wally went off to shower.

Once he was out of earshot, Skye said to the three men waiting in the living room, "After the medic is finished treating Wally, I'm going to need a couple of minutes alone with my husband."

"We'll catch a ride with Crow." Carson gave her a look that implied he knew what she wanted to tell Wally in private. "And we'll meet you at the police station." He tossed her the Hummer's keys.

"We can use my uncle's Pontiac." Skye tried to return the fob to her father-in-law. "It might not look like much, but it runs fine."

"No need." Carson grinned. "With both your vehicles totaled, I'm giving you the SUV." When Skye started to protest, he shrugged. "I already found someone who has a brand-new one sitting in his garage that's he's willing to sell to me and I don't need two."

Skye shrugged. If Wally objected to the gift, he could argue with his dad about the Hummer. She heard the shower shut off and went to lay out the clothes she'd bought for Wally after her ob-gyn appointment, thrilled he was finally here to wear them. They'd have to order him some new uniforms ASAP.

In the meantime, she grabbed Wally's duffel and dug out the uniform from the night of the tornado. Wally had changed into the spare he kept at the PD and that had been the one Charlie had laundered for them. She hadn't even thought of giving him the one in the canvas bag.

Digging it out now and grabbing the one he'd just taken off, she put both uniforms in a pile near the door to wash later. She usually had them dry-cleaned so they'd look crisper, but this was an emergency.

While Skye was emptying Wally's pants pockets, he came out of the bathroom. As if on cue, Crow entered the bedroom. He immediately instructed Wally to drop the towel and sit on the bed. Skye closed the door and joined her husband, watching carefully as the ex-medic examined him.

She winced as Crow pressed on the contusions decorating Wally's abs and chest, then blew out a relieved breath when the ex-medic declared the bruises superficial. Next, Crow inspected the raw gouges around Wally's wrist. Frowning, he cleaned them with an alcohol pad, applied antiseptic cream, and wrapped them in gauze.

"Are those from being tied up?" Skye asked from her seat next to Wally.

"Yeah." He patted her leg. "I kept trying to get out of the zip ties, and finally figured that if I got my wrists bloody enough, I could slip them off." When she shook her head, he said, "Hey. It worked."

Crow paused in treating the scrapes on Wally's face and said, "Yep. The chief here had already kicked open the basement door when we entered the house. He had the biker on the kitchen floor and was securing his hands with a bandana."

"Impressive." Skye kissed Wally's cheek, then narrowed her eyes. "So you weren't really limping because your circulation had been cut off for so long. You screwed up your back kicking open the door."

"Possibly." Wally shrugged. "I'll take a couple of ibuprofen and it'll be fine."

Skye ignored Wally, looked at Crow, and said, "He hurt his back a few months ago. It got better after two or three days of rest. Does he need to go to the hospital for it or for any of his other injuries?"

"Keep the wounds clean. The contusions aren't serious, but if he's still experiencing back pain in a day or two, he should see a doctor." Crow packed up his first aid kit. "And he should get some rest."

"Thanks so much for all your help," Skye said. "You and your team were awesome."

Wally echoed Skye's appreciation as he put on the clothes Skye handed him.

"Just doing my job. Glad it all turned out so well." The ex-medic winked at them. "No hanky-panky for a day or two."

"Seriously?" Skye rubbed her huge belly. She could swear it had grown in the last forty-eight hours. "I think we're both benched for the duration."

"Or not." Wally shot Skye a heated look. "According to your ob-gyn, we're green-lighted until you go into labor. We just need to be creative."

Giggling, Skye waited as Wally pulled on socks and laced his new tennis shoes. When she heard the motor home's outer door open and close, she got up and checked to make sure their guests were gone.

Returning to the bedroom, she put her arms around Wally and tugged him back down to sit on the edge of the bed. "Speaking of Dr. Johnson, she had some surprising news for me when I saw her on Tuesday."

"What did she say?" Wally's voice rose in alarm. "You texted that everything was okay. Is there something wrong with the baby?"

"Nope. The babies are great," Skye reassured him.

"You said 'babies'?" Wally's eyes widened and he cleared his throat. "As in more than one?"

"Absolutely." Skye studied his expression. "We're having twins."

What if he wasn't happy at the prospect of double fatherhood? It wasn't as if she could send one of the babies back.

"Oh. My. God!" Wally grabbed Skye in a bear hug. "That is positively, freaking wonderful. Do you know their sex? Are they identical?"

"I didn't ask any of that." Skye brushed a

lock of hair from Wally's forehead. "I thought we'd agreed to be surprised. Have you changed your mind?"

"No. Let's wait." Wally put his hand to his chest. "Although I'm not really sure how many more bombshells I can take."

"Me either." Skye poked him in the ribs. "No more disappearing."

"That was the mayor's fault." Wally hauled Skye to her feet. "I take it you figured out the hint I sent my dad, and talked to Dante."

"Once your father remembered it and I tracked down my uncle." Skye allowed Wally to lead her through the motor coach and out the door. "Dante's been home with the flu since the afternoon he sent you to look at the Hollister property. He didn't even know you were missing until I told him."

"Likely story," Wally teased as he helped Skye into the SUV and slid behind the wheel. "He was probably hoping that I was gone for good."

"Let's pray even Dante isn't that evil." Skye fastened her seat belt and said, "While you drive us to the station, I'll give you an update on the rest of what's happened in your absence. Hizzoner has something cooked up with the city council and you won't believe what the Dooziers tried to do."

By the time Wally was up to speed, they'd

arrived at the PD and entered the building. Skye was relieved to see that things seemed to be getting back to normal. The whiteboards for missing possessions and pets were still in place, but all the people had been located. And, always a good sign, there wasn't anyone lined up at the counter. Plus, the phones were silent.

After a brief stop in the dispatchers' office for May to hug Wally and talk excitedly about the twins, he and Skye headed into the back of the station. Quirk met them in the hallway and told them he'd notified all the proper authorities that Wally had been found.

Wally thanked Roy and then Skye watched as the two men exchanged a man hug — one arm and a lot of back thumping. She was surprised to see both guys blink away some moisture before the usual neutral cop expressions returned to their faces.

Roy cleared his throat and said, "The guy called Jackal was ready to tear the place apart, so I stashed him in the basement holding cell to cool off. Boo-Boo's with Zelda in the interrogation room. Tuck and Mr. Boyd are babysitting Tin in your office." The sergeant rubbed his neck. "None of them would give up their real names, so we'll have to wait until we have their fingerprints to identify them."

"Good job." Wally glanced at Skye. "I don't suppose you'd be willing to stay with your mother?" When she narrowed her eyes, he bargained, "You can be with me while we interview Tin and Boo-Boo, but not Jackal."

"Agreed." Skye smirked and headed to the stairs. "I would have settled for Tin."

When Skye entered Wally's office, she saw that a chair had been placed against the back wall and the biker was handcuffed to it. Tin was a big guy, well over six foot, heavily muscled. His long, dark hair was clean and the look on his handsome face was thoughtful rather than angry or mean. She didn't buy him as a hardened outlaw biker.

"I need to talk to you alone, Chief." Tin directed his statement to Wally.

Wally nodded. "Dad, Tuck, please give us the room." He looked at Tin. "My wife is the department psych consult and is staying."

"Can she keep her mouth shut?" Tin's intense gaze swept over Skye.

"*She* can speak for herself." Skye suppressed a shiver and met his penetrating stare with her own. "And one of the most important obligations of a psychologist is to maintain confidentiality."

"But you're not my therapist," Tin drawled, lifting an eyebrow.

"Good point." Skye inclined her head. "Instead, I'll give you my word."

"People break promises all the time." Tin gazed into her eyes. "The chief's father tells me you led the investigation to find your husband." He glanced at her pregnant belly. "And even physically hindered, you insisted on being present for his rescue."

"Of course." Skye twined her fingers with Wally's. "He is the love of my life and the most important person in the world to me. If the situation had been reversed, he would have come for me near death and wearing a full-body cast."

"I certainly would have, sugar." Wally's voice was husky. "My desire to get back to you was the reason I was finally able to break free and smash down that door. Nothing could stop me from returning to you and the baby." He grinned. "I mean you and the babies."

"That's what I thought." Tin nodded, a wishful expression in his eyes.

"Why are my wife's feelings for me important?" Wally asked.

"Because I'm going to trust you two with my life." Tin exhaled noisily. "And I needed to be sure that you are both capable of true loyalty."

"We are." Skye allowed Wally to ease her into one of the empty visitor chairs, then smiled at Tin. "And now I'm dying of curiosity. What's your big secret?"

"He's an undercover cop," Wally said slowly, his face lighting up with recognition. "I knew there was something odd about him. He was too concerned with my welfare, and his language patterns when he spoke to me and when he was with the gang changed significantly."

"I figured you'd picked up on that." Tin chuckled. "I kept forgetting we weren't fellow cops when we talked." He winced. "Sorry I punched you in the face. I had to make it look real."

"No worries." Wally shrugged. "I'm betting you saved me from far worse."

"Yeah." Tin twitched his shoulders. "Too bad Boo-Boo slipped past me."

"You did your best." Wally leaned a hip on his desk. "Which agency are you with?"

"It's better if you don't know." Tin met Wally's eyes without blinking.

"I'm guessing your prints won't pop," Wally said thoughtfully.

Tin shook his head. "Nope. But you running them might cause a problem, so if you haven't already put them in the system, you should lose them."

"You know I can't release you without some verification," Wally said.

"Take off my belt," Tin instructed. "Cut the stitches in the center and you'll find a card between the two pieces of leather. Use the station's landline to call that number on it, identify yourself as law enforcement, and read off the code on the back. They'll vouch for me."

After retrieving the card, Wally took a seat behind his desk, grabbed the phone, and dialed. He studied the pasteboard square, then as he waited, tapped it against his fingernail.

"If you are what you say you are" — Skye glared at Tin — "why didn't you release Wally?"

"If I hadn't been able to find a reason for the gang to keep him alive, I would have let him go." Tin twisted his lips. "But I've been undercover for a long time and I've only recently gotten into a position where I'm trusted with sensitive intel. Freeing the chief would have resulted in all that work being flushed down the toilet. I would have had to start all over with another gang."

Skye scowled. "Is the information worth more than my husband's life?"

"No," Tin growled. "But I was walking a

thin line attempting to keep him safe and not blow my cover." When Skye narrowed her eyes, he explained, "These gangs have branched out from the city and are infiltrating the countryside. They entice kids with drugs and whores to join up. And they won't let them leave once they're in. The gang starts out robbing empty houses, but they soon escalate to occupied homes where they often rape and beat their victims. They move from location to location, making it hard for local law enforcement to spot their patterns."

"Oh." Skye rubbed her belly and thought of all the mothers who had lost their babies to these monsters. "I had no idea any of that was happening."

"Few people do." Tin lifted one side of his mouth in a sardonic smile. "That's what makes catching them so tricky."

They fell silent until Wally returned the receiver to its base, took a set of keys from his top drawer, stood, and walked over to Tin. Unlocking the undercover officer's handcuffs, he helped him to his feet.

"Thanks, man." Tin rubbed his wrists and asked, "Am I free to go?"

"Yep." Wally smiled and held out his hand. "Thanks for saving my ass."

"Glad it worked out." Tin gripped Wally's

hand. "You need to make sure Jackal and Boo-Boo overhear that due to outstanding warrants, I've been shipped to another county. Then I can claim I escaped during transport."

"Will do."

Skye struggled to her feet and put her fingers on Tin's bicep. "Thank you for protecting my husband. If I can ever repay you, all you have to do is ask." She tilted her head. "Can we know your real name?"

"Spencer, ma'am." He squeezed her hand and started for the door.

Just as he gripped the knob, Wally yelled, "Wait."

Tin turned and raised a questioning eyebrow. "Forget something?"

"The first night I was held in the basement, your gang was talking about looting," Wally said. "Boo-Boo mentioned a man with a German shepherd and said something about his old lady. Were you with them when they ran into that guy?"

"No. But Veep told me about it." Tin scratched his jaw. "We had heard the people in one of the big houses in that neighborhood were on vacation, so we were only a few blocks away when the tornado went through. Veep decided that would be a perfect time to do some pillaging and we started looking inside the wrecked houses.

"We split into two groups. Veep and his crew were the ones to see the guy with the dog. Evidently, Veep spotted a flat-screen television he wanted, so they were making their way through the debris to get it when they saw the guy lying unconscious on the floor and a woman zapping him with some kind of old-fashioned cattle prod. The shepherd was biting her arm, but she never stopped. Veep's posse waited out of sight until she left, then ran in, grabbed the TV, and vamoosed."

Skye shook her head. How had a couple as in love as Bartolommeo Capuchini described Billie and Zeke Lyons ended up with the wife killing the husband? Had the huge life insurance policy been too much of a temptation? Or had Billie just been an incredible actress?

Chapter 23

"Surely no wild beast could wish a pleasanter home."

— Cowardly Lion

When Quentin and the rest of the security team arrived at the police station, Skye and Wally thanked them all for their help, then waved goodbye as Tuck and his men marched out to the parking lot. Quentin stayed behind, and after an awkward hug between the cousins, he and Wally spent a few minutes rehashing the kidnapping and rescue.

Finally, Quentin said, "Well, I'd better get going. I've got a date for brunch tomorrow morning with a former Miss Texas and I surely don't want to stand her up."

Skye teased, "It certainly must be nice not to have to hang around until there's a scheduled flight home."

"I see you're beginning to understand the

advantages of having money." Quentin pecked her on the cheek and said, "Take care of yourselves."

"You too." Wally grinned. "Watch out for those beauty queens. I hear they can be feisty."

Carson embraced his nephew and said, "Have a good trip. I'm going to stay in Scumble River a while to help out with the tornado relief efforts, so unless it's an emergency, I want you to handle anything that comes up with the company."

"Will do." Quentin touched two fingers to his forehead and walked out the station's front door.

After Quentin and the security team left, Wally and Quirk grilled the bikers. Boo-Boo's nearly hysterical ramblings didn't shed any light on either Wally's kidnapping or the Lyons murder, and Jackal demanded a lawyer, then clammed up. Once the interrogation was finished, both men were transported to the county jail to be booked and wait for their public defense attorneys.

By that time, it was nearly two a.m. and everyone was exhausted. Despite Wally's attempts to persuade his father and Skye to go home and get some rest, they had refused and waited for him. Now, as they trudged out to the parking lot, Skye felt as if she were sleepwalking.

Getting into the Hummer, Carson said, "Drop me off at the motel. Before he left for the airport, I had Quentin pick up my stuff at the motor home and leave it at the motel room I reserved for Quentin and the team."

"You didn't have to do that, Dad," Skye protested.

He winked. "I'm sure you two would like a little time alone."

"We'd be happy to have you stay with us." She glanced at Wally. "Right?"

"Thanks, Dad. We appreciate the privacy," Wally said, ignoring Skye. "It would be kind of tight with the three of us in the motor coach." He reached over and patted Skye's belly. "Or maybe I should say with the five of us. Did she tell you we're having twins?"

"Not in so many words." Carson chuckled. "But congratulations."

"It was Skye and the baby that kept me going when I was being held in that basement. No way in hell was Reid raising my child." Wally grinned. "I mean children."

"As if," Skye snorted.

Once they'd dropped Carson at Up A Lazy River, Wally and Skye drove home in silence. They dragged themselves inside, and while Skye took a shower, Wally ate the leftovers from one of May's casseroles. Then they crawled into bed and, with a sweet kiss, drifted off.

Six hours later, Skye woke with her back nestled against Wally's front. One of his arms cradled her stomach while the fingers of his free hand stroked around her belly button. And something hard was pressed against her rear end.

Blinking the sleep from her eyes, Skye purred, "Good morning to you, too, sweetheart."

"It sure is, darlin'," Wally rumbled in her ear. "How do you feel?"

"Me?" Skye pushed her hair out of her face. "I'm not the one who was beaten up and held prisoner by an outlaw biker gang."

"But you are the one who, despite hauling around two little humans inside of you, figured out where I was and saved me and the macho, ex-military guys using nothing but a laser-gun sight." Wally pressed his lips to her throat and trailed kisses down her cleavage.

"But I didn't solve the murder." She giggled when he hit a ticklish spot, then added, "Heck, I couldn't even locate the prime suspect."

"We'll find Billie Lyons today." Wally's mouth continued its journey southward.

"It's just a shame our only witnesses are on the lam."

"Not to mention criminals." Skye's voice was breathy as Wally's lips and fingers persisted in their exploration. "A jury would love that."

"Which means we'll have to convict Billie the old-fashioned way." Wally shoved off his boxer briefs. "Once we get her into the police station, we make her confess."

"How are we going to figure out where she is?" Skye watched her underwear float over the side of the bed. Considering her maternity panties were the size of a topsail, once they caught air, they soared for several feet. "The tornado has really messed things up."

"We'll work on that little problem later." Wally's mouth hovered over Skye's, his breath caressing her lips. "Much, much later."

"Crow told us not to mess around for a day or two," Skye protested halfheartedly.

Wally ignored her, divested Skye of her nightshirt, and palmed her breasts. "What were you saying, sugar?"

"I forget."

The next time Skye woke up, Wally wasn't beside her, but she heard his voice in the other room. Hoping he was on the phone and they didn't have houseguests, she heaved herself out of bed and hurried into the bathroom. She'd better get dressed. Evidently, the second honeymoon was over, and they were back at work.

Once she had put on a pair of shorts and a T-shirt, she emerged from the bedroom and saw Wally standing at the washing machine, a frown on his handsome face. Seeing Skye, he said goodbye to whomever he'd been talking to and tucked his phone into the pocket of his jeans.

Turning to her, he held up the clothes and asked, "What setting do I use on this?"

"It depends." Skye stepped toward him. "What does the tag on the shirt say?"

Wally squinted at the embroidered tag above the pocket and said, "Chief Boyd."

Rolling her eyes, Skye nudged him aside, took the clothes from his hands, and glanced inside the collar. Normally, she'd tease him about being housework-challenged and too dependent on their cleaning lady, Dorothy Snyder. But Skye was so happy to have him back. Today, she'd give him a pass and just do his laundry for him.

Once Skye had Wally's uniforms washing, she made them breakfast, then joined him at the kitchen table. He was on the phone again, and from what she could hear on his end of the telephone conversation, Quirk was briefing him on what had occurred in his absence and apologizing for the lack of attention to the Zeke Lyons murder case. Wally reassured the sergeant and informed him that he would be taking over the Lyons investigation, then disconnected and kissed Skye hello.

While she and Wally ate, she pondered what they knew about Billie Lyons. Although she'd seen the woman only once, from what everyone had told her, she felt like she had some understanding of Billie's way of thinking. So where would she go with both a dog and her mother in tow?

Hmm . . . Billie and her mother had been staying at the shelter when she'd been called to pick up the German shepherd, which probably meant both women had no other place to live. Skye hadn't been able to locate any family or close friends in the area when she'd been searching for Billie. And Aunt Millie had said Billie worked from home, editing scientific journals, so she didn't have any local colleagues.

Attempting to find a rental property that would accept a large animal would be nearly impossible. Billie could have realized that, and instead of looking for housing for her, her mother, and the dog together, she might have tried to locate something for them and the pet separately.

When May had been grumbling that it would be so much easier if Jed would just board Chocolate until they rebuilt the Labrador's pen, she'd mentioned that Linc Quillen was offering to lodge all animals displaced by the tornado free of charge at his veterinary clinic. After hearing that, Skye had meant to check out Linc's clinic but got distracted when Carson remembered Wally's message about Dante. And then with everything that happened later, her mother's comment had slipped Skye's mind.

Could it be that Billie had heard about the vet's generous offer and taken the German shepherd there? If she had, Linc probably knew her current location. Or at least had her cell phone number. Information no one else they'd asked seemed to possess.

"You have a pleased look on your face, sugar," Wally drawled, interrupting Skye's thoughts. "What's going through that pretty head of yours?"

Smiling at her gorgeous husband, Skye said, "I might have just figured out how to find Billie Lyons."

"Oh?" Wally took a sip of his coffee and waved his hand for her to continue.

"The crime scene techs authorized the

release of Zeke Lyons's dog to Billie, which means she needed to find somewhere for the German shepherd to live," Skye started. "The local disaster shelters don't allow animals, and according to Aunt Minnie, Billie and her mother don't have any nearby relatives or close friends, so . . ."

When Skye finished explaining her reasoning, Wally grinned and said, "Let's go visit Linc and see if the good doctor can help us."

While Wally cleaned up the breakfast dishes, Skye hurriedly fastened her hair into a ponytail and put on a bit of makeup, then they headed south of town. It was a blessing that none of the tornadoes that touched down in Scumble River had hit the area around the veterinary clinic.

As they pulled into the parking lot, Skye smiled at the clinic's sign, which read: PETS ARE FAMILY. WOULD YOU CHAIN YOUR GRANDMA OUTSIDE?

Getting out of the SUV, Skye patted the hood and asked, "Will you be driving the Hummer instead of your squad car from now on?"

"At least until the crime scene techs finish gathering forensic evidence from the cruiser." Wally put his hand on Skye's waist and guided her toward the clinic. "We're hoping to get fingerprints of some of the gang members."

"I'll have to return Uncle Wiley's Pontiac when he gets back to town on Sunday, so if you're not through with the Hummer by then, I'll need to rent a car."

"I've got that covered for you." Wally's smile was enigmatic.

Before Skye could question him, they pushed through the clinic's double glass doors and entered the empty waiting room. A few seconds later, a huge man with acne-scarred skin and a crew cut lumbered into sight. He wore jeans and a T-shirt with the clinic's name and paw-print logo embroidered across his massive chest. His muscular arms were decorated with tattoos and a small gold hoop hung from his earlobe.

He marched behind the front counter and growled, "We're full."

"Hi, Cal." Skye held out her hand. "You probably don't remember me, but I'm Skye Denison-Boyd and this is my husband, Wally, the chief of police. Are you still keeping an eye on the clinic for Dr. Quillen?"

"Yeah." The man eyed her palm as if it held a pile of poop, but he finally gripped her fingers for a nanosecond and muttered, "I came back to help when I heard about the tornado."

"Nice to see you again." Wally held his hand out and Cal seemed much more comfortable shaking it than he had Skye's. "Is Dr. Quillen around?"

"He's out back with some new arrivals." The guy jerked his thumb over his shoulder. "Follow that hallway to the exit and watch your step."

"So a lot of folks have brought their displaced pets here to board?" Skye asked.

"Too many." Cal crossed his gigantic arms. "Dr. Q is being run ragged."

"Has Dr. Quillen put out the word that he needs assistance?" Wally asked.

"Nah. He doesn't want to take away from the people whose property was wrecked," Cal answered, then pointing to the corridor again, he repeated, "Doc and his girlfriend are that a-way. Maybe you can talk him into asking for some folks to help."

Recognizing a dismissal when she heard one, Skye thanked the taciturn man and followed Wally down the passageway to the back of the building. When she stepped outside, she saw rows and rows of newly erected kennels, each with a canvas roof and a comfy dog bed.

Waving at Linc and his girlfriend, Abby, Skye and Wally walked toward the couple standing among the new kennels. Linc had been seeing Abby Fleming since Skye had arranged a date between the school nurse and the veterinarian a few months ago. She was thrilled that one of her matchmaking efforts had finally paid off.

Linc was an attractive man with a lean but muscled physique, and Abby, a tall blond with beautiful, blue eyes and an athletic build, was just plain dazzling. As Skye and Wally joined them, they paused before entering the next kennel.

"What brings you two out here?" Linc asked, twining his fingers with Abby's.

"I don't suppose it's to help us feed and water all these animals." Abby raised a perfectly arched eyebrow. "Or to muck out their pens."

"Sorry." Wally shook his head. "Not this time. We're looking for Billie Lyons." He turned to Linc. "Did she drop off her husband's dog here?"

"Billie Lyons." Linc rubbed his chin. "That doesn't ring a bell."

"What's the dog's name?" Abby asked, her eyes twinkling. "Linc's a lot more likely to know the animal than the owner."

"I don't think that I ever heard." Wally glanced at Skye. "How about you?"

"Nope. All I know is that it's a German shepherd."

"We've got two shepherds." Linc pointed a few kennels down. "That one is Prince and the one over in the next row is Leo."

"Leo." Skye grinned at Wally. "I'll bet Zeke *Lyons* named his dog after a lion."

"If Leo's the one, although I don't recall the name, I do remember his owner," Linc said. "She was a pretty woman in her late forties and she was accompanied by an older lady who kept encouraging the younger one to have the dog euthanized."

"That sounds like Billie and her mother," Skye said.

"Let me get Leo's identification certificate." Linc disappeared for a few seconds, then came back holding a four-by-six index card. "I can put the number into the computer to get the owner's information."

The two couples went inside, took seats in Linc's office, and then as he brought up the program, Abby asked, "Why are you trying to locate this Billie Lyons?"

Skye was a little surprised that Abby hadn't heard about the murder. Evidently, the tornadoes' repercussions were still interfering with the Scumble River grapevine. The local paper usually came out on Wednesday, but she hadn't seen a copy anywhere on her rounds yesterday. Maybe it hadn't been printed this week.

Realizing that Abby was staring at her, Skye said, "Billie's husband was found dead right after their house was destroyed in the tornado."

"How horrible." Abby's forehead wrinkled in sympathy. "The poor woman."

Skye glanced at Wally, and when he gave her a slight nod, she continued. "We haven't been able to find Billie since she was notified and we need to talk to her about the investigation."

"Investigation? Was he murdered? Is she a suspect?" Abby's eyes widened. "Why would she kill her husband?"

"There are always reasons. Some more obvious than others," Wally answered. "But since we haven't been able to speak to her —"

"Found it." Linc looked up from the computer monitor. "Looks like Billie Lyons must have rented an apartment in Bourbonnais." He read off the address. "Do you want her phone number, as well?"

"Please," Skye said. "Wally's father was able to find a lot of information on Billie and Zeke using a software program the company he works for owns, but there was no record of a cell phone and no one I spoke to had it either."

"It's probably a prepaid one." Wally

squeezed Skye's knee. "Folks who only want a cell for emergency often purchase that kind."

"If you watch mystery programs on television, you'd think only criminals use disposable phones." Abby tilted her head. "They call them burners, right?"

"Uh-huh." Wally helped Skye to her feet, then turned to Linc and said, "Thanks for the help. Is there anything we can do to give you a hand with the dogs you're boarding for the tornado victims?"

"We're currently at maximum capacity for the canines. I still have a little space for cats, but I've purchased as many portable dog kennels as I can afford, so if you know of anyone who wants to donate more of those or food or litter or other equipment . . ."

Skye tugged Wally down and whispered in his ear, "I bet your dad would be willing to help out." She'd told him all about Carson's donation to the shelter and his purchase of the Doozier stun guns.

"I might have someone." Wally held out his hand to Linc. "I'll let you know."

As Wally and Skye moved toward the door, she paused and asked, "Linc, do you recall if Billie had a dog bite on her arm?"

"I didn't see any." Linc gazed at the ceiling. "Nope. She was wearing a tank top and her arms didn't have a mark on them. At the time, I thought how lucky she was since so many people were scraped and bruised after the tornadoes."

CHAPTER 24

> "I have been wicked in my day, but I never thought a little girl like you would ever be able to melt me and end my wicked deeds."
>
> — Wicked Witch of the West

Walking down the clinic's front steps, Wally said, "If Billie doesn't have a dog bite on her arm, she can't be the woman the motorcycle gang saw zapping Zeke Lyons after the tornado."

"I was just thinking that." Skye wrinkled her nose as they headed to the clinic's parking lot. "But you still want to talk to her, right?"

"Absolutely." Wally opened the SUV door and helped Skye climb inside before rounding the vehicle and sliding into the driver's seat.

"Are you going to call Billie to come in to the police station or are we heading to

Bourbonnais?" Skye asked, fastening her seat belt.

Wally took out his cell. "Let's try calling and go from there."

His key ring, duty belt, and weapon had been found in the squad car and were still being processed by the crime scene techs, but when Tin — a.k.a. Spencer — had been arrested, he'd had Wally's phone in his pocket. After the undercover officer was released and his personal effects were returned to him, he'd returned the cell to Wally.

Skye watched as her husband dialed. It was so good to have him back. He hadn't been missing that long, but she'd been terrified that she'd never see him again. That he'd never get to hold his babies. That after all they'd been through to be with each other, in the end, they still weren't going to be able to grow old together.

A few seconds later, Skye heard Wally identify himself and say, "Mrs. Lyons, I'd like to bring you up to speed on your husband's murder investigation. Would you be able to meet me at the Scumble River Police Department?" He paused for her answer, then said, "Say in about an hour?" Another pause. "Fine. See you then."

After disconnecting, Wally turned to Skye

and said, "She's on her way."

"It didn't seem as if she was reluctant to talk to you," Skye commented as Wally put away his phone and drove toward town.

"Not at all." Wally pursed his mouth. "In fact, she sounded eager." He frowned. "I could hear her mother yelling at her in the background."

"That doesn't surprise me." Skye rubbed her belly. Minnie had returned Skye's call and given her the lowdown on Billie's mom. "From what everyone's told me, Myra Gulch is a pain in the butt. And her house was next door to her daughter's place. Can you imagine having a mother-in-law like her only a few hundred feet away?"

"Myra Gulch is Mrs. Lyons's mother?" Wally asked, and when Skye nodded, he added, "I don't think that I ever noticed Billie's maiden name. But then again, I haven't really had a chance to study the Lyons file."

"Your father and I investigated because we thought your disappearance might be connected with the murder." Skye poked his arm. "You, on the other hand, have been kind of busy with being kidnapped and all."

"I suppose." Wally's expression was still self-critical. "And you said Myra and her daughter are next-door neighbors?" Wally asked.

"That's what Aunt Minnie said." Skye wrinkled her brow. "And Bartolommeo Capuchini, the guy I talked to at the church shelter, mentioned that Myra had lived in the same house for at least forty years, so the Lyonses must have purposely moved next door." Skye tapped her chin. "Considering that Bartolommeo also said that Myra managed to prevent Billie from marrying Zeke for the past twenty years, I bet living close by was one of the ways Billie appeased her mother."

"I'm surprised your mom didn't try to make us build a house next door to her," Wally joked as he pulled into the police lot, parked the Hummer, and walked around to help Skye out of the SUV. "You know, it's funny that the last call I went on just before the tornado hit was to Myra Gulch's house. She called the police because her neighbors were playing their music too loud and their dog was barking. But when I got there, I couldn't hear a thing and she was furious." He rubbed his shoulder. "The woman threw a book at me."

"Do you think Myra phoned in a complaint about her own daughter and son-in-law?" Skye shook her head as Wally led her into the PD's front entrance. "I thought it was a bit harsh when Bartolommeo called her 'old lady Gulch,' but I'm beginning to see his point of view."

"Definitely." Wally waved to May behind the counter and she buzzed open the door leading to the back. "*Old lady* is probably the nicest thing he could call her. *Witch* with a capital *B* is probably more appropriate."

"Wait a minute." Skye stopped so abruptly, she pulled her hand from Wally's. "You mentioned that the gang member said it was Zeke's old lady zapping him. But maybe the biker said that it was *an* old lady."

"That would explain why Billie doesn't have a dog bite." Wally ushered Skye into the interrogation/coffee room. "Now we need to see if Myra has one. Do you think she'll accompany her daughter to the station?"

"If everything that I've heard about her is true, Myra will be with Billie." Skye eased into a chair and looked up at Wally. "But would a woman really kill her son-in-law just because she was upset that he married her daughter?"

"Hatred is a powerful motivator, and from everything you've told me, it sure sounds as if Myra hated Zeke." Wally headed to the soda machine and put in a five-dollar bill.

He pressed the buttons for a can of caffeine-free Diet Coke and a can of root beer. "And she wanted Billie back under her control and everything the same as it was before."

"But change is inevitable."

"Except from a vending machine." Wally frowned, his hand hovering next to the slot, waiting for his two bucks to come out. Sighing, he gave up and joined Skye at the table.

"What if Billie wasn't the one who bought the life insurance policy?" Skye took a sip of soda. "What if it was her mother?"

"Normally, I'd interview the women separately, but I think in this case, I'll make an exception." Wally narrowed his eyes. "But I do think it would be best if you sat between them. Concentrate on Billie. I have a feeling Myra won't fall for your good-cop routine."

"It's not a routine." Skye smacked Wally's biceps. "I *am* the good cop."

Wally got up from his chair, reached into the cupboard over the sink, and took down the old-fashioned tape recorder. Six months ago, the city attorney had decreed that the police had to make an audio record of all official interviews. And since the interrogation/coffee room wasn't set up with any kind of modern equipment, and there was no money in the budget to correct that issue, the police had to make do with what they had lying around.

While they waited for Billie and Myra to arrive, Wally called the company that had insured Zeke to find out the details of the policy's purchase. After he hung up, he and Skye discussed strategy. The trickiest part was reading the women their rights without tipping them off that they were suspects.

They finally agreed to have the officer on duty take care of Mirandizing them before bringing them back to Wally and Skye. Wally called Anthony in from patrolling and briefed him on the situation. He instructed him to assure Billie and Myra that it was just standard operating procedure before anyone talked to the police.

A few seconds after getting everything in place, Skye spotted Billie and Myra walking toward the front entrance and she and Wally hurried back through the door to the rear of the station. Before it closed, Anthony gave them a thumbs-up.

Several minutes ticked by and Skye was beginning to fear that Anthony was having trouble with the women when the young officer showed Billie and Myra into the interrogation room. As soon as Billie took a seat, Skye eased into the chair next to her.

Myra headed toward the seat on the other side of her daughter, but Wally pulled out the chair by Skye and said, "Here you go, Mrs. Gulch."

When she grudgingly complied, Wally took a seat facing the three women over the table.

Turning on the tape recorder, Wally announced the date and time and instructed, "Please state your full names and current addresses." After they complied, Wally said, "We have a few questions regarding Zeke's murder. In order to make you both more comfortable, we are allowing you to remain together during this conversation."

"Are we suspects?" Myra glared. "Maybe we should have a lawyer."

"Because the next of kin usually has a unique perspective, it is customary to talk to them about the victim," Wally said smoothly. "But you're free to call an attorney."

"Mother, we want to do everything we can to help the police find Zeke's killer." Billie shot her mom a firm look, then asked, "What do you want to know?"

"I understand that your husband didn't have any local family members other than yourself," Wally said.

"That's correct." Billie wiped a tear from her eye with the tissue Skye handed her. "Zeke was raised in an orphanage. He was left on the doorstep and never knew the identity of his parents."

"He was a mutt," Myra hissed. "Just like that dog of his. No papers."

Wally sent Skye a quick glance, then turned back to Billie and asked, "How would you describe Zeke's relationship with his friends and coworkers?"

"Cordial." Billie twisted the Kleenex. "He was a very private man and kind of shy."

"Not too shy to take up with you," Myra groused.

"Mrs. Gulch, you don't seem too fond of your son-in-law." Wally's tone was mild, but Billie stiffened. He raised a brow. "Did your mother and husband get along, Mrs. Lyons?"

Billie's cheeks reddened and she stuttered, "As well as could be expected."

"But that wasn't too well, right?" Skye turned in her chair so she was facing Billie and had her back to Myra. "I understand that your mother objected to your marriage."

"Uh . . ." Billie tried to look around Skye at her mom. "It was only because she loves me so much. My father deserted us when I was born and Mother was afraid that Zeke would do the same to me."

"And he did," Myra needled. "He's gone.

Leaving you with a pile of rubbish for a house and a hulking hound to feed."

"It's not his fault he was killed!" Billie cried.

"If he hadn't chosen that damn dog over you, he'd still be alive." Myra moved her chair so she could see her daughter.

"How can you be so cruel, Mother?" Billie sobbed.

Skye patted the distraught woman's arm as she wept. Then after a few seconds of silence, Wally said, "Tell me what happened right before the tornado."

"We were sitting in the living room listening to music when John, our across-the-street neighbor, knocked on the door and said that there was a tornado warning. We hadn't heard the siren." Billie sniffled. "He wanted us to take shelter in his basement, but because of his son's allergy, Leo would have to stay at home. Zeke sent me with John but said he couldn't leave Leo alone."

"And that was the last time you saw him alive?" Skye asked softly.

Billie nodded.

"Do you have a basement, Mrs. Gulch?" Wally asked abruptly, staring at the older woman.

"No." Myra scowled. "And I wasn't leaving my house open to looters. I took cover in my bathtub."

"That was so dangerous, Mother." Billie put her hand on her chest. "That old cattle prod of Grandpa Gulch's wouldn't help you if someone had a gun."

Skye and Wally exchanged meaningful looks and Wally said, "Mrs. Gulch, please remove your sweater."

Despite the heat and humidity outside, the older woman wore a light cardigan.

"I will not," Myra snapped.

"Is that because you don't want us to see the bite marks on your arm?" Wally asked.

"How did you know about those?" Billie's gaze darted from Wally to her mother. "She got those from a stray when she came to find me at John's house."

"No." Wally crossed his arms. "Leo bit her when she was using that cattle prod of hers on your husband."

"No," Billie gasped. "Mother, tell them you didn't do that to Zeke."

"Of course I didn't," Myra bellowed. "Don't be more stupid than usual."

"The bite marks are why she tried so hard to convince you to put Leo down." Wally took Billie's hand. "Once he was euthanized, he'd be cremated and we wouldn't be able to match the teeth marks forensically."

"Mother?" Billie's voice wavered and she jerked her fingers from Wally's. "That's not true, is it?"

"After all that I've done for you, you don't trust me?" Myra's lips thinned.

Billie shook her head. "No. I do." She looked at Skye and said, "You can't believe my own mother would harm the man I loved."

"It's not what I believe." Skye patted her back. "It's all about the evidence." She pretended to think, then said, "I know. If the cattle prod you mentioned doesn't match the marks on Mr. Lyons's chest, and if Leo's teeth don't match her wound, we can prove it isn't your mom."

"The cattle prod is back at the apartment and Leo is at Dr. Quillen's clinic." Billie nodded. "I can go get the prod and you can have Mother's arm checked."

"Are you crazy?" Myra roared. "The cops don't care if I'm really guilty. They just want to close out their case. If you hand over that cattle prod, they'll just fake the evidence. And no one is touching my arm."

"Well" — Billie wavered, her gaze flickering back and forth from Skye to Myra — "maybe Mom's right and I shouldn't."

"We can get a search warrant," Wally said. "And it will include your arm, Mrs. Gulch."

"You can't let them do this to me," Myra shrieked. "I've always protected you."

"That's not quite true," Skye said softly. "Are you aware that your mother took out a half-a-million-dollar life insurance policy on your husband two months ago?"

"No." Billie's voice quavered. "How is that possible? I thought you could only buy life insurance on yourself."

"Actually," Wally said, "it can be purchased on your spouse, your child, your business partner, or your parents. We figure that your mother filled out the forms, claiming to be you, when she bought the one on Mr. Lyons." He stared at Myra. "And that misrepresentation means the contract is considered void from the date of issue."

"How do you know Mother is the one who bought it?" Billie asked.

"Did you purchase it?" Skye asked.

"No." Billie's voice was so soft, Skye barely heard her denial.

"That's what we figured." Wally put his hands palms down on the table. "We know it was your mother because she's the one paying the premiums. That gives her motivation, the fact she was alone after the tornado gives her opportunity, and her knowledge of Zeke's heart condition and the cattle prod gives her means."

Myra glowered for several seconds, then said, "It's not what it looks like."

"Oh?" Skye glanced at Wally. Where had they heard that before?

"I didn't mean to kill him." Myra straightened. "I went over to check to see if he was okay, and when he came at me in the dark, I thought he was a looter."

"Why didn't you get help once you saw it was Mr. Lyons? Why did you shock him over and over again?" Wally asked. "And why did you lie about your dog bite?"

"I was afraid Billie would never forgive me." Myra looked sad. "She's all I have in the world."

"Why did you take out the life insurance policy?" Skye asked.

"Billie needed to be protected if anything happened to Zeke," Myra said quickly and then crossed her arms. "He wasn't a young man."

"Did you know there were witnesses to you zapping your son-in-law?" Wally asked conversationally.

"No." Myra wrinkled her brow, then must have decided to tough it out. "If that were true, I'd be arrested, not sitting here."

"Yep. Those looters you were so afraid of told me all about how you just kept zapping him." Wally leaned back. "Even when Leo was biting you, you kept shocking Zeke."

"I . . ." Myra gulped, a look of panic on her face. "A jury will believe me over some criminal."

"Maybe." Skye shrugged. "But we also have the evidence. Mr. Lyons was zapped more than once. And then there's the half-million-dollar insurance policy."

"Uh. I . . ." Myra wrinkled here brow, then smiled triumphantly. "I'm just a frail old woman. I wouldn't be able to overpower a grown man."

"You could with a long-handled cattle prod." Wally's voice was knife-edged. "Especially if he wasn't expecting you to attack him."

"That doesn't prove anything!" Myra screamed. "You're twisting everything. Billie, tell them!"

"How could you do it, Mother?" Billie asked. "I loved him." She got up and walked to the door. "I'll never forgive you. Never."

"You just couldn't bear the thought of your daughter being married." Skye's tone was sympathetic. "You loved her and wanted her with you."

"I . . . I . . ." Myra scrubbed her eyes with her fists. "Maybe I do need a lawyer."

"Only if you want to escalate the proceedings." Wally hooked his thumbs in his belt loops. "But you do have a right to counsel," he said carefully. "However, then you won't be able to tell us your side of the story."

Skye added, "And Billie will hate you. You won't be able to tell her about the mitigating circumstances of the situation."

Wally was quiet, allowing Myra to think about what had been said, then asked, "Do you want to call your attorney?"

"No. I guess not." Myra sighed, obviously realizing she was running out of options.

"Well, you can anytime," Skye added. She didn't want the judge to throw out her confession because Myra's rights hadn't been upheld.

"Okay." Myra slumped. "That man was taking my daughter away from me. He'd promised they'd live next door, but I found out he was planning to retire in a few years and wanted to move somewhere warm."

"That must have made you really angry," Skye murmured encouragingly.

"It did." Myra jerked up her chin. "When I confronted him, he said I could go with them. But I've lived here my whole life. I didn't want to move."

"So you started planning his death," Wally said.

"And that's when you bought the life insurance?" Skye guessed.

"Yes," Myra admitted. "But I wasn't sure how to get rid of him."

Wally pounced. "But the tornado gave you the perfect opportunity."

"And now you've lost Billie," Skye said, staring into Myra's eyes. "You killed a man for nothing."

Myra collapsed against the back of the chair. It was clear she had given up. She buried her face in her hands. "Tell Billie I'm sorry," Myra sobbed. "I just wanted us to be together like we used to be."

Skye and Wally exchanged a look. In front of them was a perfect illustration of what not to do as a parent. While Wally wrapped up the questioning and had Myra write out her confession, Skye rubbed her belly and prayed she and Wally would get things right with their children.

Four hours later, the search warrants had been executed, the evidence secured, and Myra's case had been turned over to the city attorney.

It was nearly seven o'clock when Skye and Wally finally were able to leave the PD and head home. Skye was not only exhausted, but starving as well. And Wally looked ready to collapse. The stress of the past several days had finally caught up with them.

As they walked up the steps of the motor

coach, Wally said, "I thought Myra Gulch would be a tougher nut to crack."

"Once she realized that she'd lost her daughter, she just didn't care anymore." Skye's smile was grim.

"And we did have the cattle prod, bite marks, and insurance policy," Wally added. "With all that against her, she really had no choice."

"I'm so sick of people saying they have no choice." Skye blew out a long breath. "Myra's choice should have been to be a good mother, rather than a selfish one."

"It's a shame her daughter and son-in-law ended up paying the price." Wally kissed Skye's temple. "Which is why we will put our kids first."

"Too bad we can't protect them from all the witches in this world." Skye rested her hand on her stomach. "I guess we just have to make sure they know that there's no place like home."

EPILOGUE

"And oh, Aunt Em! I'm so glad to be at home again!"

— Dorothy

Six weeks later

Skye stood in the open doorway of the motor coach that she and Wally now called home and tugged a pink sweatshirt over her head. It was the largest size available, but it still fit snugly over her baby belly, and as her fingers traced the black lettering stretched across the fabric, she mouthed the printed words: WE'RE SCUMBLE RIVER STRONG.

With the sudden drop in temperature, she was glad her father-in-law had opted for the hoodies versus the T-shirts when he bought a gross of the shirts to support the relief-effort fund-raiser. Carson had then randomly handed out most of them to the kids who'd attended the first school assembly.

It had been a tough autumn for the Scumble Riverites, but everyone had pulled together and the town was beginning to rebuild. Hundreds of volunteers had been bussed in to tackle clearing the twelve zones decimated by the tornadoes. Nine hundred structures had sustained significant damage.

Dante had declared a civil emergency, allowing the town government to seek resources and spend the money needed for the cleanup. Evidently, whatever he had been plotting had been put on hold, and Skye hoped that the person taking Zeke Lyons's spot on the council would be a stronger advocate for all the citizens, rather than just Dante's cronies.

The schools hadn't been as badly damaged as the board had at first feared, and with a bit shuffling, they'd been able to resume classes after only a ten-day delay. Both winter and spring breaks had to be shortened, but they wouldn't have to extend the year into the summer months.

Skye had been thrilled at how easily the school psych intern had adjusted. She and Piper had worked together as if they'd been a team forever. The first week school had been back in session, they'd held more counseling groups than either of them had ever led in the past.

The tornado-devastated students and staff had continued to need sessions for quite a while, but the demand had tapered off by last Friday, when Skye officially went on maternity leave. Although it had been a relief to have the past week to prepare for the babies, she couldn't resist calling every day for an update. Nevertheless, she was confident that, between the special-ed co-op psychologist and Piper, the kids, parents, and faculty would be well served.

Resting a hip against the doorframe, Skye blinked back tears as the construction crew finished hauling away the last debris of what had been her first home with Wally. Even the foundation had had to be removed, and the only thing left was a huge hole in the ground.

So far, Mrs. Griggs's ghost hadn't put in an appearance and Skye wasn't sure if she was happy or sad about the spirit's absence. Maybe, once the new house was built, Mrs. Griggs would return.

A loud meow startled Skye from her musings and she said, "I just fed you."

She peered over her stomach and raised a brow at the black cat doing figure eights around her jean-clad ankles. Frannie and Justin had returned Bingo before heading back to school, and surprisingly, the usually finicky feline had adjusted with minimal fuss to his new life in the motor coach.

Just before Skye's young friends had left, Justin had hugged her and whispered, "Thanks for getting help for Mom and Dad. The aide starts next week and will come on Mondays and Wednesdays to make sure they have the basics."

Skye had been relieved that the assistance had been put in place so quickly. It would have been a shame for Justin to sit out a semester waiting for his parents to get the support they needed.

Shortly after Frannie and Justin's departure, Skye had gotten a gleeful call from Linc. Carson had arranged for all the kennels and supplies the veterinarian needed to shelter the animals left homeless from the tornadoes. She'd been able to evade the vet's questions about the mysterious donor, but at some point, she and Wally would need to figure out a way of revealing his father's fortune.

Skye had a feeling that when the babies arrived, there just wouldn't be a way of hiding his wealth from the town. Maybe the best thing would be to have Kathryn Steele interview Wally about Carson's generosity for the newspaper. *The Star*'s owner would handle the story in a tasteful manner.

Shoving that concern away for another day, Skye watched as the last of construction trucks disappeared from view and Wally's squad car pulled into the driveway. Skye glanced at her watch. It was after five and she hadn't even thought about dinner yet.

Biting her lip, Skye turned to head into the kitchen, but before she reached the fridge, there was a sudden rush of warm water pouring down her inner thighs. *Well, heck!* Apparently, the contractions she'd been experiencing over the last several hours weren't Braxton-Hicks after all.

A few seconds later, when Wally walked through the door, Skye hadn't moved. He started to speak, but she pointed to the puddle on the floor and his face drained of all color.

After a frozen instant, Wally stepped closer, put his arm around her, and asked, "How close are your contractions?"

"I'm not really sure." Skye bit her lip. "Maybe twenty minutes. I didn't realize they were the real deal. Should we wait and see?"

"Absolutely not!" Shooting her an anxious look, he said, "Do you want to change or just go like that?"

"I'm not going to the hospital in wet pants."

"I'll call Dr. Johnson while you get dressed."

Skye nodded and darted into the bedroom. She grabbed a pair of yoga pants from the closet, then as she shimmied out of her jeans, a contraction gripped her and she yelped.

Wally raced into the room and wrapped an arm around her back and waist. "Breathe through it, sugar."

Skye felt Wally panting with her and the warmth of his embrace helped ease her panic.

"That one was the worst so far," Skye said after the pain lessened.

"What can I do?"

"Help me get these on." Skye shoved the pants into his hands.

Once she was decent, she snatched her purse from the dresser and Wally grabbed her suitcase. Walking outside, he tried to steer her toward his police cruiser, but she turned toward Wally's gift to her — a shiny, silver Mercedes.

"We are taking my car. I love it and I'm riding in it to the hospital." Skye stared at Wally, daring him to object.

"But I can use the lights and siren if we

take the cruiser."

"No."

Wally opened his mouth to argue, but apparently, her stubborn glare changed his mind. He helped her into the luxury SUV, ran around the hood, and leaped behind the wheel.

As he sped toward Kankakee, Skye cried out when another contraction hit. She held her belly and panted.

"Shit!" Wally glanced at his watch. "That was only eight minutes from the last one."

"I'll text my parents, your dad, Charlie, Trixie, and Vince." Skye dug her cell from her purse.

"Good plan."

Skye finished her texts, then screamed, "I need to push!"

"Hold on to it, sugar." Wally pressed down on the accelerator. Five minutes later, he pulled up to the hospital's emergency entrance and laid on the horn.

When a man dressed in scrubs rushed out the door, Wally shouted, "My wife's contractions are three minutes apart and she feels like she needs to push."

"Be right back," the man said as he raced into the hospital.

A few seconds later, the attendant returned with a wheelchair and Wally helped

Skye into it. He accompanied her as she was propelled toward the birthing center. A nurse met them in the hall and took their information. They had preregistered for one of the Labor/Delivery/Recovery suites and they were quickly ushered into a room.

Once Skye was in a hospital gown, her pulse, blood pressure, and temperature were taken and a monitor was placed on her stomach to check for uterine contractions and assess the baby's heart rate. Skye was lying on the bed, panting through another contraction, when her ob-gyn arrived.

The doctor pulled up a stool and said, "I'm going to examine your cervix to determine how far labor has progressed."

"It feels as if my insides are coming out." Sweat dripped down Skye's face.

"You can do this, darlin'." Wally stroked her wet hair away from her forehead and held her hand, continuing to murmur soothingly into her ear.

"I feel such an intense pressure," Skye sobbed. "Like I have no control over what's happening."

"You're dilated to ten centimeters," Dr. Johnson announced. "And the baby's crowning." She shot Skye and Wally a smile. "You guys made it here just in time."

Skye grunted her agreement. The pain had

become so bad she couldn't speak. Wally's face was pale and his brown eyes shone with concern.

Dr. Johnson looked at her. "Skye, you can push now."

Bearing down as hard as she could, Skye felt as if she were caught in a bad remake of *Alien* and her stomach would burst open at any minute.

When Wally stroked her cheek, she knocked his hand away and hissed, "Don't touch me." After a few more rounds of pushing, she added, "Ever again."

A couple of minutes later, the first baby was born, and his sister appeared ten minutes later. Dr. Johnson instructed Wally on how to cut the umbilical cords, and once that was successfully accomplished, the nurse took the infants to clean them while the doctor finished with Skye.

After Skye had on a new gown and the bedding was changed, Wally helped her sit up. The nurse placed Skye's new daughter in her arms and a second nurse handed Wally his son. Then, finally, the four of them were alone.

"Thank you, darlin'." Wally wiped the moisture from his cheeks as he gazed adoringly at his son. "I never thought I could be this happy."

"Me either," Skye murmured, looking at their daughter with the same tears of joy in her eyes. "Thank you for giving me the life I never even knew that I wanted."

Ten minutes later, Wally said, "We should probably let my dad and your parents come meet their grandchildren."

"I suppose." Skye squirmed. "Mom is none too happy that I wouldn't let her in here for the delivery. Or that we still haven't picked out names."

"She'll get over it as soon as she has an armful of baby." Wally grinned.

May, Jed, and Carson spent several hours with their children and grandchildren. Charlie, Trixie, Owen, Vince, and Loretta also popped in to visit. But finally the nurse shooed everyone away. Once they were all gone and the babies were in their bassinets, Wally sat in a recliner next to Skye and held her hand.

"It almost feels as if we've just been through another tornado." Wally sighed. "So much has gone on these past couple of months."

"But it's not what happens to us that's important." Skye stared at her wonderful husband. "It's what we do about it and what we learn from it." She squeezed his fingers. "And I've learned that I don't care about things. All I care about is having our family together."

"Me too." He brought her hand to his mouth and kissed her palm. "Me too."

ACKNOWLEDGMENTS

A huge thanks to Cindy Killian, Sarah Whitt Reed, and Margaret Adame Trott for sharing their labor and delivery experiences. Skye needed all the help she could get!

ABOUT THE AUTHOR

Denise Swanson is the *New York Times* bestselling author of the Scumble River mysteries and the Devereaux's Dime Store mysteries, as well as many contemporary romances. She worked as a school psychologist for twenty-two years before quitting to write full-time. She lives in rural Illinois with her husband. Visit her online on Facebook, Twitter, and Pinterest.

The employees of Thorndike Press hope you have enjoyed this Large Print book. All our Thorndike, Wheeler, and Kennebec Large Print titles are designed for easy reading, and all our books are made to last. Other Thorndike Press Large Print books are available at your library, through selected bookstores, or directly from us.

For information about titles, please call:

(800) 223-1244

or visit our website at:

gale.com/thorndike

To share your comments, please write:

Publisher
Thorndike Press
10 Water St., Suite 310
Waterville, ME 04901